Someone beyond the university, certainly. And she wouldn't be the target of Arab martial-arts masters. University of Sydney professors didn't strike her as the types to bring in hired assassins.

She stepped into another chamber, this one much smaller than the first one. It smelled ghastly, and a pan of the light showed why. The ceiling had spiderweb cracks in it. Water had trickled through and ruined the goods arrayed on the floor—long-rotted animal hides, bodies wrapped in cloth, which from their outlines looked to be nothing more than skeletons, jars that had been filled with grain and other foodstuffs and that now contained only mold.

"Ugh," Annja pronounced. Now it was definitely time to leave.

She spun and blinked furiously, meeting another beam of light—this one aimed right at her eyes.

"Put your flashlight down and put your hands up!"

Because the light had practically blinded her, Annja couldn't see the speaker, but she guessed it was the man she'd followed. He'd gotten behind her and hidden, waited for the right time to approach.

"Drop it now!" he ordered.

Annja had no choice but to comply.

Titles in this series:

ROGUE Angel

Alex Archer

ETERNAL JOURNEY

A GOLD EAGLE BOOK FROM

WORLDWIDE®

TORONTO • NEW YORK • LONDON
AMSTERDAM • PARIS • SYDNEY • HAMBURG
STOCKHOLM • ATHENS • TOKYO • MILAN
MADRID • WARSAW • BUDAPEST • AUCKLAND

Recycling programs
for this product may
not exist in your area.

First edition March 2009

ISBN-13: 978-0-373-62135-4
ISBN-10:   0-373-62135-3

ETERNAL JOURNEY

Special thanks and acknowledgment to
Jean Rabe for her contribution to this work.

Printed in U.S.A.

The
LEGEND

...THE ENGLISH COMMANDER TOOK
JOAN'S SWORD AND RAISED IT HIGH.

The broadsword, plain and unadorned,
gleamed in the firelight. He put the tip against
the ground and his foot at the center of the blade.
The broadsword shattered, fragments falling
into the mud. The crowd surged forward,
peasant and soldier, and snatched the shards
from the trampled mud. The commander tossed
the hilt deep into the crowd.
Smoke almost obscured Joan, but she continued
praying till the end, until finally the flames climbed
her body and she sagged against the restraints.

Joan of Arc died that fateful day in France,
but her legend and sword are reborn....

PROLOGUE

Henenu's heart raced as he watched the slab fall and split, so much of it crumbling into worthless gravel. He swore that he could feel the last pulse leaving his body as he dropped to his knees, eyes locked on the ruined stone. The prayer that he'd painstakingly carved on its polished surface to honor the mistress to the entrance of the valley was destroyed.

All those long, long hours wasted.

His brother and five other men had been fitting the slab in place above the temple entrance. It was to be the crowning piece to the structure they'd all labored so hard to build.

"Fools, you!" Henenu spit when he regained his breath. "The mother goddess curse you all and send your souls to a dark place for your clumsiness!" Then softly he added, "Curse the lot of us for coming to this escapeless hole."

He ground his fist against the earth so hard his knuckles bled, closed his eyes and begged the mother goddess's forgiveness. He promised to carve another, more magnificent slab—one that would be placed by all of his men. There would be no risk of failure next time.

"A fool, me," he said. Henenu directed his anger inward now. "The fault is with me. The blame is all mine."

Perhaps the mother goddess was furious that they had spent their time erecting buildings rather than trying to get home. No, Henenu thought, they had tried so often to rebuild the boats and sail away, and had been thwarted at each attempt.

Perhaps this temple was not large enough, and in her irritation at the slight the mistress to the entrance of the valley had caused the stone to break, displaying her displeasure.

Certainly this was not as large as her temple in Henenu's home city. He looked at the building through narrowed eyes, seeing the sharp angles and planes and the squat, wide steps that led up to an entranceway that yawned black like the maw of a hungry beast. It was a beautiful building.

Again he stared at the broken slab and felt his chest grow tight.

Stone was plentiful in this land, and so Henenu could order more pieces cut, knock down a wall and make the temple larger. That might appease the mother goddess. But his men were not as numerous as the builders he'd commanded back home. It had taken several years to accomplish this much.

And what would appeasing the goddess bring them?

A bigger temple would not grant the promise of a rich

afterlife. This land they'd found would forever prevent them from joining the gods.

This land would consign them to the abyss.

"Brother." Khentemsemet had come down the temple steps and stood in front of Henenu, bowing respectfully and blocking the view to the entrance and the ruined slab. "The responsibility—I take it, Henenu. My fingers ached in weakness, and I lost my hold on the prayer stone. I will accept whatever punishment you—"

Henenu rose and shook his head, looked around his younger brother and to the temple entrance again. His ire had cooled somewhat, seeing Khentemsemet's penitent face and tear-filled eyes, and he let out a low breath that sounded like dry leaves rustling in a lazy wind. "No punishment, brother. I will carve another slab."

"The mother goddess…"

"It was merely a piece of rock, dear Khentemsemet."

"But, Henenu…"

"The next prayer I inscribe to Hathor, our mother goddess, will be more eloquent," Henenu said. "In it I will pay better homage to she who is the wife of Horus. She is our only mother goddess."

Khentemsemet's shoulders relaxed and he turned to regard the temple, his eyes avoiding the broken stone. The setting sun painted the walls a molten bronze, and the shimmering waves of heat that rose from the ground made the carved images on the building's sides appear to move. The majority of creatures and the men and women depicted had cows' heads or ears or horns. Hathor's was the largest. Her bovine visage was enfolded in a sun-shaped disk, and her arms stretched up as if she were trying to grab her beloved Horus, the god of the sky and the noon sun.

Similar figures were displayed on the handful of smaller buildings that spread away to the north, the etchings all deep, as there was little age to the structures and the wind had not had a proper chance to weather the stone.

A few of the images on the temple were incongruous to the rest; they were smaller than the carved Egyptian deities, and they formed a line like a border along the base. They were of quadrupeds with large, muscular back legs, tiny front legs, long tails, and pouches where young ones poked out their heads.

Henenu and Khentemsemet looked to the west to see a quartet of the sun-tinged animals hop across the horizon.

"This escapeless hole," Henenu pronounced again. "It will keep us from ascending."

1

A wide-brimmed hat the color of wet sand shielded the archaeologist's eyes from the sun and made it difficult for the cameraman to get a good shot of his face. The man worked steadily and carefully, sifting dirt and picking out what looked like unremarkable shards of pottery, all the while oblivious to the film crew around him.

"Wes, look up once in a while, okay?" Annja Creed stood back far enough so her shadow would not encroach. "We've been over this a few times," she reminded her colleague.

"Yeah, yeah. No worries." The archaeologist tipped his head up and smiled, showing an even row of bright white teeth that contrasted sharply with his well-tanned skin and scruffy beard. He winked at her.

"Ah, sometimes I don't know Christmas from Bourke Street, Miss Creed," he replied. "I get my head into this and I forget all else."

Annja put Wes somewhere between thirty-five and fifty, his hair graying, but his face unlined and his eyes bright. He was dressed in the traditional khaki pants most archaeologists wore, but his shirt was a brilliant lake-blue, new and with sharp creases; he'd worn a new shirt each day of the shoot, and had polished his shoes. He'd stubbornly refused to give his age and many other details about his personal life, saying, "I don't need the world to know all of that, Miss Creed. I'm not important. This site is, though."

She could have gotten all the biographical information she wanted for her piece from the foundation funding the dig—about Dr. Wesley Michaels, his wife and the handful of other archaeologists. She could have gotten Wes's age, weight, favorite beverage, and even the name of his first pet if she'd pressed. But he was right…the site deserved the spotlight.

"Besides, don't you have enough pictures of me, Miss Creed? I thought you finished up yesterday." Wes gave her another wink and returned to his sifting, the angle of his hat again obscuring his face.

Annja loved to hear Wes talk. He had a thick Australian accent, perhaps exaggerated for her benefit.

"Just about finished, Dr. Michaels," the cameraman pronounced. "A few more pans, Annja, and it'll be a wrap, as they say."

"Thanks, Oliver." Annja pointed to the north. "Could you get some more on the skeletons, please. That fellow working over there by himself. He's uncovered quite a bit this morning. You can see the whole skull now."

Oliver made a face. "More bone shots. Sure."

The archaeologists labored in a long bowl-like depression, concentrating on a section of midden at the base of a hill, a layer of soil that was stained dark by the decomposition of refuse left behind by people who lived a long time ago. The southern section had fragments of stone tools, bits of crude jewelry and pottery chips, the latter of which obviously fascinated Wes. He was attentive with even the smallest piece.

Annja watched him with detached envy. It was a fascinating dig, and a part of her wished she was working it, not just hosting a television segment highlighting the site. Three and a half days of filming and interviews for a one-hour slot on *Chasing History's Monsters*. She held back a laugh; there'd been no monsters here in this desolate stretch in a forest preserve northwest of Sydney, but she knew her producer would fabricate one. He'd come up with some beast that supposedly either lured the ancient Egyptians to Australia or prevented them from leaving—some creature that had enough myths and legends swirling around it to attract good viewing numbers.

The features of the midden drew Annja's thoughts back. Discolorations spoke of the human impact here, such as spots where posts had been set for houses and hearths had been dug for cooking. Most fascinating were the unearthed stones covered with carvings.

Egyptian hieroglyphs, these archaeologists were certain. Others disputed it, claiming they were merely unusual aboriginal petroglyphs. She'd seen plenty of petroglyphs in books and on various Internet sites, and pictographs—paintings on rocks that usually held some religious meaning. She had to side with Wes. They certainly did look like Egyptian hieroglyphs. One of the more distinct carvings was of a slight woman with the head of a cow. One of her arms was stretched above her head; the other arm had been chopped off when the stone broke.

"Hathor," Wes had explained. "The wife of Horus. She was an ancient goddess, dating to dynastic times, maybe earlier. Nothing aboriginal about her and Horus."

Annja and her crew had agreed not to give the exact location of the dig. Wes and the foundation had been adamant about that. They had enough problems with errant hikers trudging over out of curiosity. Too much publicity would mean they'd have to up their security to protect against looters and tourists, and that would cut into what Wes called a "damn scant budget."

There was a second dig about a mile away, on the other side of the ridge in a lightly wooded section. Smaller and not nearly as interesting as this, Annja thought, though certainly part of the same ancient city. University of Sydney graduate students were working there to uncover more hieroglyphs. A third Egyptian dig was taking place near Brisbane, and Annja had lobbied to visit that site, too, as it was the most recent. But her producer cited timing and money, and so she had grudgingly settled solely on Dr. Michaels's team.

"This is all considered *fringe* archaeology anyway," Doug Morrell had argued, because not all the experts agreed it was Egyptian. Not worth too much airtime, but certainly worth some, he had said. Normally, the hint of some monster triggered her assignment. This time, it was a leak that a rival television show was going to send a team to the dig. Doug had admitted wanting the scoop on the place.

Annja breathed deep, smelling the age of the things being unearthed, the dryness of the ground and the tinge of sweat from the archaeologists. She thought maybe she'd come back here on her own before the year was out and see what progress had been made.

Wes Michaels hoped to get the results of some radio-carbon dating before Annja and her crew finished. Using the known half-life of carbon 14, and measuring the amount of undecayed carbon in a plant specimen his wife had uncovered at the bottom of a bowl, Wes hoped to determine the age of the features of this site. Annja knew geochronology would also help—dating artifacts by the age of the geological formation they were discovered in. But those test results were still hanging.

Wes had explained to Annja that a handful of curators and computer programmers were cataloging what had already been taken away from the site and were storing them in a museum in Sydney. He had offered to show her some of the more interesting specimens locked away there. She thought maybe she'd take him up on that during her return trip.

"Fringe nothing, Miss Creed. I'm not an Egyptologist, but I don't need to be to tell me that's indeed Hathor." Wes held up a curved piece of pottery on which was painted a complete image of the cow-headed woman. "Look, she's on several pieces here."

Annja watched her cameraman work at the far end of the midden, where an archaeologist who looked little more than a teenager continued to brush the dirt away from a skeleton. The rest of her crew was packing up.

"What do you know of Hathor?" Annja knelt next to Wes Michaels and noted his gaze lingering on her lithe form. He might be a married man, she thought, but that didn't prevent him from looking.

"The mistress of turquoise, she was called. Mistress of the entrance to the valley, queen of the west, lady of the sycamore, lady of all the gods, the gold of the gods. There were more than a few names for her." Wes returned his gaze to the pottery piece. "Goddess of women, music, beauty, love, joy…all the important things in this world were her purview. They believed she blessed women with fertility. Some say the Greeks recognized her, as well, some sort of relation to Aphrodite."

"The primal mother," Jennifer said as she joined them. Hair tucked under a bushman's hat, and nose smeared with sunscreen, she was equally difficult to pin an age to. Annja thought she was overly thin, elbows and wrist bones protruding. "Hathor was said to have some erotic significance to the Egyptian culture." She playfully nudged her husband.

"Say no more. Say no more," he shot back.

Jennifer continued, "Her symbols include the *sistra*. It's sort of a rattle, and we've found two of them here. Hathor was especially prominent in Ta-Netjer."

"The Land of God," Wes translated.

"Which is modern-day Dendra in northern Egypt." Jennifer pointed to another image of Hathor on a stone. "Her priests were male and female, dancers, musicians. Some were midwives, and it was said Hathor's oracles could interpret people's dreams."

Wes passed Annja the pottery piece he'd been studying. "Careful with it," he instructed. Then he shook his head and frowned, realizing he need make no such admonition to her.

"Primal mother, you called her?" Annja mused.

Wes opened his mouth to answer, but Jennifer clicked her teeth, as much as telling him this question was hers to field. "The Egyptians believed that the world began when the great floods retreated, and at that time Hathor slipped from the reeds and stood on the first patch of dry ground. The first day of the ancient year was considered her birthday, and they celebrated it with a lavish festival. Before dawn, they'd tote her statue onto the roof of her temple at Dendra."

Annja nodded. "So that the rays of Horus, her husband, could shine on the statue, thus representing the marriage of the sun and the sky."

Jennifer beamed at Annja's knowledge. "But it wasn't all light," she said.

"No." Annja scowled. "If I remember my studies, she had a few dark roles, too. Some say she was also the goddess Sekhmet, and in that guise she exacted a blood toll on mankind." She returned the pottery piece to Wes. "A temple at Kom el-Hism in the Middle Kingdom was dedicated to Sekhmet-Hathor." Maybe there was the monster angle. Sekhmet down under, Annja mused.

"Indeed!" Jennifer said. "In one of Tutankhamen's shrines, they discovered a carving that tells how Hathor became Sekhmet at her father's, Ra's, urging. She nearly wiped out humanity, but she finally went back to being Hathor and stopped the massacre. A smart one, you are, Miss Creed. Too bad you can't stay longer."

Annja politely ignored the invitation. "Wasn't Hathor said to accept the dead at the gates of the west?"

"Now, that role wasn't dark!" Wes snorted. "The goddess greeted them at the gates with bread and beer. Hope it was a pint of Tooheys."

Annja couldn't help but laugh with him. "I *will* be back," she told him. "Without a cameraman."

After a few moments she drifted away to another section of the dig, leaving Wes and his wife to discuss the pottery shards and the mother goddess. "And maybe I'll try a Tooheys myself tonight," Annja called back to them.

Three members of the five-man film crew were leaving on a red-eye flight. But she and Oliver were scheduled to fly out the next day around noon. So tonight she'd settle back with her laptop in her hotel room in Sydney—after a good meal, of course, and that Tooheys—and search her favorite archaeology Web sites for more tidbits about Hathor. Maybe she'd search the fringe sites, too.

She made a mental note to also look into the Brisbane dig. The theories she'd already read about the Australian sites suggested that thousands of years ago Egyptians had sailed here looking for gold, and that the aboriginals who lived here at the time were said to have heard the *beating hearts* of all the ships, likely the drums that kept the oarsmen in time.

Could Wes Michaels come up with enough evidence to silence the skeptics and prove that the Egyptians really did reach Australian soil before Captain Cook?

Lost in thought, Annja nearly tripped over one of the archaeologists.

"No room for bludgers here, eh, cobber?" A lanky archaeologist raised his eyebrows when Annja caught herself from falling. His face was as smooth and flat as a shovel, and it glistened with sweat in the late-afternoon sun. It wasn't a warm day, it being early fall in Australia, but his shirt was heavy and long-sleeved, and the sweat stains were dark under his arms.

"No bludgers," Annja admitted. It was Australian slang for a layabout, someone who let others do the work for him.

"Your cameraman caught Josie napping yesterday, Miss Creed, and that's been sitting in my craw. I complained to Dr. Michaels about it, but I bet he didn't say anything to you. Did he?"

Annja shook her head.

"It'll make us all look like lazy louts. Not one of us is a bludger. Josie's just got a touch of the flu is all. Still under it, she is." He wiped the back of his hand across his forehead, smearing the dirt.

Annja offered the archaeologist a weak smile. "Oliver's just wrapping," she said. "We're heading back to Sydney within the hour."

"He didn't need to film Josie taking a little snooze," the man persisted. He gestured to the largest tree at the dig site, a fifty-yard tall stringybark that was mostly dead. Josie, the oldest archaeologist, was sitting against the trunk. "Josie there is gonna make us all look—"

"I wouldn't worry about it." Annja poked out her lower lip and let out a long breath that fluttered her hair. "It's a one-hour show, and we're interested in the hieroglyphics, nothing else." Annja wouldn't go so far as to promise that the snoozing archaeologist wouldn't appear in the segment. She'd long ago learned not to make any promises regarding *Chasing History's Monsters*.

"One hour's all?" the man asked.

She nodded. She'd thought she'd explained that to everyone.

"Dr. Michaels'll be mad as a cut snake, Miss Creed. I'll wager he figures that as many days as you've been out here you were putting together some sort of series like those Alaskan crab fishermen have. Make him a local celebrity. Get him all kinds of publicity on the National Geographic Channel or…"

Annja feigned interest in something on the rise and headed in that direction. "One hour is all," she called out. There was a tinge of irritation in her voice—both at the archaeologist's complaints and the shortness of the segment. This site was worthy of much more than a one-hour piece—many of the places she visited were worthy of more. But television had its limits, she realized. She just didn't have to like them.

She spied Oliver at the top of the ridge, taking a few shots of the student dig in the distance. Probably going to compare its small size to the professional dig here…if there was room, she thought. "Yep. Only one bloody hour," she mumbled.

2

Annja got up early, packed her suitcase and jogged down six flights in the hotel tower to knock on Oliver's door. The cameraman had a room on the smoking floor, and the nicotine that permeated the walls set her nose to wrinkling and settled uncomfortably in her mouth.

"C'mon, Ollie. Answer the door. It stinks out here. Get up. C'mon," she shouted.

She'd slept poorly, snatching only minutes here and there, her dreams filled with fire and with the notion of the mother goddess's other self nearly wiping out humankind. How would one of Hathor's oracles interpret such nightmares?

"I need coffee, Oliver. C'mon. Let's get some food." She intended to coax the notoriously late-sleeping cameraman to join her for breakfast, but he wouldn't stir. The rest of the crew gone on the red-eye. She knocked once more and then resigned herself to breakfasting alone.

"Good thing Oliver's sleeping in," she whispered several minutes later as she perused the menu in the restaurant off the lobby. The cup of coffee in front of her had so far done nothing to rejuvenate her. "I don't have to hold back ordering." She was famished and decided it was better that her cameraman didn't see her gorge herself.

"I'll have the creamy Bircher muesli with kiwis, and the strawberry-and-blueberry soy shake for starters," she told the waiter. "Give me a little time with that, then I'll have the free-range eggs, three of them poached on whole wheat, with tarragon hollandaise sauce, a slice of this baker's special—" she pointed to a line on the menu "—banana-and-macadamia nut cake—better make that two slices—and a side of chipolata sausage and onions. Oh, and bring more coffee."

There were a lot of words in her order, but not terribly much food, she thought, looking at the beautiful presentation that was shortly set before her.

On second thought, it was a lot of food, she decided when she was halfway through. Good thing that she was eating alone. Aside from Oliver not seeing this mountain she was inhaling, the solitude let her think about one of the esoteric archaeology sites she'd visited via her laptop last night.

Wes Michaels had told her not a single mummy had been found so far at any of the Australian digs, which was one of the factors that led some of his contemporaries to argue they were not Egyptian finds. But in ancient times only the pharaoh and his family were so preserved; it was believed important for their journey to the afterlife, where they would join with the gods. The regular folk had no chance of ascending that high. In later centuries, however, the wealthy were also mummified, and some time after that it became common practice for Egyptians from all levels of society—including their cats.

So, Annja thought, based on the age of the site north of Sydney, there'd either been no relatives to a pharaoh there worth mummifying, or something had wiped all of them out in one fell swoop before a single body could be preserved.

"Hathor's wrath? The monster the segment needs? Or maybe there was no natron," she mused aloud. Jennifer had mentioned the lack of natron yesterday, and Annja, knowing nothing about it, did a little surfing and learned that natron was a naturally occurring mix of soda ash and sodium bicarbonate, salt and sodium sulfate. The Egyptians used it in their mummification process. No natron, no mummies.

And if a body was not preserved, the Egyptians believed the soul that had inhabited it could well be consigned to a wretched afterlife.

"Like being damned, I guess," Annja said as she played with the salt shaker. "Not a pretty thought if you're an ancient Egyptian. No natron, no heaven."

She shoveled down the rest of her breakfast, put her hands on her stomach and leaned back in the chair, tipped her head up and studied the ceiling. She wouldn't need to eat anything on the plane. "Maybe I won't eat until next Tuesday," she said. "Ooph. Talk about my eyes being bigger than…" She let her words trail off when she saw a table of tourists watching her.

Annja sat straight and glanced at her watch. She'd

spent more than an hour in the restaurant, and that left only two hours before she and Oliver had to catch the shuttle to the airport. Time for a quick swim to work off some of the calories, she thought—not that she'd ever needed to worry about her weight or had ever bothered to count calories.

"Excellent tucker," she told the waiter on her way out, using the Australian slang for food.

She stopped in her room to dig her bathing suit out of the suitcase and put it on. Had she more time, she would have visited one of the city's beaches, even though it might be a little on the cool side. She'd seen one of the largest out the window of her plane coming in, and it looked so beautiful and inviting. All the more reason for a return trip, she thought. She really did intend to come back, and not just for the Michaels dig.

Everyone she'd met in Australia had been so friendly, and only a scattered few of them had recognized her as a celebrity from *Chasing History's Monsters*. She hadn't had time to visit Circular Quay or ride the ferries, or to get down to the Canberra military museum she'd heard so much about.

Annja rarely had time to do any tourist activities during her globe-hopping. She'd stay a few extra days now if she could, but her schedule was too tight. From here she was going home to New York, where she would put the polish on the fringe piece, as it had been labeled. Two days after that she'd be on a flight to Peru for her next assignment.

Fossils of five-foot-tall penguins with long spearlike beaks had been found in the mountains, dating back forty million years. Her producer postulated that there was a link between the giant penguins and odd-sized skeletons with overlarge craniums that came from much later periods. "Mutant Creatures of the Peaks," Doug intended to call the segment. She suppressed a giggle.

She threw a towel over her shoulder, snugged into the only pair of jeans she'd brought and stuck her wallet in the back pocket; out of habit she never left her money in her hotel room. She slipped into her flip-flops, which she made a mental note to toss when she was done rather than repack them, and headed out, pausing in front of the mirror. It amazed her that she could look this good given the way she often stuffed herself silly. But then lately the problem had been keeping her weight up; she was so active, between jetting here and there for *Chasing History's Monsters* and fighting the assorted clusters of toughs she'd encountered since inheriting Joan of Arc's sword. She tucked her hair behind her ears. Dark brown, it glistened in the sunlight streaming through her hotel room window. She remembered how pale it used to make her look, contrasting sharply with her then-scholar's complexion. Now her skin was ruddy from all the hours outdoors, and her white bikini top made her look even more tanned.

"I look pretty good." Annja, for once, wasn't embarrassed to admit it.

Maybe Oliver was up finally and would join her for a dip. If he wasn't awake, she'd roust him and drag him along. No use her being the only one with something sodden in the suitcase.

She took the stairs again, this time at a slow pace, as

she didn't want to stub her toes or catch her flip-flops on the metal strips edging each step. She knocked louder at his door this time.

"Come on, Ollie." A pause. "Ollie!"

She let out a sigh, the air whistling between her teeth.

Oliver wasn't the best of company, but still…breakfast alone, a swim alone. A swim would benefit him more than her. She pounded on the door, then after a moment tried the knob.

The mechanism that registered the keycard had been sprung, and the door opened.

"Ollie?"

Annja stared at the spotless, empty room.

The bed was made, as if he hadn't slept in it. No suitcase, no mussed towels in the bathroom.

Her breath hissed out. So he'd taken the red-eye back with the others. A seat must have opened up. He could have told her, though, she thought angrily.

"You should have told me," she said, shaking her head. But she knew Ollie wasn't the most considerate sort. An excellent cameraman, he was less than excellent in the social department.

"Breakfast alone, swim alone. Fine." Annja stepped back into the hall and was about to close the door when something caught her notice. She pushed the door wide and tiptoed in, nearly tripping when her flip-flops caught in the thick carpet.

There, at the foot of the bed, near the hem of the quilt, was a spot of blood.

3

It's probably nothing, Annja told herself. But the hairs on her arm prickled and indicated otherwise. She crept around Oliver's room and this time eyed everything in a more careful light.

Yes, the bed was made. But there was a crease in the middle that a good hotel maid would have smoothed flat. The chair by the lamp had been moved from its usual spot because the depressions in the carpet showed where it usually rested. The lamp shade was slightly askew, too.

Annja sniffed the air, finding only the smell of cigarettes and a touch of flowery spray that the cleaning staff no doubt used to help mask the smell of cigarettes.

She looked in the bathroom. Not a single rumpled towel, and the glasses were turned upside down on doilies, as if Ollie hadn't used them. No toothbrush by the sink, no razor, no toiletry bag. No smudges on the faucet or mirror. No heavy towel on the floor to act as a bath mat, and no spots of water anywhere that would indicate someone had used the room recently. She pushed aside the shower curtain and saw that the tub was dry. The sink basin was dry, too, evidence to her that Ollie hadn't been in here for at least a few hours.

Annja sucked in a breath and went to the closet. It was empty, too, save for a fluffy white robe, an ironing board propped up against the back wall and an iron and extra feather pillow on the top shelf. Next she checked the drawers, not sure why she was doing this, and all the while trying to tell herself that indeed Oliver had caught the red-eye.

Telling herself that the blood spot was nothing.

"Oliver's just fine," she said. Then she noticed that one of the knobs was missing from the television.

"I'm operating on too wild an imagination and too little sleep. That's all." But her words weren't working to quell her rising fears. She reached for the phone and called the front desk. "Hello. Has Oliver Vylan checked out? Room 312? No? Thanks."

She slapped the heel of her hand against her forehead. "Just call Oliver," she said. Annja knew his cell phone number by heart and quickly punched the buttons. One ring. Two. "C'mon, Oliver. Answer."

If he was on the plane, maybe he couldn't, she thought. At certain times some airlines wouldn't let you use your cell phone. They'd flown American. She'd remembered using her cell phone all the time on American flights.

Eight rings. His voice mail message came on.

"Oliver, this is Annja. Call me." She let her voice sound

urgent, so he'd return the call right away. She'd have to go up to her room and grab her cell phone in case he did call.

She depressed the switch hook and started dialing Doug Morrell. Halfway through, she stopped. The time difference, she thought. "To hell with the hours." She finished the number and let the phone ring, then left another message when an answering machine kicked in. "Doug, this is Annja. Has Oliver checked in with you? Call me, please."

The blood spot could be something.

She called the front desk again. "Hello. Would you please contact the police." Annja didn't know the Sydney equivalent of 911, or she would have handled that herself. "Send them up here as soon they arrive. And send someone from hotel security now, to Oliver Vylan's room. Yes, room 312. I believe something…bad…has happened to him." She replaced the phone in the cradle, ignoring the questions of the now nervous front-desk woman.

Had Oliver gone pub-crawling? she wondered.

He'd mentioned that possibility at dinner last night. Had he gotten himself into trouble at one of the bars? Had he come back bloodied from being on the receiving end of someone's fist? That might explain the blood spot. But it wouldn't explain his absence. While her cameraman wasn't the politest of fellows, she hadn't known him to be the type to get into a brawl, nor was he the type to drink to excess. But then how well did she know him? They'd worked together for several months, but never socialized more than sharing meals after shoots. He had family in New York, she recalled from conversations, two sisters, and he had a fiancée he mentioned often. Annja didn't want to have to call any of them to report bad news.

"Oh, think, Annja! Calm down." He could well be in the restaurant having breakfast! And the lack of suitcase and camera equipment might mean that he left them with the concierge in preparation for checking out.

There might be nothing wrong at all.

She let out a tentative sigh of relief and called the restaurant and described Oliver. "Are you sure he's not there? Check one more time, please. It's important."

She felt her chest growing tight with worry and her heart racing. She was used to danger and had come to accept being shot at and kicked, but she would never get used to people around her finding trouble. The fatigue she'd felt from lack of sleep rolled off her, and again her eyes locked on the blood spot. Her breath caught.

The maître d' came back on the line and interrupted her thoughts.

"You're certain he's not there? Yes. Thank you," Annja said dully, and hung up the phone. "Oliver, what's happened to you? What sort of trouble did you manage to find?"

She could have gone with him on the pub crawl, hadn't really needed to turn in so early to surf the archaeology Web sites. *Should* have gone with him, she admonished herself, stopped him from drinking too much, getting into a fight, getting blood on the carpet of his hotel room, from worrying her so.

She knelt at the foot of the bed, fingers hovering above the blood spot, senses registering the smell of nicotine that clung to the carpet and the quilt.

Leave the spot alone, she told herself. You've called the police. Don't interfere. Let them... She touched the edge of the spot anyway, finding it congealed but not crusty. Maybe only an hour or two old, she guessed. Maybe Oliver had been here when she knocked the first time before going to breakfast. Maybe if she'd been persistent then she would have found him safe.

"Should have tried the door then." She chewed on her lower lip. "Ollie, Ollie, what trouble did you—?" She heard the elevator open out in the hall. "Police can't have gotten here this quick," she muttered. She jumped up, thoughts brightening. Maybe it was Oliver, coming back to the room to make sure he hadn't left anything. Annja darted outside and nearly bumped into a long-nosed man with a hotel security badge on his dark blue suit coat.

"You're the one who—"

"Called the front desk? Yes, I—"

"Reported trouble with one of our guests? A Mr. Oliver Vylan from the United States?" He didn't have as pleasing an accent as the archaeologists she'd spent the past few days with. He sounded more British than Aussie, though there were similarities to both accents.

"Oliver Vylan, yes. My cameraman. He's gone missing," Annja said.

She stood there only a moment more, looking between the open hotel room door and the security man, and then she stepped around him and to the elevator and thumbed the up button.

"He's gone missing, I say again, and I'm worried," she continued. "I found a spot of blood. It's at the foot of the bed." She was certain now that some harm had come to

Oliver, and that despite her best thoughts the cameraman wasn't ready to check out and head to the airport.

"Miss..." The security man beckoned, clearly wanting more information about the situation.

"Creed. Annja Creed, room 914. I'll be right back. I have to go get my cell phone." Annja slipped into the elevator and pressed the button for the ninth floor, shifting back and forth on the balls of her feet, her flip-flops making squeaky sounds. "After I call home one more time. Try to call Ollie again." And after I worry some more, she thought. "Ollie, Ollie, Ollie, what's happened to you?"

The airport? Maybe she should call American just to make sure that he hadn't caught the red-eye flight to LaGuardia. One final time she told herself that all this worry was for nothing, and that she was wasting the hotel security man's time and soon the police's time. She prayed she was wasting everyone's time and that Oliver was all right.

But he wasn't all right, she confirmed when the elevator doors opened onto her floor and she stepped out. At the end of the hall, the door to her room was open, and a thumping, bumping, crashing sound came from within. Someone was ransacking the place.

Annja didn't panic. Danger was nothing new to her. In fact, it had been her constant companion since she inherited her sword and began her battle against whatever the forces of darkness decided to throw at her.

She reached for that sword now, touching the pommel with her mind and calling it from the ephemeral pocket of nothingness where it resided. She felt her fingers close on it, then just as quickly she dismissed it. Assess the situation first, she admonished herself. Don't let worry rule you. She sprinted down the hall, flip-flops slapping against the soles of her feet as she went. She vaguely registered a door opening behind her, and then another, heard the curious whispers of hotel guests poking their heads out.

A heartbeat more and she was in the doorway of her room, staring at three dark-clad men who were tearing her things apart.

"That's the woman," the tallest of them said. He was standing on her shattered laptop. "That's the one who was with the photographer. Kill her!"

4

Situation assessed, Annja thought. She mentally called for her sword again, in the same instant drawing it back as she leaped into the room, bringing the blade down decisively at the first man she came to, a swarthy, barrel-chested thug with deep wrinkles around his eyes. He was just beyond the doorway—the other two were farther back in the room, and he snarled at her and spit and fumbled at his back.

He was going for a gun, she knew instinctively, and she managed to turn her sword at the last second so she struck him hard in the side of the head with the flat of the blade, knocking him senseless. She would try to take them alive, at least one of them, she decided. Dead, they certainly couldn't tell her what they'd done to her cameraman…or what any of this was about.

The barrel-chested man shook his head and continued to fumble at the small of his back. She released one hand from the sword and struck his throat with her palm, watching his eyes bulge. He was the oldest and appeared the most out of shape, the least threat, she judged. She turned her attention to the other two.

The slightest was a young man standing close to the window. He'd been pulling things out of her suitcase and tossing them every which way.

What was he searching for?

He'd dropped a pair of her shoes and gaped at her when she'd entered. He said something softly in a foreign language. She didn't catch any of it, but she registered that his face was severely pockmarked, as if he'd had an illness or a bad case of acne in his youth.

The tallest, the one who had danced on her laptop, was near the desk. "Kill her!" he repeated. "Kill her!"

Clearly the leader, Annja thought.

"Are those the only words you know?" Annja instantly regretted her quip as he cursed and dug his heel into what was left of the hard drive.

The barrel-chested one, still doubled over from the second blow she'd delivered, made an attempt to regain his wind, but eased back against the wall and looked almost helplessly to the leader.

At first glance Annja had thought them all in some sort of uniform, but that wasn't the case. Each wore black pants, the tallest in tight-fitting jeans, with the other two in slacks that one might wear to an office. The tallest had on a black polo shirt, with something embroidered over the pocket. He was moving now, and so she couldn't read it because the fabric bunched. The wiry one wore a simple black T-shirt, while the wheezing man had a sport shirt with the buttons pulled tight across his middle. Two wore black leather shoes, the wiry one in a pair of new-looking gray running shoes.

All of them were slightly dark skinned, but not black or suntanned.

Not Aussies or aboriginals. Arabs? she wondered.

The barrel-chested man finally caught his breath, bolted upright and grabbed her arm, still grimacing in pain from her blows. His grip was strong and he maliciously dug in his fingers.

"She's got a sword!" he hollered.

The tall one growled as he pulled a gun from his waistband. "I think we all can see that, Zuka!"

Zuka—she had the name of one, not that the tidbit was very useful at the moment. An unusual name, though.

"What should I do, Sute?"

Two names now. Annja knew Sute was an Egyptian name, a derivative of Sutekh, the name of the evil god of chaos said to have slain Osiris.

"Surrender, all of you," Annja said, though perhaps too softly for the wiry one to hear.

"Kill her, I said! Kill her and we'll be gone from here!"

Annja's hotel room was not a small one, but it was confining to fight in, which worked to her advantage, as the men could not circle her. Zuka, the barrel-chested man, pulled her toward him, fingers digging in even harder. She didn't resist. In fact, using his momentum, she slammed herself against him, pinning him to the wall. Once more the breath was knocked from him, but he stubbornly refused to release his grip.

Better he hold on to her, she thought, as that was keeping him from drawing a gun.

She drove her heel down on his instep and jabbed her right elbow into his gut. He wasn't a soft man, she realized, just big, but neither was he well trained in physical combat. She slung him around just as the tall man fired.

The gun had a silencer, making a spitting sound followed almost instantly by the soft thud of the bullet striking Zuka, whom she'd inadvertently used as a shield. He sagged against her, and she jumped back, losing a flip-flop and bumping into the door frame.

The tall man fired again, grazing Annja's shoulder. Then she was moving, thrusting the stinging pain to the back of her mind and bringing the sword around until it was aimed at his heart.

"Thrice damn you!" he cursed. His gun jammed, and he threw it at her.

Annja sidestepped the hurled gun and adjusted the grip on her sword.

"You will join Zuka, Annja Creed. Join him in hell, as my master commands!" In a flash the man reached behind his back again, retrieving a second gun as she lunged forward, the sword's blade gleaming in the sun coming in through the window. A streak of flashing silver hit the barrel and knocked the gun away. "The pit for you, Annja Creed!"

Why? she wondered as she dropped beneath a punch aimed at her face. Why the pit for me? What have I done to you? I don't even know you. And who is your master?

Then everything seemed to speed up, and she dismissed her questions and concentrated only on the fight. The tall man backed away to buy himself a moment, kicking aside pieces of her laptop and drawing a dagger. Small, it was nonetheless deadly.

The wiry one had a gun, too, but it wasn't aimed at her. He was looking beyond Annja and to the doorway behind her, his hands shaking. She couldn't risk a glance over her shoulder, but from the sound of hushed voices she could tell that curious hotel guests had spilled out into the hall and were looking inside.

"Get out of here!" she called to them.

"The police," someone said, a young man from the tone of his voice. "Someone should call them."

"I hear sirens," another said.

"Bloke's got a gun," a third said. "And the sheila's got a sword!"

There was a scream as the wiry man started firing.

Annja spun like a top and instinctively darted close to the man called Sute, plunging her sword into his stomach before he could use the dagger. A curse died on his lips as the blade slipped from his hand.

There were more screams, and Annja pulled her sword free and whirled as the wiry man vaulted past her and across the bed, nearly tangling his feet in the covers. He was firing his gun into the crowd gathered in the hallway. The shots were wild, intended to scatter the people, she could tell. But one of the spectators outside her door had been hit and was twitching and gasping in pain and disbelief. A few people hovered over him, but the rest fled toward the elevators, shouting and screaming, their feet thundering dully against the carpeted floor.

The wiry man took advantage of the panic and rushed into the hallway, turning down the far corner, away from the panicked people and waving his gun to keep anyone from following him.

"Call an ambulance!" Annja shouted. "Someone call an ambulance!" She knew that she had to catch the wiry man to find out what happened to Ollie…and to find out why these men had attacked her. She couldn't afford to wait for the police and paramedics and risk this one getting away.

She registered everything in a single glance as she leaped over the wounded man. There were four people still outside her door, two of them kneeling by the wounded man, another standing in shock, staring at the bloody sword in her hand. The downed man had been hit high in the right side of his chest. There was a good chance he would survive if help came quickly. She could do nothing to aid him.

But if she'd reacted faster to the three men ransacking her room, killed the first outright rather than trying to subdue him, the bystander might not have been hit in the first place. Her breath caught at the thought.

She saw a police officer step out of the elevator and wedge his way through the panicked hotel guests. Shouts hinted there were more police behind him. In that instant she willed the sword away. The police didn't need to see a woman with a sword; she knew it would distract them from the true villains. Also, they would want her statement right now. Her target darted around the corner of an intersecting hallway, and from the clanking sound she could tell he'd pushed open the door to the stairwell. She churned after him, the flip-flop on her left foot slapping madly, her bare right foot striking the well-worn carpet.

She'd catch up to the young man, question him and then she'd return to her hotel room, hand him over to the police and answer their questions. If the gawkers mentioned a sword…well, there'd be no sign of such a weapon. And, as always, she'd deny using one.

She turned the corner and thrust the heel of her hand against the door. It flew open, striking the wall behind it with a resonant clang. She heard footsteps and followed him down the stairs, taking three steps at a time. Above and behind her people were shouting, one in a commanding voice that could have belonged to one of the police officers.

"Take everyone's name," she heard.

"What's this about a woman with a sword?" another asked.

"Who are these men? Seen them before?"

Then the door clanged shut and deadened everything save for the rapid click-clacking of her target's feet.

One landing later she caught sight of him. Leaning against the railing, he fired upward, the bullets ricocheting harmlessly off the bottoms of the steps above him and the wall. Then he vaulted over the railing, dropping to the next lower level, and she did the same, only a few dozen steps behind him now.

Annja was so determined to catch him that she gritted her teeth and ignored the biting pain in her shoulder and the ache of her bare foot—she was scraping it against the rough sandpaper-like metal strips that had been nailed to the steps. From somewhere above her a door clanged open, followed by curious shouts. The police or hotel security, she suspected, come to join in the chase. She ignored those noises, too, and increased her speed.

A superb athlete, Annja knew the only reason she

hadn't yet caught the young man was that he was obviously in excellent shape and he was in shoes that gave him better traction on these stairs. But she would catch him.

Just another minute, she told herself.

Annja was just beyond the landing for the fifth floor when the door clanged open directly behind her. *Police* was her first thought, but the spitting sound of a silenced gun ended that notion. She glanced over her shoulder, the gesture nearly costing her balance, as the toe of her flip-flop caught on a metal strip. She kicked off the shoe and dropped to a crouch as the gun continued to spit bullets.

Two guns, she corrected herself, as she spun to face the new adversaries. Two men had burst onto the fifth-floor landing, these also dressed in black.

The color of the day, she thought.

But these men looked a little different, with broad shoulders and thick arms, like bodybuilders or professional muscle. They conversed rapidly in a language she didn't recognize as they continued to fire. Annja somersaulted down to the fourth-floor landing, then rounded the stairwell and headed for the third floor.

The wiry man stood down there, blocking her way and holding his gun out, both hands clamped so tight his knuckles looked pale. His fingers trembled, and sweat beaded heavily on his face.

"Stop!" he commanded.

"Why? So I'll be an easier target?" Annja flattened herself against the outer stairwell wall as he squeezed the trigger. The staccato shots were loud. More spitting came from the two silenced guns above her, bullets striking the concrete wall just above her head.

She willed the sword to her, the mental gesture coming easily. The hilt fit into her grip as if it were an extension of her arm. Her fingers held it tight as she pushed off from the step, body arcing down as if she was diving off the side of a pool. She tucked herself into a ball and rolled, straightening her legs when they pointed down to the third-floor landing and feeling the impact of the wiry man's face against the balls of her feet. His cheekbones cracked from the impact.

Annja dissected the sounds—the man's painful gasp, his gun clattering to the floor, his body following it with a dull thud, more gunfire from above, bullets striking the concrete, several bullets striking the torso of the wiry man, from whom she just pushed herself off. She continued down the next flight of stairs, registering that the third floor was where Oliver had stayed.

The two men raced behind her, chattering in a foreign language. Annja was fluent in many languages—French, Spanish, Portuguese, Italian, Romanian—and she had some command of Russian. What the men spoke wasn't any of them. She couldn't understand a single word, save the few English terms sprinkled in—*American, photographer,* and *Creed.*

This had to have something to do with the dig, but what? And what about the other members of her crew who had left on the red-eye? Had they truly left? Or had these men gotten to them?

No, they were safe, she told herself. She would've heard something at breakfast about shootings or kidnappings, or would've picked up on trouble at the hotel. No, these men hadn't gotten to the hotel in time to stop the rest of her crew. Just in time to stop Oliver. And now they were trying to stop her.

More doors clanged opened and closed from floors above, and more shouts followed. Two guns discharged, these without silencers. The police, Annja was certain, hoping they would nail one of the men pursuing her.

But only shoot one, she prayed; she wanted one alive to question.

Halfway down to the first floor, she stopped and whirled as more gunfire erupted. It was followed by the sound of a body tumbling down the stairs. A heartbeat later, only one dark-clad man appeared on the steps above her, one hand on the railing to balance himself, the other holding a gun—a Glock 17. Odd that something like that would register, Annja thought, given the dire situation.

She feinted to her right, toward the outer wall of the stairwell, then dipped and pivoted to her left. He fired at where'd she'd stood a breath before. Pushing off the step, she flew up at him, executing a hammering block when his leg came out to defend himself.

"What is this about?" she shouted. "What have you done with Oliver?"

He grunted and tried to draw a bead on her, shooting the railing instead. Only one step below him now, she grabbed his raised leg and tugged, setting him off balance. Agile, he didn't fall. He swept the gun at her, the barrel striking her face. He brought it back for a second strike and pulled the trigger in the same motion. Annja reacted with an inward parry, a *kenpo* blocking method.

One hand wrapped around the hilt of her sword, she opened her other hand and redirected his next blow by riding with the force of his swing. He hadn't anticipated that and scrambled to maintain his hold on the gun.

"Kiai!" Annja shouted, as she used her diaphragm to purge the air from her body. The *kenpo* technique fortified her body and clearly shook the man. She rammed the heel of her hand into his stomach and felt his breath rush out. "I don't want to kill you," she said to herself as much as to him. "Though that's clearly what you intend for me."

But why do you want to kill me?

"There's one more shooter down there!" This came from well above her. "Call it in that one's dead."

Annja had to finish this quickly. Having the police here was all well and good, she thought, but they would tangle her up for hours in questioning. She needed to call Doug, alert the crew who took the red-eye that they might be in danger for God knows what reason and try to call Ollie again. She desperately wanted to sort all this out before letting the authorities commandeer her time.

"Kiai!" she repeated, following it this time with a swipe of her sword. The blade sheered into the man's fingers, forcing him to release the gun.

He grabbed his injured hand with his good one and stared at her, his eyes angry daggers.

"Gahba!" he spat at her. *"Kelbeh!"*

"No doubt you're calling me something terrible," she said.

"Khanzeera al matina!" Clearly in pain, the man nonetheless refused to quit. He lashed out with one leg, and then the other, clipping Annja once but causing her no real harm.

She had been a superb athlete before acquiring the sword. She'd since become even better, drawing on its power and honing her skills to an almost unbelievable level. That she'd lived through all this so far—and so much more in other countries before this—was a testament to her training and determination.

"I…said…I…don't…want…to…kill…you!" The words steamed out as if she were a kettle left too long on the stove. "But you're not going to be able to answer my questions, are you? Know any English?"

The police nearing, she again dismissed the sword, in the same motion reaching up and grabbing her attacker's shirt, pulling him toward her and finally setting him off balance.

She lifted him and spun him so he was on the step below her now. Then she pushed him and rode him down the rest of the steps like a bobsled, the back of his head cracking hard and making her wince. For a moment, she feared she might have indeed killed him, but he spit at her and feebly tried to knock her off him.

She jammed her knee into his stomach.

"Where is Oliver? What have you done with him?"

"He saw! You saw!" the man cried, finally speaking so she could understand him. She shook him, and his head rolled to the side.

"Saw what? What did we see?"

"I see them!" Again this came from above. "The woman and a man. The man might be dead. She's throttling him!"

"He's not dead." Annja groaned and pushed herself off him and jumped down the last few steps and out the exit door, the footsteps of the police clacking behind her. A heartbeat later she was in the lobby. A heartbeat more and she was through the revolving doors and onto the sidewalk, sucking in the cool fall air.

I should stop and talk to the police right now, she thought. Clear this up, tell them about Oliver. She couldn't get any more out of her attacker until he came to, and that would be under police guard in a local hospital—and that would be provided he could speak enough English to make sense. The police would take her in, too, as she was disheveled and bloodied, and no doubt they'd connect her to the reports of a woman in jeans and a bikini top swinging a sword. She'd work through it all; she had before. She'd done nothing wrong.

But it would take time.

Maybe the police would let her call her producer first, or try Oliver again.

Not likely.

But necessary, she decided as she ran, her bare feet striking the cool concrete and sending needles of pain into her because she'd scraped them raw against those metal strips. She had to tell Doug about the attack and ask him to check on the rest of the crew. He needs to know what's going on. I need to figure out what's going on.

What had she and Ollie seen?

I need to think! Leaving the scene of the crime wasn't a good thing, she knew, but she needed space.

Annja spied a pay phone on the street corner. She sped toward it. Just past the hotel parking lot, it cast a shadow on the sidewalk that looked like the pendulum of a clock. She hoped she had enough coins to make it work.

The breeze was cool and tugged the bad scents from

her as she ran, the smoke from Oliver's hotel room, the cordite from the gunshots, the blood. The breeze carried the smell of car and bus exhaust and of redfish that was grilling in a restaurant nearby.

People on the sidewalk called out to her, most in concern, seeing blood run from her shoulder and from her face where the gun had struck her. But some called to the police, as much as telling her that at least one officer had come out of the hotel in search of her or anyone else involved in the mayhem.

"One phone call," she said to herself. "Just one and then I'm yours until this is all resolved."

Her hand closed on the receiver and she lifted it, reached for her wallet and cursed. The phone cord had been cut. Sydney had its vandals just like anywhere else. She dropped the receiver and whirled, expecting to see a police officer jogging up to her, but instead spying another dark-clad man cutting through the pedestrians.

He drew a gun, and the passersby screamed and parted, giving him a clear shot at Annja.

"How many of you?" she hollered as she dropped into a catlike pose. She mentally reached for her sword, but stopped herself. Too many spectators, and in broad daylight she couldn't risk it. Her life was one big secret, and it didn't need to be exposed on a sidewalk in downtown Sydney. "Just how blasted many of you are after me?"

A bullet whispered through the air from behind her, striking the side of the pay phone and letting her know another assailant was near. She sprung up, past the phone and off the sidewalk, over the curb and onto the street, where a bus was just pulling away.

The driver was closing the doors in a panic, not wanting his passengers endangered. She managed to squeeze on.

"A brass button," he told her, oblivious to the fact that she'd been the target of the shooters. The door hissed closed behind her.

"We're being shot at! Just get this bus moving for the love of God!" she shouted.

The bus lurched out into traffic as the wail of a multitude of sirens cut through the air.

She found a small coin in her wallet, tugged it out, held it up and then dropped it in the slot. The Australian dollar was about the size of a U.S. dime, but thicker, nicknamed a brass button.

"Here? Happy?" She mentally rebuked herself for being snide to the man.

"You're hurt, miss?" The driver noted the blood, but didn't keep his eyes on her; he was intent on speeding away from the scene.

"I'm fine. Really." Annja threaded her way down the center of the bus to the back, sagging into an empty seat and avoiding the curious stares of the dozen passengers.

"Pig's arse!" said an elderly woman who peered over the back of her seat to ogle Annja.

"You're bleedin'," another passenger pointed out. "And you're in your underwear."

"It's a bikini top," Annja fumed.

"Pig's you're fine," the elderly woman persisted.

Annja closed her eyes and pictured Oliver. "I'll wager I'm in better shape than my cameraman," she said.

5

Annja heard the sirens' wail subside as the bus moved farther from her hotel. She sensed the other passengers staring at her. She knew she certainly must be something to look at—a fright in jeans, a bikini top, blood spatters everywhere and filthy bare feet. She tucked her feet up under her and felt the bottoms with her fingers. The skin was practically shredded on the heels.

Shoes, she needed shoes and socks, she thought, a long-sleeved shirt and maybe a sweater. And her cell phone—any phone—so she could call Doug and try Oliver again. She needed to call the police, too.

She needed to think.

Annja let the bus rock her, hoping it would relax her, but instead she felt more anxious. In her mind's eye she saw Oliver's empty room and the spot of blood. She saw the faces of the men who'd attacked her, their hard, cold eyes, and then the lifeless bodies of the ones she'd killed.

The tall one called Sute loomed large in her memory. Something about him bothered her—beyond her killing him. She didn't regret what she'd done. She'd had no choice. Sadly, killing had become somewhat common-place in her life. At least she hadn't become so inured to it that she didn't feel anything. She felt sorry for the dead men's families. And she was sorry she had not been able to capture one and ask him questions.

She focused on the sounds around her and tried to clear her mind. The spot of blood faded, and instead she called up the image of Hathor on the piece of pottery Wes Michaels had passed to her. Smooth and warm, she re-membered the shard feeling, somehow, comforting.

The sirens had receded completely now.

She heard someone on the street hollering for a cab, heard a vendor calling to passersby, "Avos! Ripe avos here." A car horn was honking, music spilling out a window. The roar of a piece of construction equipment was the loudest; on the shuttle to the hotel a few days ago she'd noted a parking garage going up and an old furni-ture store being torn down. They must be passing that spot, she thought.

A few moments later the bus slowed, then squeaked and belched exhaust before shuddering to a stop. She could tell they were at a traffic light from the clacking of heels and chattering of all the people crossing the street.

The smells of the city intensified. From herself, the scents of blood and sweat hung heavy in her nostrils. There were warring perfumes from the women in the seats ahead of her. Added to that were the acrid aromas of the bus's fumes and those from other cars, and the general miasma of any big city's pollution. She thought she might have picked up a tinge of salt from the ocean, as Sydney was on the coast, but she suspected that was her imagination.

What have I done? Leaving a crime scene? she wondered. She respected the authorities, had certainly dealt with them in many foreign countries, and if she'd stayed in the hotel she wouldn't have encountered the two thugs on the sidewalk. Seven in total, all dressed in black, all foreign and all wanting to kill her.

Again she saw the face of the tall one.

They probably killed Oliver because of whatever he'd seen. And they'd dumped his body somewhere.

"And they think I saw it, too," she whispered. "Saw what he did. But just what did we see?"

She dismissed the etched image of the goddess Hathor and her missing arm where the shard was broken, and Annja tried to replay the past several days in her mind, focusing on what Wes Michaels had uncovered at the dig.

There was nothing extraordinarily valuable, she thought, although extraordinary in the fact there were Egyptian relics on Australian soil. Nothing on the scale of Nefertiti's resting place, she thought, or King Tut's tomb.

Nothing worth killing over, certainly.

"I'm missing something," she mused. "Something important, obviously. What did I see?"

One of the bus's rear wheels hit a pothole and bounced her harshly against the seat.

"Got a bingle over there!" This came from the elderly woman two seats ahead.

Annja opened her eyes just as the bus found another pothole, this one even deeper. Her teeth clacked together, and she managed to bite both the inside of her cheek and her tongue.

Something else to add to the list of aches, she thought.

"Yep, it's a big bingle, all right!" This came from another passenger, a middle-aged man who got up out of his seat and pressed his face to the window for a better look. "Someone's goin' to the hospital, I'll bet."

"A bingle?" Annja asked.

"An accident." A young woman with a streak of pink in a shock of otherwise jet-black hair had sidled back to sit across the aisle from Annja. She was dressed in tight green leather pants and a purple shirt that was a little too short for her long arms, and red tennis shoes without laces—everything clashing. She pointed out the window at a late-model station wagon that had plowed into the back of something that looked like a Mini Cooper. "Probably some tourist not used to driving on the left. Both cars are cactus."

Cactus? Dead, Annja guessed. The bus had slowed, no doubt so the driver could get a good look, too. Steam was pouring out of the station wagon, the hood crumpled and the left front tire caved under, and the driver of what was left of the little car held his head in his hands. There was a man in black on the corner, staring at the bus.

One of the men who'd chased her? One of their associates? Or was it her imagination taking a vivid turn?

Annja turned so she could get a better look at him. No, he didn't look anything like the others. Blond hair and a pale complexion, listening to something on an iPod, nothing to worry over, she told herself. She let out a sigh of relief, and then froze. Running along the sidewalk and pushing his way through the people watching the bingle, was a swarthy-looking man dressed in black. She made a move to rise, intending to jump off the bus and confront him. But the bus wheezed away into traffic, and she lost sight of him.

A loud cough startled her. "I said, you're a tourist, too, ain'tcha?" the woman with the pink streak asked.

"Yes." Annja gave a slight smile and nodded. The gesture hurt; her face was sore from where the gun had struck her, and a headache was starting to crescendo behind her eyes. She wanted to get a look in the mirror to assess the damage, especially to check out her shoulder wound. Her skin felt tight and warm there. Again she cursed herself for bolting instead of speaking with the police and getting a little medical attention.

"Get in a fight?" Pink Streak persisted. "A car accident?"

No, I always look like this, Annja mentally retorted. "Some men chased me."

"Oh! Yeah, I saw." She popped a stick of gum in her mouth and started chewing noisily, grabbing the seat back when the bus lurched around a corner a little too sharply.

Annja had no trouble balancing herself.

"Guy on the sidewalk, shooting at you. I saw him just before the bus left the stop. All *Die Hard* and *Lethal Weapon* like. Wow, you know. None of my bizzo, really, but why was he after you? I mean, you look pretty spunk and all. Was he wanting to have a go at you? Did you pinch something of his?"

Annja shook her head. "I didn't steal anything. And I don't know why they were after me," she said honestly.

"Yeah, you don't look like the pinching type. Where you from?" Pink Streak was looking Annja up and down more closely. "You look familiar."

"New York." Again Annja was honest.

"Never been there." Pink Streak smacked her gum, made a face at the old woman two seats up, said, "Mind your bizzo," then slapped her palm against her leg. "TV. That's it. I've seen you on TV."

Annja inwardly groaned. She'd not expected the punk girl to have watched something like *Chasing History's Monsters*.

"A model, I bet, a tall poppy, you! Got the body for it, you have, and…"

Annja opened her mouth to reply, but the hiss of the bus drowned her out. It eased to the curb and the doors opened.

"Darlinghurst!" the driver called out.

Annja got up and hurried down the aisle.

"Watch yourself!" Pink Streak called after her. "Keep to Potts Point!"

Potts Point? Annja had no idea what that was, or where. However, within a heartbeat she did know where she stood.

Kings Cross. Annja realized it the moment she stepped onto the sidewalk and looked down the street. She'd grabbed a stack of pamphlets the first morning she ate breakfast in the hotel restaurant—something to look at while she waited for her food. The first pamphlet she'd skimmed was about Kings Cross. She recognized some of the buildings pictured in the advertisement. The waiter told her the Cross was painted by the Australian media as the drug and red light district of the entire continent, but that it had cleaned up its image in the past two decades. The waiter also said it was a must-see spot, one of the most densely populated areas on the continent, and was admittedly a bit of a tourist trap.

It certainly was colorful. Even on this sunny day, neon lights glowed bright and hung from practically every building. Convenience Store, one read, 24 Hours. Annja noted there were a lot of 24 Hours signs. Many of the businesses on both sides of the tree-lined street—and along the street behind her, she noted with a glance over her shoulder—were a mix of adult bookshops, dingy-looking nightclubs, seedy bars, burlesque shows and strip clubs. There were some trendy cafés and respectable-looking shops here and there, but the neon of their bawdy neighbors clashed with their sedate exteriors.

Adult Gifts, one neon sign advertised. Live Nude Dancers, another read.

"Like anyone would want to see dead nude dancers," Annja muttered.

The ground floor of the buildings mostly looked the same—dark, shadowed by awnings and overhangs, lit at the edges by the neon. The second and third levels were glossy black stone sitting next to bricks painted white and pink that stood out across from fronts festooned in pale yellow, beige, orchid and a surprisingly subdued orange. Apartments, Annja guessed, or maybe offices for the places below. Window boxes were filled with flowers that were holding on in the still reasonable weather. Iron grates covered up some of the widows, looking artful while being protective.

She spied a sign that read Backpackers Welcome, hanging lopsidedly over a weathered wooden door. On a storefront window next to it flyers were taped announcing AIDS testing, health clinics and a place where intravenous drug users could inject themselves under supervision.

The sidewalks were filled with people. Many were tourists; she could tell by their attire and the way they gaped openmouthed at some of the establishments. Some were regulars to the businesses, she noted, because of their obvious familiarity with the neighborhood. A drunk leaned against a sex-toy shop window a few businesses down; he stared at Annja and smiled, showing a smattering of yellowed teeth. At the next shop two heavily made-up girls in skimpy skirts and high boots chatted with a pair of well-dressed businessmen.

She spied a heavily tattooed man. A purple-and-green serpent twisting down his arm and wrapping around his wrist was the mildest of the images. A gaunt-looking fellow in black leather, skin pulled so tight across his face his head looked skeletal, stopped to talk to the tattooed man and passed him a small white envelope.

"Satan made Sydney," Annja whispered. Mark Twain was sometimes credited with saying that after he took a world tour in 1895 and passed through Australia. Annja had read plenty of Twain and knew the quote was wrongly attributed. "But Satan might have had a hand in crafting Kings Cross," she said to herself.

Annja shivered. Her feet were sore. She looked down to see that the sidewalk was made of a patchwork of maroon bricks, grime and discarded cigarette butts looking to be the mortar. She wrapped her arms around herself and looked for a pay phone. One more attempt to call Oliver and Doug. Then she'd make a call to the police and come up with a reason why she'd run from the hotel. The police had to know who she was, from the tag on her luggage or from checking with the hotel.

The convenience store first, and then she'd make some calls, she decided, starting across the walk when the signal changed. In the block running east she saw that no cars were allowed on the street, that it was limited to pedestrian and bicycle traffic. A frumpy-looking woman on a ten-speed stopped and stared. Annja would not have been out of place, given the wild assortment of people and their dress in this neighborhood, but the blood spatters and bare feet were raising eyebrows.

No Shirt, No Shoes, No Service, the sign on the convenience store said. Annja ignored it and went inside, tugging down her jeans so they hid the tops of her feet. A banner at the back said Chemist, so she headed for it. She knew it meant the equivalent of a pharmacist, and the things she needed would be there. She spied an aisle with ribbons and hair ties, and went down it, finding a bin with fuzzy socks at the end. She rooted through it and selected a purple pair that looked the least fuzzy, then bought gauze, alcohol, first-aid tape and a pair of scissors.

She ignored the clerk's concerned expression, took her purchases outside and darted through the doorway of a tiny Japanese restaurant.

The restroom was the dirtiest she'd seen in some time, and Annja couldn't help but wrinkle her nose at the myriad disagreeable smells. The air was at the same time thick and close, and she sat on the back of the toilet and put her feet on the seat as she cleaned them with the alcohol.

"Wow, that hurts," she whispered. "What a horrible day this has been."

Day? She suspected not much more than an hour had passed since she'd found Oliver's room empty.

She worked quickly, wanting to get out of there and get to the task of solving this wretched mystery. Her feet bandaged, she slipped the socks over them, then went to the sink. The mirror was chipped and filmy, and Annja was thankful for that, as it helped to mask her appearance. She thoroughly cleaned her shoulder where the bullet had grazed it.

"Thank God he wasn't a better shot." The wound was superficial, but it had bled enough to make a good bit of her bikini top pink.

After scrubbing the dirt off the little piece of soap she found, she washed the blood off her arm and tried to get some of it out of her top, and then she dried off with some paper towels and smoothed her hair behind her ears. She splashed her face and gingerly touched her scraped cheek. It would be bruising soon.

Annja stared at her hazy reflection. Her eyes, amber-green, showed neither anger nor sadness. But when she blinked and moistened them they showed that she was suddenly deep in thought. A few moments more and she tossed the paper towels onto the top of the overflowing trashcan and left the restroom, pausing at the take-out counter to order a small coffee and swallow it down.

She was so very tired and hoped the caffeine would at least give her a psychological boost.

Out on the street again, she stopped in a boutique that accepted American credit cards and bought the only pair of shoes that fit—baby-blue leather sneakers with silver laces—and a long-sleeved silky beige shirt with an aboriginal design of a kangaroo splayed across the front.

Feeling better than she had since breakfast, she headed toward a pay phone on the far corner of the block. It was near the famous El Alamein Fountain, a huge globelike water display that she would have considered pretty were her circumstances different.

Annja hadn't taken more than a dozen steps when a man with a hand like a ham grabbed her arm and pulled her into a shadowed doorway.

6

Jon looked as if he wasn't quite old enough to drive, but he was a second-year graduate student in anthropology with an emphasis in archaeology. His round baby face and mass of curly red hair hid some of his years, as did the fact he'd made no attempt to move out of his parents' house and didn't care that all his friends knew it. He sat cross-legged on a small rug he'd brought with him—a futile effort to keep the dirt off his pants—and he stared at a slab of stone he'd just brushed off.

The first image in the upper left corner was of a cane crooked to the right, with a tilted square sitting halfway up from its base. Next to it were four circles stacked on top of each other, like a snowman without features, and a legless creature that looked like a cross between a walrus and a dog. There was also a setting sun, a cow-headed man holding an ankh, a three-legged owl, parallel wavy lines, stiff-looking birds, a narrow pyramid and a heavily lashed eye. The symbols were at the same time crude and elegant, and he tentatively touched the walrus-dog.

"Amazing," he breathed. "Thousands of years old. This is just glorious."

The images had been weathered by the salty sea air and the dirt that had shifted above them for centuries. Still, there wasn't a single figure that couldn't be made out. Translating them was another matter.

"Hey, Jon-Jon. No one at the uni could make much of that last piece you dug up." This came from Cindy, a class-mate whose sun-leathered face made her look quite a bit older than her twenty-four years. She leaned over Jon's back to get a better look at the slab, hands on his shoulders and breasts grazing the top of his head. Unlike Jon, she'd made no attempt to keep the dirt off her clothes, which had been eggshell-white when she started the day's work.

"None of the profs at the uni could figure out any story from it," she continued. "But they were using newer translation texts." She pushed off Jon and came around to squat in front of him, the slab between them.

Despite the cooling weather, she'd worn shorts. Jon stared at her knees.

"Doc figured it out, though," Cindy said. "The only prof who could. He showed me his notes this morning. They're on the clipboard over by the cooler if you want to take a look."

Jon dropped his gaze to the slab. "I want to finish here first."

The wind gusted and Cindy made a *brrring* sound. Jon looked at her knees again and noted the goose bumps.

"I'll tell you what his notes say, then." She let a pause settle between them, to let Jon know that what she was about to say was important. "Doc used the old translation guides on the slabs, says they talk about an expedition looking for yellow metal. That would be gold. Says they were also looking for a new world to explore. Says an oracle of Hathor directed them to come this way. Who cares about an oracle's vision. Think about it…gold!"

Jon looked her in the face now. Cindy was pretty, definitely, and with plenty of curves. But there were creases around her eyes and at the corners of her lips…too much time spent suntanning, and the pale blond color she chose to dye her hair was unflattering and brittle looking.

"Yeah, gold," he said. "I know. The Egyptians used gold on some of their sarcophaguses."

She licked her lips. "So anyway, Doc says your slab goes on to say that while the Egyptians were exploring around here, their leader was bitten by a poisonous snake and died. Prof thinks maybe there's a tomb around here somewhere, and that maybe it's on this side of the ridge. Maybe somewhere down through the crevice."

"So it'd be our find," Jon said, suddenly very interested. "The uni's, I mean. Not Dr. Michaels and his team over yonder." He scratched at his skin. "It'd be a kick if the uni found a tomb, while Dr. Michaels and his so-called professional team picked the wrong spot to dig."

She smiled, the invisible braces on her teeth showing. "Doc wants us to keep quiet about it. Not to traipse over the hill and breathe a word to Dr. Michaels. Not to—"

"I could write my thesis on—"

Cindy made a growling sound. "I don't care who gets

credit for what, Jon, or if the uni makes headlines. I don't give a rat's ass about your thesis."

Jon cocked his head.

"Don't you get it?" She dropped her voice to a conspiratorial whisper. "Gold. If the Egyptians were looking for gold…and found it…well, it's probably buried in the tomb."

Jon groaned. Just when it looked as if Cindy was taking archaeology seriously her magpie complex kicked in.

"Gold, treasure. Maybe some pretty little pieces don't have to be cataloged. Know what I mean? Maybe I might just get compensated, and then some, for all the clothes and shoes I've ruined on this blasted project. 'Sides, we both know I'm not going to get an A out of this. I'll be lucky if I pass. I figure I might as well get something." *Like gold*, she mouthed.

Jon watched her sashay away, hips swinging more than they needed to. He groaned again. How did she ever make it this far at the university? There were twelve graduate students assigned to this dig. Next semester it would be a different twelve. A part of him hoped it would be next semester's batch that uncovered the tomb; he didn't want to deal with Cindy's sticky fingers.

"I should report you," Jon muttered. "I should tell." But that would be juvenile, he decided. He returned his attention to the slab, then pulled a notebook out of his pocket and fluttered the pages to knock the dirt out. He thumbed through his scrawl about this particular site.

Originally it had been heavily overgrown with vegetation and rock. The soil line had been higher. It was considered a tertiary site, compared to the larger site Dr.

Michaels's professional crew was digging just over the rise. There'd been previous excavation attempts at the very spot where Jon sat, but nothing much had come of it—not even when a philanthropist had brought in expensive laser scanning equipment. That was why the university in Sydney had been given the go-ahead to send their graduate students to this place. There were some interesting pieces, but nothing spectacular was expected to be found. It was just a place to train would-be archaeologists.

To Jon's knowledge, this was the first time the university had been involved in something considered a fringe project. Even some of the professors scoffed at the notion of Egyptians on Australian soil. But Jon knew it was more than likely Egyptians actually had come here—beyond the evidence that was directly in front of him.

Australia appeared on a Greek map dated earlier than 200 years B.C., and Sumerian and Mayan writings referenced a lost land in the Pacific. Then, more than twenty years ago archaeologists in Fayum, Egypt, discovered fossils of kangaroos. And eighty years ago things looking suspiciously like boomerangs were found in Tutankhamen's tomb.

So ancient peoples from far away, worlds away, knew about Australia, and in Jon's view certainly *had* been here…even before the aborigines.

Especially the Egyptians.

"Fringe nothing," Jon grumbled. "This is all fair dinkum. And screw the gold. Hello award-winning thesis and a free ride in some doctorate program." Maybe Dr. Michaels across the ridge would beg him to join that team. "Indiana Jones, eat your ever loving heart out."

A "harrumph" startled Jon and made him bolt upright to his feet.

"Doc, sorry. Didn't hear you."

Jon knew their project head detested the Indiana Jones films.

"Cindy said she told you about my translations."

"Um, yeah." Jon was always nervous around instructors.

"Walk with me," the professor said.

"Sure."

Doc was a small man, at little more than five feet and slender. Most of the students dwarfed him. He was a tidy man, somehow staying clean despite sifting and digging alongside his charges. Jon admired him because Doc didn't ask the students to do anything he wouldn't do himself.

He was always in a broad-brimmed hat to shield his face from the sun. He had several in his jeep, and was wearing an olive-green one today with a tie that disappeared into his thick black beard. Jon guessed that Doc dyed the beard since the short and always neatly combed hair on his head was a mix of gray and black.

Doc rubbed his hands together as they walked and pursed his lips in a pensive expression. He mumbled about seeking more funding from the university, perhaps in the form of grants; the words were meant for himself, and Jon politely pretended not to listen.

Their course took them past the students around the sifting table and beyond the tents where they passed the nights. They came to a rock cleft, where a piece of split sandstone had formed a crevice. Spikes held a rope ladder that led down into it. The crevice couldn't be seen from a distance. Because of the sandstone and the shadows that extended from the ridge, you almost had to be on top of it to notice.

Jon hoped he was being given permission to climb down. Doc was careful about the university's liability, and only allowed students down there under careful supervision. There were more hieroglyphics down there. A lot more.

"Tomorrow," Doc told him. "You and I and Cindy…"

Jon made a face.

"You and I and Matthew will go down and take many more photographs, bring some things up. There's important work to do."

"We could go down now." Jon couldn't keep the excitement out of his voice.

"Tomorrow, when we've a full day of it." Doc's voice was kind but stern. "I've got some lights coming in the morning that will make it much easier to see. I need the light to better translate."

Jon anxiously shifted back and forth on the balls of his feet. "I just knew you'd be able to translate that first tablet. And the one I'm still cleaning. You'll read that one, too."

Doc nodded. "These hieroglyphics," he began. He tipped his head up and inhaled the cool fall air, and his gaze followed a noisy flock of birds heading west, farther into the forest preserve. "They are very ancient, archaic, from the early dynasties. Most Egyptologists would not be able to translate them, Jon. They're all schooled to read what's called Middle Egyptian. Very few—myself one of them—can read the formative styles."

"Because these hieroglyphics look a little like Phoenician and Sumerian," Jon supplied, puffing out his chest a little.

Doc nodded. "And that's one of the reasons not everyone thinks these hieroglyphics are Egyptian."

"So much the fools, them," Jon said.

"Fools indeed," Doc agreed.

"Think I'm gonna dux this class, Doc?" Jon cringed, realizing he shouldn't be asking something like this so soon in the session.

Doc crossed his arms and placed his hands on his elbows. He didn't answer.

"Presumptuous of me, huh?" Jon rocked back on his heels and shook his head. "Sorry."

"You'll *dux* this class," Doc said after a moment. "We both know you're my best student."

Jon's eyes gleamed and he opened his mouth to say something else, but stopped when he heard a muffled chirping sound. Doc disentangled his arms and reached into the deep pocket of his jacket. He retrieved a satellite phone and thumbed a button.

"If you'll excuse me, Jon." Doc continued walking.

I'm gonna ace this, Jon thought. He happily headed back to clean his slab.

DOC WAITED until he was well out of earshot of any of the students, then he held the phone to his ear.

"This must be important." He paused and swallowed hard. "Had better be important to bother me here while I am with the students." He cocked his head and listened intently. Then he dropped his voice. "Annja Creed? The American? You have her, yes?"

He scowled, all the lines of his face drawing together so that his expression looked pinched and pained.

The voice on the other end came through. "She escaped us, but we killed her cameraman. He put up little fight, and no one will find his body."

"Go on," Doc said.

"We have his cameras and his computer. They're on the way to your office now."

The lines on his face deepened.

"I put them in a packing crate, just as you told me, labeled it so anyone looking will think it's filled with books."

"What else?"

"The rest of the television people, they left before we got to the hotel."

Doc clicked his tongue against his teeth, waiting for the speaker to finish.

"Likely they are of no consequence. It was the cameraman and Annja Creed. They're the only ones who saw."

"And you let her get away."

A hiss of static came across the phone.

"Yes, she got away. Sir…Master. She had a sword. She killed Zuka and Sute and—"

"Where is Annja Creed now?"

There was another hiss of static.

"Where, I say?"

"Master, she got on a bus. I could not read the words. I do not know its destination. The police came to the hotel, and we had to leave. We could not take the bodies with us, Zuka and Sute and…"

Doc held the phone away from him and stared at it, the shadow cast by the big brim of his hat obscuring the buttons. Finally, he brought it back to his ear.

"I suggest you find her or you may also be among the

casualties." He ended the connection and replaced the phone in his pocket, stood quietly and stared at the rise that separated the two digs. After several minutes he turned and retraced his steps, stopping at the slab Jon still busily and carefully cleaned.

"You can translate this, right?" Jon didn't look up; he fixed his gaze on Doc's shoes.

"Of course," Doc returned. "Let me read it to you."

7

"American, yes?" The man who'd tugged Annja into the doorway released her and beamed, revealing a large gold tooth amid a mouthful of polished white ones.

She'd nearly struck him, her reflexes were that honed and she'd become so used to being threatened. But she'd caught herself and relaxed her hands. She stepped back, ready to offer a verbal jab instead.

He was too quick for her and continued, "A lovely day this is, American lady. A tourist, I can tell. I know tourists." He smiled even broader. "I like tourists!"

His eyes twinkled merrily, somehow putting her at ease. He was overdressed in a purple tuxedo so dark in the shadows it looked black, with lavender satin piping up the legs and an emerald-green cummerbund that bulged slightly with his paunch. He had makeup on; his long, narrow face was paler than his neck and hands, a little rouge was visible on his cheeks and he batted eyelashes that had to be false, judging by their exaggerated length and curl. Annja thought he looked like a circus clown going to some formal affair.

"How do you know I'm American?" Annja had intended to ask why he'd rudely tugged her off the sidewalk, but the other question came out first.

"I'm not your average Cross *spruiker,* you know! I've got keen eyes. I can tell Americans." He clapped his hands. "Besides, you don't have the look of a local, or a pommy. English," he translated for her benefit. "You don't have your chin tipped up to catch the better air, and you don't have that English swagger, if you know what I mean." He paused. "And you're walking alone. Americans don't seem to require company in the Cross. Brave and curious, the lot of you are."

She raised an eyebrow, a little taken aback by the odd-looking fellow, but deciding he posed no threat.

"And since you're curious, and obviously a tourist, you simply must come in and see the show." He waved with a flourish to the door behind him. "What say you, mate?"

She shook her head. "I have to make a phone call."

"There's a phone in the lobby." He pointed to the sign above the door. The Purple Pussycat.

She caught a whiff of him, a cologne that was musky and flowery and would have been overpowering were she not outside on the sidewalk where the scents from the Japanese restaurant next door intruded. Her feet ached, and the headache that had started on the bus was getting worse.

She could sit for a few moments, inside this place, collect her thoughts and then call Doug and the police on the pay phone he mentioned. She wanted to rest her feet briefly.

"A spectacular show we have this late morning," he persisted. "And it's just about to start. You wouldn't want to miss the opening number."

Annja had a sense that he used the same spiel on anyone who came close enough for him to grab.

"Old Broadway show tunes, like you've never heard them before. Better than Broadway, because they're Australian."

"How much?" she asked.

"For you, dear lady, only eight dollars."

"And for everyone else?" She offered him a weak smile.

"Eight dollars." This time he bowed as he gestured grandly to the door, the color of which nearly matched his tuxedo.

Just a few minutes, she told herself, to rest my feet and to think. God, but I need to think. And thinking wasn't happening out here on the sidewalk, and hadn't been possible on the bus.

He opened the door, and she went inside, instantly assaulted by more smells—incense, perfume, fried potatoes, popcorn, something terribly sugary. They all warred for her attention. She went to the counter. It was stainless steel and glass, reminiscent of one from an old movie theater she'd attended once in a while near the orphanage in New Orleans where she grew up.

An elderly woman with a heart-shaped face and a tired expression emerged from behind the popcorn machine.

"G'day!"

Annja took in the rest of the lobby, hoping to find a

bench to sit on, and seeing nothing but movie-style posters of women in flouncy gowns. She spied the pay phone, an old thing…or perhaps it was made to look old. The place definitely had a retro ambience, as if she'd stepped back into 1940 or 1950.

"One ticket?" The woman's voice was high and soft, sounding like crystal wind chimes. "Eight dollars. Show's about to start. You'd best hurry to get a good seat."

Annja retrieved a five-dollar bill and three one-dollar coins out of her wallet, pausing to look at the face on the bill before she passed it over. Australian money was much more colorful than American, and the bills had a parchment feel to them.

"Popcorn?" the woman asked.

Annja shook her head.

"Iced coffee? Soda? Perhaps—"

"No, thank you." Annja headed toward a heavy curtain, above which a sign said Auditorium. She'd collect her thoughts for a few minutes. Rest her feet. Try to lessen the pounding in her head. Then she'd come back out to make the calls.

She looked at the time before going inside. On the wall behind the concession counter was a large purple cat with a twitching tail, its belly the clock. Less than an hour had passed since the men had tried to kill her at the hotel.

She pushed aside the curtain and let the darkness swallow her.

It took a few moments for her eyes to adjust. She stood in an aisle that stretched between two banks of movie-theater-style seats. The only light was what spilled out beneath the hem of the closed curtain at the stage down front. Her eyes picked through the shadows, seeing only a dozen other people inside an auditorium that could hold well over one hundred. Most of them were close to the stage. Annja selected a seat in the last row. The seats were upholstered in dark red velveteen, though some of the cushions had been replaced and covered with various colors of vinyl. The seat squeaked when she sat, causing the other patrons to turn around and try to spot the newcomer. She leaned against the high back and it squeaked again.

The floor was carpeted, the nap worn thin and the pattern lost where sections of the canvas backing showed through. It was clean—Annja was struck by the cleanliness of the place. There was still the hint of popcorn in the air and a vague fustiness just because of the age of the building. But there was nothing objectionable.

She tipped her head back and closed her eyes. Annja knew several martial-arts relaxation techniques, any of which would help the tension melt away as she balanced and centered herself. She breathed deep and slow, imagining a point of light in the distance and focusing on it.

Suddenly speakers crackled on the walls and George M. Cohan's "Give My Regards to Broadway" began playing, with "Remember me to Kings Cross" in place of "Remember me to Herald Square."

Her eyes opened wide as the curtains parted and a single bright spotlight struck a lanky torch singer in a black sequined gown. The woman threw her head back and began singing "If He Walked into My Life" from *Mame*. Something didn't seem quite right about the singer, and so Annja leaned forward and studied the woman.

Not a woman, Annja decided after a moment. The singer sported an Adam's apple, as did the next one who came out singing "Whatever Lola Wants," from *Damn Yankees*. Annja recognized this warbler as the man in the purple tuxedo who'd lured her into this place. Female impersonators, the lot of them, and they weren't terrible, Annja decided, a bargain for eight bucks. She watched only one more number—an eight-member chorus line singing about a "singular sensation," before she closed her eyes and resumed her breathing exercise and focused on an imagined speck of light.

What did Oliver see? What did I see? What relic was so valuable someone would kill for it?

She forced out the sound—the taped orchestra coming from the speakers, the lyrics being crooned by the singers on the stage, the click-clack of the tap shoes, the muffled cough of someone several rows ahead of her. There was only her breath now, regular and relaxing, almost hypnotic. She put herself in a trance and started to relive the past few days.

ANNJA HAD TRAVELED considerably, but primarily to Europe, as her main interest in history was there. She'd never been to Australia before and had been immediately struck by the similarities to the United States and England in the way the people dressed and the city looked. The more closely she observed everything, however, the more pleasant differences she noted, and she had a yearning to come back for a longer stay.

She'd had barely enough time to throw her bag in the hotel room and head out to the dig the first day. The shooting schedule would be fairly tight. There were forms to sign in the van—the standard one for liability, stating that the dig financiers would not be held accountable if she was injured at the site. And then there was an agreement that she would not disclose the precise spot where the archaeologists worked.

"Oh, there's enough folks already who know the general vicinity," Wes Michaels had told her. "Some of the local papers have done features on us before. But we've not had any television coverage."

It was clear from the beginning that he was dressing up a little for the camera; she'd spotted his wife cutting off the price tag from his shirt. Annja was pleased he bothered to buy something new.

On the ride to the site she had noticed the country-side air. It was achingly clean, with just a hint of salt from the ocean. The closer the van got to the dig, the more other scents intruded…from the trees primarily, as the site was in a forest preserve, and from the earth the archaeologists had been peeling away to get to the relics beneath.

One of the first things Dr. Michaels and his wife had uncovered was still at the site because of its size and because the corporation funding the project hadn't yet decided whether to leave it there for posterity or bring it back to Sydney for storage. It was a carving of an ape, or something that looked like a squatting ape, taller than a man and as broad across as two, and chiseled out of a stone that had a high iron content.

"The Egyptian god Thoth, probably," Wes had said. "My best guess, anyway. Three thousand years old or thereabouts. Looks similar to one found on the old Wolvi Road property some forty years back. Folks scoffed back then, too."

He showed her a smaller, similar statue that Oliver shot as it was being crated up. It was badly weathered from time and the sea air, and she could barely make out the cross of life clutched in the ape's fingers.

"Thoth was sometimes depicted as an ape," Wes had explained. "Then about two thousand years after this one was made they started carving Thoth as a bird-headed man. Like I said, Miss Creed, I'm not an Egyptologist. But I'm a damn good archaeologist. I know my stuff."

Annja liked him immediately.

"Our best find," Jennifer said, "is a cross of life. Wes wasn't sure it should go on your television program, but I've talked him into it. Haven't crated it yet—kept it out just for you."

Oliver was quick to record it, and Annja was equally quick to admire it. This cross of life, or Egyptian ankh, as some called it, was made of jade and had survived the weather and shifting earth that the years had heaped upon it. It was easily three or four pounds and carved from a single piece. Annja whistled lowly when—with gloved hands—she was allowed to hold it.

Wes chattered animatedly while she examined it. "In Toowomba years back they found more than a dozen granite stones with inscriptions in Phoenician. I read that one translated roughly into 'Here is the place to worship Ra or worship the sun.'"

Jennifer continued. "Thirty years ago a man named Gilroy found some Egyptian symbols scattered in with

aboriginal cave art, not terribly far from where an
Egyptian sun disk was found carved in a cliff face. There
was a faint outline of a chariot, too, but you can hardly
see it anymore."

"And if you're talking about aboriginals," Wes cut in,
"there's records of a cult in New South Wales that wor-
shipped Biame, a sky-being. Biame has lots of parallels
to Thoth. There's some aboriginal rock art near the
Hawkesbury River that has some folks looking like
ancient Egyptians. Fringe nothing."

Jennifer nudged her husband. "Tell her the good part,
Wesley, about Grafton. She might not have read about
him. I'm sure she didn't have time to read everything."

Annja had to concentrate on the couple's exchange, as
it was difficult to think of anything but the piece of jade
in her hands.

Wes snorted. "Almost eighty years ago, there was an
anthropologist from around here, name of Sir Grafton
Elliot-Smith. He found some remains in a New Zealand
cave and said the skull belonged to an Egyptian, said it
was at least two thousand years old." He spit at the ground
and twisted the ball of his foot atop the spot. "Grafton's
papers were in the science library in Canberra but they
disappeared a few decades ago."

Annja reluctantly set the jade ankh in the padding
material in the crate. "Beautiful," she said. "That piece
is truly beautiful."

AGAIN, ALL ANNJA HEARD was her breathing, slow and
regular, hypnotic. The jade ankh could be worth a fortune
because of its age, its Egyptian ties and above all simply

because of its size and weight. It was a true museum piece on many levels.

She replayed other things from the site—carvings on pieces of pots and vases, an intact vase that was worth more than a tidy sum, cow-headed figurines, simple tools, the skeleton. They hadn't dated those bones. What if the skeleton wasn't ancient? What if it was some murder victim? What if Oliver's disappearance and the attack on her had nothing to do with the dig? She mentally chastised herself for letting her imagination run so wild.

No, it has to be the dig. Think, think, think. Annja scolded. What did I see?

Again her thoughts returned to the hefty piece of jade.

"Definitely beautiful," she whispered. "One of a kind."

But enough to kill over…and just because she and Oliver had seen it?

"No," she stated with authority. Annja shook her head, the gesture rousing her fully from her trance. Valuable? Most certainly, that ankh was. But not beyond price, and not worth Oliver's life, she felt deep in her gut. "It was something else we saw. But what?"

"Shh!"

She saw the craggy face of a pudgy man sitting directly in front of her. He'd turned around and set a doughy finger to his lips.

"Shh!" he repeated.

Annja had been so focused on her recollections of the dig that she'd shut out everything around her. The music coming from speakers intruded now. It was boisterous, and something she was not familiar with—not any Broadway tune she'd heard.

The female impersonators on the stage were in various states of dress and were performing a bawdy number. A heavy-set singer trying to cram too many pounds into a red dress that screamed at the seams was rushing back and forth, trailing a lime-green feather boa. The audience laughed, and Annja realized it was a comedy number.

The audience?

Annja gasped. When she'd entered the auditorium she'd counted one dozen people. Now there were easily five times that many. She'd concentrated so hard on her recollections of the dig site that she hadn't heard all these people come in, hadn't heard the numbers change or the scenery wheeled onto the stage.

The trance had helped her, though, even if she wasn't satisfied that the jade ankh was the object behind today's mayhem. The trance had chased away her headache, and her feet were not nearly so sore. Her stomach was another matter; it softly rumbled its hunger, and her throat was dry with thirst.

"Sorry," she whispered to the craggy-faced man. "I'm leaving."

She made her way to the aisle, feeling a little stiff from not moving in a while. Beyond the curtains the lobby was lit brighter than when she came in, and a different woman was behind the counter. Annja stared. Different was right—that was a man dressed as a woman.

She looked to the pay phone. Someone was on it, talking and gesturing with her free hand.

Annja sighed. She could wait for that conversation to finish, or she could use the pay phone at the end of the street.

"What did I see? What did Oliver see?" she whispered. She paced in a tight circle, putting her hands under her armpits. It was chillier in the lobby than it had been when she came in. "What? Who? Who did I see? Who?" She stopped and stared at the poster of a man dressed like Marilyn Monroe. "Who, indeed?" One of the men who'd attacked her, the tall one who'd been called Sute, was familiar somehow. She'd seen him before and only now realized it. "He was at the dig," she exclaimed.

Annja bolted from the Purple Pussycat and stopped in her tracks on a rain-slick sidewalk bathed in night and neon lights.

Quite a few hours had passed since she'd stepped in for the late-morning show. In her trance, she'd fallen asleep.

8

"Brrr," Annja said. Indeed it was chilly. The sun going down, and the fall evening made her wish she'd bought a sweater in the boutique—which a glance down the street confirmed was closed now. She'd picked the blouse because it was pretty without being flashy and it would serve as a fine Australian souvenir. But at the moment, it certainly wasn't functional. The rain added to her shivers and sent her back inside the Purple Pussycat and to the concession stand. She'd noticed something earlier, hanging on the wall next to the cat timepiece.

"Miss, the eight-o'clock show started awhile ago. There's another one at ten, and—"

"That jacket," Annja said. "I'll have one of those. A medium, please." She was thankful they accepted American credit cards, because the price tag—sixty bucks or thereabout in American dollars—would have practically emptied her wallet.

She shrugged into it, finding the shoulders a perfect fit and the sleeves just a tad long. But there were elastic bands around the wrists, and so she pronounced the fit, "Good and warm, thanks." It was purple, of course, satin, and the shiny metallic threads and seed beads on the back spelled out *Pussycat*. A smaller logo was embroidered over the breast pocket. It was lined more heavily than a windbreaker, and reasonably well-made for a wearable advertisement. Still, it just looked—tacky—and was something she intended to leave behind when all of this was done.

"Oliver," she mused. "Someone needs to call your fiancée. But what to tell the woman? That I'm convinced the love of your life and my best cameraman has been murdered?" Annja still didn't want to be the someone delivering the bad news. "And someone needs to find your body, Oliver, find out just what happened. Someone needs to pay."

She zipped up the jacket and turned, just in time to see the woman on the pay phone finish her call to. Annja darted over and grabbed the receiver before it hit the cradle, even though there was no one else in the lobby to contest her for it.

Staring at the numbers, she realized she didn't have enough coins to call Oliver's cell phone—it was a New York area code and would count as an international call. Instead, she got the operator and placed a collect call to Oliver's cell phone. It didn't even ring this time. Next came a collect call to her producer. Once again she got Doug's voice mail. Then she dug out her coins and pulled Wes Michaels's card from her wallet. She stabbed in the numbers for his cell phone and growled from deep in her throat when a message played that the subscriber was out of range.

Should have realized that, she thought. No cell towers near the place. There was a satellite phone at the dig site; she'd seen one of the archaeologists with it. But she didn't have the number for it, and she was certain she couldn't get it through directory information.

"A fool I've been." Annja was still angry at herself for falling asleep in the auditorium. She'd needed the rest, had slept so very little the night before, and the fight in the hotel had been taxing. Still, she knew she shouldn't have allowed herself any respite, should have called the police, as she was doing now.

"Hello? I'm calling about the—" she searched for the correct words "—the bodies that were found at the Sheraton on the Park hotel this morning. Yes, the Sheraton on Elizabeth Street. I was—"

The desk officer stopped her from continuing. Annja tapped her foot and politely listened to him.

"Miss, I can put you through to media relations and—"

"No, you don't understand, sir. I'm not a news reporter looking for a quote. I was there…. Yes, that's right. I was there at the hotel."

The desk officer interrupted her again. "Miss, the media-relations spokesman will be able to—"

"No, I'm really not a reporter. Honest. I'm a witness, almost a victim, actually. More than just a witness to the whole thing. I was shot at, and I—"

Once more the desk officer cut her off, and Annja realized he must be getting a lot of phone calls about the incident and was skeptical about her involvement. Perhaps they got a lot of crank calls.

"No, sir. I did not speak with the police at the scene. Listen to me. Please." Annja blew a breath out between her teeth. "Can you transfer me, please, to one of the officers working on the case?" She knew they would either be at the station or still at the hotel. Police in any country didn't quit easily. "Sergeant Griffith, yes, that will be fine. I'd like to speak with Sergeant Griffith. Thank you."

Music she'd expect to hear in an elevator came on the line, and she tapped her foot faster. One minute passed. Two minutes. She looked at the pussycat clock. Three minutes, and the god-awful hold music changed to a tune equally bad. She turned back to stare at the number pad on the phone.

Then someone tapped on her shoulder.

"I need to make a call. How much longer are you going to be?"

Annja turned, seeing the woman who had been on the phone earlier.

"It's important," the woman persisted.

"So's this," Annja quietly retorted. Patience. Be polite, no need to cause a scene.

"This is very important!" the woman shouted.

Annja sucked in a breath and slammed the receiver down, deciding a trip to the police station was a better alternative than listening to hold music for who knew how long. A trip to the station was in order…right after she returned to the dig. If the men had indeed tried to kill her because of something she'd seen, it was possible Dr. Michaels and his team were also in danger.

She raised the collar on her jacket and returned to the sidewalk, dozens of thoughts swirling through her head—Oliver, the police, Dr. Michaels, the jade ankh, the tall man she recognized from the dig site.

"Sute," she said, remembering the name one of her other attackers had called him. She'd spotted him shortly before they left the site, when she'd walked up the ridge to get Oliver. He was getting a distance shot of the student dig, and Annja looked through the camera to see it closer. Sute was there, with three more men who might have been her attackers. She only recognized Sute because of his height and lankiness. There were others at the dig, students and an older gentleman, small, who might have been a teacher. Another fellow who stood apart from the rest.

Remember, Annja told herself. What…who…did you see?

And there were tents, indicating that, like Dr. Michaels and his archaeologists, the students stayed at the site overnight.

"Who are you, Sute? Who *were* you?" She corrected herself. Annja glanced down at the bricks. The neon lights reflected on the water held in the mortar, looking like colorful electric snakes slithering away in all directions from her blue shoes.

Despite the rain, the Cross was crowded. *Friday night, no wonder,* she thought. Friday nights in most big cities bustled. It was hard to tell the tourists from the locals now, most of them wearing a raincoat or carrying an umbrella, heads down as they walked or turned toward companions they talked to. The night masked nationalities and ages, blending everything together like a watercolor painting that had smeared.

Across the street two lovers huddled under the overhang of a youth hostel. They were locked in a kiss and ignored the passersby who paused to watch or taunt. One shouted, "Get a room!" before guffawing and moving on.

Someone paused under the awning near them, and appeared to look across the street directly at Annja. There were too many shadows to see more than his outline or to be really sure if he was looking at her. Maybe he was simply standing out of the rain and waiting for a cab. But she had the sensation that she was being watched, an unpleasant tingling that she'd come to recognize as a precursor to trouble.

She took a step forward, considering crossing the street and getting a good look at the man. But a car splashed by, and when it had passed, the man was gone. The two lovers continued kissing.

Maybe she could find a policeman walking a beat here. Maybe he could put her through right away to this Sergeant Griffith. Maybe Griffith would call Oliver's fiancée and deliver the unfortunate news. Maybe he already had.

"They're looking for me," she mused, thinking of both the police and the men who'd tried to kill her. Perhaps the man she'd just spotted across the street had been shooting at her at the hotel. More likely he was just an innocuous visitor to the Cross.

The police were looking for her because her hotel room had been ransacked and she was nowhere to be found, had missed her flight. The police would have checked the airport, the hospitals, too, probably thought she was kidnapped or dead.

The dark-clad men were looking because she'd seen something she wasn't supposed to.

The sounds of the Cross had intensified with nightfall, all of it bouncing off the shop walls—distant horns and sirens; the patter of the rain on the awnings, against the street and against the shoulders of people who scurried from one nightclub to the next; and the music. Annja could hear the strains of an unfamiliar tune spilling out the doorway of the Purple Pussycat behind her, and she picked out a stereo playing loudly from an upper apartment nearby. There was a jazz group across the street and to the east of the lovers, a figure she could barely see through the window wailing away on a trumpet, an old Louis Armstrong number. She wished her circumstances were different and that she could go inside the jazz club, sit and listen to the group. She'd gained quite an appreciation for good jazz growing up in New Orleans.

After a moment, Annja forced the sounds and sights to the back of her mind and brought her most urgent concern to the forefront. How could she get out to the dig? Renting a car was the only option, a four-wheel drive would be best. Likely most of the rental-car places were at the airport, so Annja would have to take a cab out there. She started looking for one.

Instead, her eyes lit on a black-cherry-colored Harley-Davidson Night Train. It gleamed in the lights of a trendy bistro. Expensive in the United States, and even more expensive here because of import fees, its owner must be someone reasonably well-off, she guessed.

She couldn't just steal it. *Shouldn't*, she told herself. No matter how desperate she considered her situation. Still, she headed toward it. The bike would solve her transportation problem and would get her out to the dig. It could travel the off-road part of the trip better than an average car.

A minute later and she was standing beside it, fingers stretching out to touch the leather handgrip.

Theft? She didn't need that heaped on top of everything else, though God knew she'd done other things she wasn't proud of out of necessity. No doubt the police already considered her tied in with what happened at the hotel. She didn't need this added to it.

But lives could depend on her reaching the dig. Wes Michaels, his wife, Jennifer, and the other archaeologists out there might be in danger—if they weren't already dead. Maybe the students at the tertiary dig were in danger, too.

"I can't call out there," she said. "No cell tower." Again she cursed herself for falling asleep in the Purple Pussycat. "I should have done a lot of things differently."

Theft was a minor thing, really, she thought as her hand closed on the grip, in the grand scheme of today's events and…

"Hey, get away from my bike!"

9

Annja released the handgrip, skittered back a step and bumped into a rangy young man in a black leather jacket, chains hanging from epaulets on the shoulders. She put him at twenty-five, maybe, his face lineless and his dark eyes wide and bright. She was tall, but he towered over her, at least six-four, she guessed. His head was shaved, and he had a tattoo of an angry-looking gargoyle on the right side of his forehead, the tail twisting down and getting lost in a bushy eyebrow that was pierced with a thin silver hoop. A small diamond stud pierced his nose, and larger diamonds glittered on his earlobes. He had on black jeans and black leather chaps. But his shirt was a pale shade of rose that added what Annja thought was an out-of-place splash of color.

"Oh, sorry," he said after looking her up and down. "I thought you were going to steal my bike or something.

Didn't mean to bark at you. I'm a little overly protective of my precious there."

You were right to bark at me. I *was* going to steal *it,* Annja thought.

The biker squinted and cupped his hand over his eyes, showing a gold pinkie ring set with a diamond that was at least three carats. "I recognize you," he said cheerfully.

Annja sagged. First the odd-looking girl on the bus, and now the tall, bald biker decorated with diamonds.

"You're from *Chasing History's Monsters*. You're Annja Creed—the archaeologist!"

He grinned broadly and thrust out his hand. "I watch your program all the time. I'm addicted to the History Channel, Discovery, National Geographic, you name it. Can I get a picture, of me and you? That'd be ace."

Without waiting for her answer, he turned to a middle-aged man behind him, also wearing a leather jacket. The fellow had a tousled mop of dishwater-blond hair and looked put off by the request. "Get a pic of us, Nate. This is Annja Creed."

The bald biker sidled up next to Annja and hesitantly put his arm around her shoulder. He was polite, careful not to squeeze her or to seem too friendly. Nate produced a thin digital camera from his pocket and shook his head.

"Dark out here, and even with the flash, there's no guarantee." He took four pictures from slightly different angles and replaced the camera. "We goin' in? Bet Max's been waitin' for a half hour already." He nodded to the bar a few doors south of the bike. "It's a soaker out here, raining hard enough to choke a frog. We goin' in?"

Annja thought it wasn't raining all that hard.

The bald biker didn't answer his friend. Instead, he again stepped in front of Annja, still grinning. "Thanks for letting me get a pic. So you're here filming something, right? I mean, not in the Cross, but here." He gestured with his right hand. "In Oz. Filming something for TV."

"Finished yesterday," she said.

He touched his thumb to his chin and looked thoughtful, as if he wanted to keep engaging her in conversation but wasn't sure what else to say. She noticed he had tattoos on the fingers of his left hand that were made to look like rings.

"Listen, sir…"

"Darioush," he supplied. When he saw her raised eyebrow, he added, "It's Persian. My mother traces her roots back to Persia. It means 'ancient king.' Friends call me Dari." He paused. "You can call me Dari."

Nate was frowning and looking from Dari to the bar and back again, finally folding his arms in front of his chest. Annja wondered if they were a couple. Nate's T-shirt was pink and had five lions sprawled in the center, all of them male.

The pedestrians had stopped moving and crowded around them, some of them taking down their umbrellas so they could get a better look. Annja heard whispers.

"What's going on? Why aren't we moving?"

"Some celebrity, I think. In the purple jacket."

"Don't know who she is. Somebody important, though. Look at her Harley. That's a sexy bike."

"She look familiar to you? I think I might have seen her somewhere."

Nate leaned over to a woman in a blue rain slicker and

made a face. "That sheila there, she's on the television. National Geographic or something historical. Dari's smitten. And that's Dari's bike, not hers."

Out of the corner of her eye, Annja saw two men at the edge of the crowd. They had dark complexions, and something was familiar about the one with the broader shoulders.

Dari slid a step to his left so he stood directly between Annja and Nate. "I think my favorite segment was the one you did on the goat suckers of Mexico. I caught it in reruns, too, and then I ordered the DVD."

"The *chupacabras?*" Annja asked, as she'd made no reference to goat suckers on the segment but guessed that's what he was talking about. She kept her eyes on the two men, who appeared perturbed that they'd been bottlenecked on the sidewalk. Still, she thought they could have gone around by going into the street.

Dari nodded vigorously. "Yes, that's it. The goat-headed vampires of Chilpancingo. And then there was the show you did on—"

Annja held her hand out like a traffic cop stopping cars. "I'm sorry. I'd love to talk, Dari, but I'm in a terrible hurry and—"

The man with the broad shoulders pushed himself into the middle of the crowd.

"Oh, sorry. No worries. I didn't mean to tie you up here, getting drenched out in the rain and all, catching a cold. Probably got some steak dinner planned and—"

She shook her head. "The segment I finished here, I have to get back to the site." She swallowed hard and opted for a shortened version of the truth, lowering her voice and moving so close to Dari that she could smell his aftershave. "Look, I have to get out there now. *Right now.* It's important. Some of the people I interviewed yesterday could be in danger. I can't call them. There's no cell service there. My cameraman is missing, and some very bad people are after me. I can't tell you any more than that."

She lost sight of the broad-shouldered man, but his companion remained at the edge of the cluster. She felt for the sword in her mind, ready to summon it if necessary.

"Can't explain," she whispered. "Not here. Not in front of all these people."

"What's she saying?" asked the woman in the blue slicker.

If she drew her sword, if the two men were among those after her, some innocent person in the crowd could get hurt. The image of the hotel patron shot in the hallway flashed in her mind.

"I didn't mean to hold you up, Miss Creed," Dari said. "I hope no one gets hurt. Thank you for stopping, though. The pictures—"

"I'd like to borrow your Harley, Dari. I need to get out there, like I said, to the site, and—"

"Huh?"

"I can't tell you exactly where I'm going, but I have to go now." Annja remembered the form she signed and her promise to Wes Michaels. "Please trust me. I just need to borrow your motorcycle for a little while. Right now, I need it. I promise that I'll…"

The other man was forcing his way into the crowd, too, his dark eyes locked on hers, his mouth in a tight line. She couldn't see his hands. Was he carrying a weapon?

Suddenly she spotted the broad-shouldered one. His face was lit by a blinking neon Tooheys sign. He was one of the men on the sidewalk outside of the hotel who had shot at her; she was sure of it.

She knew she had to be careful or a lot of innocent people could get hurt.

Dari gestured to the bike. "Hop on. I'll take you wherever you want to go, Annja Creed." He made a move to get on the bike, but Nate grabbed his arm and sputtered. Dari shook him off and said, "Later. C'mon, Annja, I said I'll take you." He sat astride the bike and leaned forward, giving her plenty of room to get on.

The two men were stalled, as some people in the crowd pushed back, not wanting to give up their spots so close to a celebrity.

"No, let me rent your bike. This might not be safe, where I'm going. And I'll not jeopardize you." Annja was adamant that an innocent bystander not get involved. "I'll give you fifty now and when I return, I'll give you more."

Dari chuckled. "I don't let anyone drive my precious here, and I've only ever let Nate ride on it before." He patted the seat behind him. "But for Annja Creed... C'mon, if you're in such a hurry." He paused. "And if you don't mind getting a little more drenched."

The two men shoved the people directly in front of them, and the gathering on the sidewalk surged forward, just as a tall man under an awning said, "I know where I've seen her. She's from that funny video program! The California model!"

The woman in the blue slicker shouted, "Gun!"

Annja threw a leg over the bike and grabbed Dari around the waist. "Move it, now! North of Sydney, that's we're going."

Dari reached to the right side of the bike, pulled the choke lever toward him and turned the key. The headlight and instrument cluster—the tachometer and speedometer—came on and glowed green, and the belly of the bike roared to life, belching exhaust as they pulled away from the curb.

"A hundred kilometers or thereabouts and into a forest preserve!" Annja shouted, her fingers clutched on his jacket. "Once we're out of the Cross, you can pull over and I'll go it alone."

She looked over her shoulder just in time to see the two men reach the curb, the people parting around them amid more cries of "Gun!" She thought they'd shoot at her, but Dari, seemingly oblivious to the threat, had deked around a double-parked car and whisked them out of sight.

Twice in a public place men had come after her. What or who was so blasted important that she'd seen that someone wanted her dead for it? It had to be damn important to risk such a public assassination, she thought.

Oliver had taken some shots of whatever, or whoever, it was. She felt certain of that. But his camera and video cards were probably destroyed.

She realized the men could have tracked her to the Cross through the bus routes, and when they couldn't find her in daylight, they must have kept watch in case she emerged from somewhere. She realized it was fortunate they didn't find her snoozing in the Purple Pussycat—she'd have been a defenseless target. Joan's sword would have had to find another owner to wield it.

"Was that a car backfire or a gunshot?" Dari shouted.

"Gunshot," Annja answered, but she didn't say it loud enough for him to hear.

Annja noted the bike's controls—the front and rear brake levers, the throttle, and the engine cutoff switch. The ignition was in the center of the steering column. It would be easy for her to run it—and she would. She noticed that there was less than a quarter tank of gas; they'd have to stop soon, probably before they were out of the city, and she'd talk him out of the bike then by talking some sense into him.

The Harley was only a few years old and rode smoothly, the tires new enough that they had easy traction on the rain-slick road. Dari wove in and out between sluggish cars, the drivers of which were slowing to look at the various sights in the neighborhoods surrounding the Cross. He spoke to her as he went, but she didn't understand him—there were too many other sounds, including the rain that *rat-a-tat-tat*ted against her purple satin jacket.

Her hair was plastered against the sides of her head by the time they'd crossed the bay and left the harbor sights behind. Dari chose a four-lane route that ran past North Sydney, Neutral Bay and Crow's Nest. The traffic was heavy. Then he took a two-lane road that went through Northbridge and near Willoughby. He was talking again, louder, and this time she heard him.

"Nate's gonna have the wobbly boot on before the night's out. Told me he was gonna drink a whole bottle of Bundy to celebrate a promotion. But he won't be drinking with the flies—Max is supposed to be there.

Someone'll give him a ride home, though, no worries. Be a mite touchy in the morning, me leaving him there, but he'll get over it."

A stretch of road opened up where the traffic was lighter, and Dari sped up. "Nate, he only watches sitcoms and reality shows. Hasn't seen one of your programs, always has something better to do, he says. No real appreciation for history. Me? I majored in it, did my thesis on medieval European cook shops actually. Studied a year in Wales, another in London, and practically lived in the Imperial War Museum. I just got me one of those big flat-panel TVs so I could watch the History Channel in high-def."

He started talking about his favorite exhibits at the Imperial War Museum and at the War Museum in Canberra, and Annja let his voice trail away and focused on the cry of some night bird she couldn't see and the shush of cars behind them rolling over the wet pavement.

Dari worked the clutch lever on the left handgrip, pushing up with the toe of his left foot and down with his heel, changing gears. He rolled the right handgrip toward him, activating the throttle and giving the bike a little more speed. He accelerated evenly, tickling the drive train and showing off his skills and the bike. As the road turned, Dari leaned left, practically closing the throttle, then opening it again on the straightaway and accelerating again. He used the brake when the rain suddenly picked up and the bike sluiced through a puddle.

She had to admit that he was good, and began to rethink whether she'd talk the bike out of him at the gas station. He wasn't afraid to use the front brake, which some riders avoided over concern that the wheel would lock up. From her own motorcycle course, she knew that the front brake was responsible for well more than half of the vehicle's stopping power. Dari pressed the brake lever quickly, like a person driving a car might tap the brake with his foot. She leaned with him on the next turn.

"Needs petrol. But there's a servo over there," he hollered, nodding to a station in the distance on the opposite side of the road. "I should've brought my helmet, or at least a hat, eh? Didn't think I'd be going more than a dozen blocks, though, when the night started." He laughed. "Good thing I'm bald, eh? Otherwise my hair would be wet."

He pulled up to the closest pump, which was under an aluminum roof. He turned off the bike and pocketed the keys, ran a hand over his head, brushing the water off. The rain was loud against the aluminum, sounding like muted machine-gun fire.

"I've got a card," he said, pulling out his wallet.

Annja shook her head, droplets flying from her hair and pelting him. "This is on me." She'd briefly entertained letting him gas up the bike and then riding off on it when he went in to pay. But she decided not to separate him from his "precious," and to continue to take advantage of his good driving.

She headed for the attendant as she got her wallet out. "Want anything to drink?" she called over her shoulder. She was terribly thirsty, and she was hungry, too. She hadn't eaten since that morning's feast.

"I'm fine," he hollered back.

She stuffed two candy bars in her pocket, devoured a

third and slugged down a small carton of iced coffee before she got on the bike behind him again.

"Think I can get your autograph later?" Dari asked. "If the rain stops, and if we can find something to write on?"

"It's the least I can do," Annja said.

"Hold on." He revved the bike. "Gotta chuck a yewy out of here to get us pointed north again."

A U-turn, Annja mentally translated as the tires softly squealed, the Harley puffed exhaust and the rain increased its tempo.

10

Dr. Gahiji Hamam, or Doc, as his graduate students affectionately called him, perused the memo on his desk. "For your approval," it said, meaning he needed to sign off on it if he accepted the course description.

Please mark any corrections in ink and initial.

Egyptian archaeology, faculty of arts, eight credit points. Department: of Near Eastern Archaeology. Prerequisites—twelve junior credit points in classical civilization, ancient history or archaeology. Four hours of lectures per week. Assessment—two one-hour tests, two two-hour exams, two three-thousand-word essays. This unit provides an in-depth introduction to the rich and varied cultures of ancient Egypt. It includes the regional impact, engineering developments, religion and death practices.

Hamam retrieved a pen from a wooden cup on his desk, signed the memo and tossed it in his Out basket. He didn't care what they listed in their course brochure; he would not be there to teach it. A visiting professor from Egypt—a native who traced his ancestry back to the great Khufu, or Cheops, Kheops or Suphis I, as some referred to the ruler—Hamam had agreed to his lucrative three-year posting for far grander reasons than to educate dozens of doomed youths. If everything went as planned, he would not need to fulfill the rest of this year, and he could get about his real business.

He would miss some of the students here, certainly Jon, Cindy and Harris and Matthew especially, a mix of sincerity and eagerness, and in Cindy's case a vacuous attractiveness that pleasantly distracted him. More than that, he would miss being in the field north of Sydney and getting his hands dirty in the sifting trays. But Hamam was sixty, and as time moved ever faster he vowed to spend less of it on academic pursuits and more of it on his efforts to join with the gods.

The chance to unearth Egyptian relics had lured him here, tugged him from his comfortable estate on the outskirts of Cairo. He wouldn't have come had it not been for the fringe digs local archaeologists worked and that the esoteric archaeology Web sites detailed. He had wanted one of the sites for himself, and the easiest avenue to that had been through the University of Sydney. He'd made that part of the condition of his temporary employment here, that he be put in charge of the university's tertiary dig in the forest preserve.

Hamam liked Sydney. He'd visited the city several

times, first when he was fresh from his doctoral program in Egypt and on holiday. He'd used his credentials to visit the records area of the science library in Canberra, where he carefully procured Sir Grafton Elliot-Smith's papers on a two-thousand-year-old mummy Grafton had discovered in New Zealand. Hamam had acquired other important relics and reports then, and on subsequent visits, as well. He knew where to spread money around so that financially strapped curators and security guards looked the other way. Hamam had been born to money, and he didn't hesitate to spend it to get what he wanted.

Occasionally he left a body in his wake, but he was careful no finger of blame was ever pointed in his direction. He would never be traced to the cameraman who had been incinerated, nor could they link him to the upcoming deaths of Annja Creed and his students.

Hamam was a very cautious man.

He liked Sydney for its mild climate, and the agreeable dampness of its ocean breezes. He was fond of the university, too, as he considered it one of the best institutes of higher learning in the world. And it boasted the Nicholson Museum right on campus. He'd been to the museum's *Exhibition Egypt: The Black Land* more times than he cared to count. It displayed sarcophagi, sculptures and three complete mummies. Wings were devoted to life before the pharaohs, gods, mummification and his favorite—the afterlife.

He could instantly visualize a beautiful limestone relief of a door lintel depicting Ptolemy I. And there was the cartouche of Akhenaton and Nefertiti that he coveted. The little museum had the most Egyptian artifacts of any display in Australia, and rivaled in quality some of the collections he'd seen in Egypt and elsewhere.

Its holdings included relics from 5000 B.C. up to nearly 400 A.D.—such as pottery gathered from the Egyptian sites of Abydos, el-Mahasna, el-Amrah, Diospolis Parva, and Oasr Ibrim. There were New Kingdom sculptures, including a head of Ramses II in remarkable condition and a diorite rendering of Horemheb, the man believed to be Tutankhamen's regent.

Hamam had researched the museum, named for Sir Charles Nicholson, an eccentric collector who purchased many relics from dealers in Cairo and who subsequently donated the lion's share of them to the university, which in turned named the museum for him. Other antiquities in the museum were bought from the Egypt Exploration Fund—now called the Egypt Exploration Society—in London in the late nineteenth century. There wasn't a single piece in the museum that Hamam would not want in his own private collection.

Hamam's office was just off Science Road on the university campus, even though archaeology was placed in the arts-and-ideas division. He'd requested this office, one of a half-dozen vacant for him to choose from, because it was the most remote of the lot. He'd thought it would be the quietest of his options, and it was, on the northeast border of the campus. The bulk of the university was spread to the south of him. There was little traffic here in comparison to the other campus streets, which were busier and more brightly lit.

He leaned back in his chair, which he had pronounced

adequate but not well designed for a small man's stature. He'd requested a different chair a month back, and had not followed up on it. Like the university he'd once taught at in Cairo, professors had to become a nuisance with their want lists to gain even a modicum of office essentials. Hamam would have purchased a chair to his specifications, but it went against his principles to use his own money for something like that. Besides, he spent relatively little time there.

Hamam listened to the heating system kick on, the hum of white noise that was almost too soothing; he found himself drifting off. He shook out his hands and unbuttoned his jacket, thrust two fingers between his shirt collar and his neck to help loosen his tie—little activities to rouse him. He much preferred the more casual dress of the dig site, but he'd just come from dinner with the vice chancellor and the dean of graduate studies, and so he had had to wear his best.

"Oh, bother," he muttered when the strains of a piano concerto wafted under his door. The night janitor for the building loved classical music and played it when he buffed the floors—loud enough to be heard over the infernal machine he pushed down the hall every third night. At least the racket would help to keep him awake. And the smell—he hated the scents of the disinfectant and the cleansers that swirled in the wake of the janitor. But the smell would help, too.

Hamam decided he would not grieve at the night janitor's demise.

With a stifled yawn Hamam turned his attention to a

series of photographs on his desk. The first showed the slab that Jon had uncovered that morning. Hamam read the inscribed text.

The snake bit two times. And because of the snake, the Mighty One of Lower Egypt has left the living. We are trapped here, our boat damaged beyond repair. So we must go forward.

He looked at the next picture, of a slab uncovered earlier.

The snake struck and we gave yolks from lizard and bird eggs and prayed to the Hidden One that our ruler might live.

Hamam knew this predated the other slab in the story. The next picture was of a damaged slab, and it described the burial of the Egyptian who had brought his fellows to Australia. Hamam translated the text.

We walked to the chamber where there were stones from all around. The chamber was properly aligned with the Western Heavens.

He tapped his finger on the edge of the desk, trying to fill in the gaps where the rest of the story had broken away with the chipped slab. "Something about three doors to eternity, a royal tomb and a holy offering," he muttered.

He gathered the pictures and put them in the bottom

drawer, beneath a stack of file folders. "Enough of this. Maybe Jon will find more for me to translate tomorrow."

Hamam grimaced as the concerto became louder and competed with the whoosh of the floor polisher. He stared at the crack under his door and waited until a shadow passed across it and the music grew distant. The accursed janitor had moved on. Then Hamam stretched forward and reached for the phone at the far corner of his desk, tugging it close. From a narrow drawer he pulled out a personal directory and searched for the numbers he wanted.

"Pizza," the entry read. He pushed the numbers.

"Janko? This is Hamam. I want to make sure that the tanker truck has been secured.… Good, good. We may need it sooner than originally planned."

Another call went to a number at an entry labeled "Sister," though Hamam had been an only child. He didn't worry that it was an international call and that the department head might remind him that personal calls made from the offices were to be local, unless it was an emergency. Hamam considered this an emergency of sorts, and anyone who might object to this expense would not be terribly long for the world.

The phone rang several times, and he nearly hung up before it was answered by a sleepy-voiced man.

"The test will be conducted soon," Hamam told the man. "Nearly all is ready. And if things go as planned, Cairo will be next."

He replaced the phone in the cradle and stepped to the narrow window. The other offices he could have selected were larger and had bigger windows that opened out onto a usually bustling campus. He drew back the shade. It was raining softly. The lights were dim on this side of the building, and reflected ghostly off the wet concrete.

"Cairo next," Hamam repeated, his voice a purr. "Then I will have what I need to join the gods."

11

For a few minutes it looked as if the rain was going to ease off. Annja hoped Dari would really open up the throttle then and make better time. But lightning flashed on the horizon, turning the black sky gray because of the frequency of the strikes. Thunder rocked the ground, the trembles coming up through the pavement and into her feet.

The wind gusted at the same time, sending the rain sideways. Dari, obviously a careful driver, slowed the bike and kept to the middle of the left lane. Ahead, cars were pulling off to the sides of the road, waiting for the worst of the weather to abate.

Dari started to do the same thing, then muttered, "Oh, the hell with it," and kept going. He said something else, but it was lost in the next boom of thunder.

They'd left the outskirts of the city, and when Annja glanced behind her she could see only a thin haze of twinkling lights, reminding her of fireflies floating to the ground in a farm field.

Annja was soaked to her skin, and knew Dari must be equally miserable. She remembered that he mentioned her catching a cold when they'd stood on the sidewalk in Kings Cross. At the time she thought the rain not even a mild annoyance. Now she thought that a cold could be a good bet.

"Whew!" Dari shouted as they continued north. "Smells like someone lost their lunch!"

A putrid odor rose all around them. Squinting, Annja saw a great expanse of mud to the west—some field that had been liberally spread with a sludgy fertilizer. She wrinkled her nose and gripped Dari tighter when the bike slid across the center lane and then came back again. He adjusted their course and said something else to her, but she still couldn't hear him over the storm.

It amazed her, sometimes, how strangers could be so helpful and considerate—like Dari leaving his evening of partying to take a stranger to a place she hadn't divulged yet…and in a nasty thunderstorm. She'd have to pay him back for this, maybe send him a set of autographed DVDs from *Chasing History's Monsters*. He'd probably like that, and it was the absolute least she could do.

They'd traveled thirty miles when traffic became nonexistent and they basically had the slippery highway to themselves.

After another ten miles the rain finally stopped. A car raced up behind them, spraying water from its wheel wells and splashing Dari and Annja as it passed.

"Next bloke that does that, I'll give him a gobful!" Dari fumed.

Annja saw another car behind them, this one keeping its distance and following them as they changed lanes. For a heartbeat she wondered if it carried some of the men who'd shot at her, like the two on the sidewalk in the Cross. After another mile, the car faded back and took an exit.

Another few miles later the bike sputtered and lurched and nearly pitched them to the pavement. Dari caught it and took the brunt of their weight on his left leg. He and Annja got off, and he walked the bike to the shoulder. He fiddled in a small pack at the back and produced a thin, stunted flashlight that he flicked on and held between his teeth as he knelt by the bike and ran his fingers over it.

Annja didn't say anything, just watched him as he looked at the engine. His fingers worked quickly and carefully, and soon he was shaking his head, the gesture bouncing the light across the black-cherry bike. Finally, he took the flashlight out of his mouth and turned it off.

He was angry. She could tell that from his breathing. She couldn't see much else, as they were on a stretch of highway with no lights from nearby communities. Dari got himself under control and shook his head again.

"My precious is cactus, at least for the time being."

Annja waited for him to continue, knowing she wouldn't have to ask him what was wrong.

"Damn connecting rod broke and went through the cylinder wall. Fixable, sure. But not right now, not out here in the night. Cactus, it is. I didn't bring a cell phone." He looked to her.

"I don't have one, either," she said.

"So we walk," he said. He turned back to the south. "I

figure we've went…oh, I dunno…sixty-five, seventy klicks, maybe a little more. Certainly more than halfway to wherever it is we were going."

"To an archaeological dig in a forest preserve," Annja said.

"The Egyptian one?" he asked.

She blinked. "You know about that?"

"Yeah, I said I was a history freak, and I subscribe to *Archaeology Today* and I've bookmarked all the esoteric and fringe sites. Been by it one day several months past— not much to look at, though. There was an article in one of the local papers. The site down in Brisbane is further along, and there's a lot more to see there." He continued to prattle about Egyptians in Australia and that some people believed the Mayans made it there, too, and the Phoenicians—who a local archaeologist claimed established a trading center on the Queensland coast.

"So why do you think the archaeologists are in danger?" He stuck the flashlight in his pocket and then moved the bike farther off the road and behind a row of scrubby bushes, where it couldn't easily be seen from the highway. "They find something? Something that the wrong sorts of people might want bad enough to kill for?"

Annja thrust her fingers in her jeans pockets, discovering in the process that her wallet was every bit as soggy as the rest of her. "I don't know." She proceeded to tell him about the men shooting at her, and that her cameraman was missing and that it all had to be something related to the dig. She usually kept the dangerous pieces of her life private, but she figured she owed Dari some explanation. She made no mention of her sword, of course, or that she'd killed some of the men in the hotel.

They started walking north. "There's a couple of small woop woops ahead, off an exit, and—"

"Excuse me?" Annja had no trouble keeping up with him, despite his long legs and impatient gait. In fact, she could have easily passed him by.

"Woop woop. You know, a small town. You say some fellow's from Woop Woop and you know he's from a place you Seppos, I mean Americans, call the sticks."

"Woop woop," Annja repeated.

"So's we walk to a woop woop and call somebody to come get us, get a garage to come pick up my precious." He paused, and added, "No worries, eh? I've got lots of friends in the Cross. Some of them don't get pissed on Friday nights."

Annja nodded.

"We'll get you a ride out to that dig somehow."

She didn't know what to say. And so she said nothing, a silence settling between them as she picked up the pace and he matched it. After about a half hour an exit sign, barely lit, came into view at the edge of their vision. But they didn't have to take it.

Dari had flagged down a pickup, which he called a "ute," or utility vehicle, and begged the driver for a lift to the nearest town off the next exit. It had been the only vehicle they'd seen on this side of the road for some time. The truck was a white Toyota Hilux that was rusted in spots. The sign on the side read Brumby Paint Co., Parramatta, NSW.

"Actually," Annja interrupted, sidling up to the window,

"if you could drop Dari off at a…woop woop, and take me north of here, say to the forest preserve, I would be ever thankful. I'll give you a twenty for your trouble."

"Both of us to the preserve," Dari said. Then softer, he said to her, "I'm not leaving you alone in the wilderness, Annja Creed."

"Yeah, I'm going past the preserve," the driver admitted. "But it'll cost you thirty." He leaned over and held out his hand, and Annja produced three damp ten-dollar bills, scowling to note she was nearly broke now.

The driver was a thin man on the far side of middle age, dressed in paint-speckled coveralls and wearing a faded baseball cap with the logo half-loose and flopped forward so Annja couldn't read it.

He stuffed the money in his front pocket. "Yeah, I'll drop you off there if you want." He crooked a thumb to the bed of the truck. "An odd pair, the two of you. I'd ask what you're doing out here in the middle of the night, but I'm not sure I want to know. Back there with the both of you. Don't want you getting my cab wet."

Annja and Dari climbed in the back and wedged themselves between cans of paint, folded canvas tarps and two extension ladders—all of which were wet. Annja noticed that the driver had rolled up his windows and locked both of his doors—trusting enough to give them a ride, but not too trusting.

"You really don't need to tag along," Annja told Dari. She pulled the hair away from her face and twisted it into a bun at the back of her head. "I wasn't kidding when I said this could be dangerous. I'd prefer not to worry about myself *and* you."

Dari shrugged. "There might be no problems at this dig, you know."

"I know."

"Then you'd have nothing to worry about. Things'll be all apples."

"But if there is—"

"I'll keep my head low, Annja. Some of my friends are planning a birthday party for me next weekend, and I'd prefer not to miss it." He grinned, the expression lost on her as she couldn't see his face for the stack of paint cans. "And I can well look out for myself."

"You really don't have to—"

"Yes, I do," he cut in. "Wouldn't be right for me to leave a lady in distress, you know. Besides, if this turns all exciting, I wouldn't want to miss it. I'll have quite the tale to tell. Maybe even be a part of history rather than just reading about it, you know."

"Sorry about your bike," she said after a few miles had passed. She fished around in the pocket of her jacket and pulled out the two candy bars she'd bought at the gas station. The wrappers were so wet they flaked away when she tried to peel them, and she chewed on the soggy candy quickly. She would have offered Dari one, were it in better condition and not smearing all over her fingers. Her next words were muffled while she finished eating, "I know bikes like that are terribly expensive here and—"

"No worries again. I can afford it. I own three op shops." He chuckled. "That would be thrift stores to you—opportunity shops. Took out a loan for the first one when I turned eighteen. Folks thought I was touched, but

I paid the bank back in less than a year. There's first-rate money in secondhand goods. Thinking about putting up another one, building this one from scratch." He paused and tipped his head back, eyes fixed on the stars poking through the thinning clouds. "I can well afford that bike, and to fix it."

He proceeded to regale her with stories about his first few years in business. She'd guessed right; he was twenty-five, soon to turn twenty-six. And she'd also guessed right on he and Nate being a couple. Nate managed one of the op shops.

The truck finally slowed and pulled to the side. The driver rolled the window down a crack.

"Here you go," he said, thrumming his fingers against the steering wheel.

"Can't you take us a little farther north?" Annja called. "To one of the main roads into the preserve?"

He shook his head. "Out with you. I was good enough to bring you this far." He thrummed his fingers harder until they got out of the truck bed. "Enjoy yourselves in the woods."'

He sped away, leaving Annja and Dari staring at a narrow muddy road that led into the trees.

"Surprised he saw this," Dari muttered. It was dark and unmarked and looked entirely eerie. "If my bike hadn't went belly up I could've got us to a better spot. Taken us right in there. It's gonna be a couple of klicks hiking to the dig, you know?"

There was just enough starlight that Annja could see thick ruts from tires on the road. "Someone else found this road, too."

"Recent," Dari said, noticing the tracks. "Maybe there'll be some of this trouble you're worried about." He touched her on the shoulder. "Hey, why didn't the police come out here with you? What with you getting shot at and all, being a celebrity, and worried about the archaeologists? You'd think they would have driven you out here in a divvy van, lights all a-flashing."

Annja didn't answer. Checking her bearings, she realized they were on the side of the preserve with the Michaels site. So while she'd have to cut through the woods to get there, at least she wouldn't have to climb the ridge in this darkness. Letting out a low breath, she started jogging, her feet slapping against the mud in time with her heart.

Dari took a couple of deep breaths and hurried after her.

12

The road—if it could be called that—where the painter had dropped them off was not one of the main routes into the preserve. It wound its way, slick like a wet snake, through white stringybark trees, and then ended at a rusting service shed. Parked outside the shed was a black SUV, the vehicle responsible for the tracks Annja had spotted. The SUV glistened in the moonlight, the water beaded up on it as if it had been freshly waxed. The cloud cover had all but disappeared, so she could easily make out that no one was inside it and that the shed was padlocked. Still, she crept closer to the SUV just to be cautious, holding her hand behind her to indicate that Dari should stay back.

She felt the hood, and while it wasn't warm, it wasn't as cool as the air around her—suggesting that the SUV had been there a little while, but not terribly long.

She peered in through the windows, unable to see

much, but noting that it didn't look lived in. There were no empty soda cans or paper bags, no napkins or maps stuffed above the visors. Very neat, and very locked, with a security light on inside that indicated an alarm would howl if she jimmied a door open. She studied the ground. Besides hers, there were two sets of prints, both with pronounced grooves to indicate hiking boots.

"Maybe Dr. Michaels's car," she mused, having not paid attention to what sort of vehicles the archaeologists had driven to the site. There'd been none parked directly near where they were working. They'd parked along another service road about a quarter mile back from the dig, one that she and Oliver had taken to do the shoot. Maybe Dr. Michaels parked elsewhere from time to time. Maybe this was his.

But she doubted it.

She had sized up Wes as a bit of an eccentric and had thought any vehicle of his would be littered with maps and boxes of papers and books. "Maybe one of the other archaeologists."

"What?" Dari had held back and couldn't quite hear her.

"Shh." Annja put a finger to her lips. "I was just speculating who this belonged to."

Dari shrugged. "I've no idea." He slogged closer and looked at the tailpipe. "It's pretty new. And pretty expensive. A rental, I'd reckon. See the sticker?"

She joined him and squinted. The words were lost in the darkness, but she recognized the shape of the logo. Annja doubted one of the crew would have rented an expensive SUV to drive out here.

"Not good," she whispered.

"A bad feeling, eh?" Dari was looking into the trees. "Which way from here to this dig? Like I said, it's been some months since I was out here—and it was daylight then."

Annja wasn't certain. Though she'd been out here on three separate days for the shoot, they'd taken a different service road. She studied the boot prints again, and then started following them.

The breeze was strong and rattled the tops of the trees, sending drops down from the recent rain. Hardy beetles fell on them, too, and Annja carefully brushed them off. The most common trees were the white stringybarks. But there were also ironwoods, smooth-barked apples, white mahogany and a giant that Dari whispered was called a gray box. There were shrubs everywhere, but in the shadows of the trees their details were largely lost and Annja couldn't identify them.

The tracks led down a narrow path, likely a game trail made by deer and wild pigs, Annja guessed. Where the path became thin and almost nonexistent, the men did not walk single file as she thought most would. One walked to the right of the path, smashing ground cover as he went.

Definitely not one of the archaeologists, she decided. All the people she'd interviewed at the dig site professed a love of this preserve and would not have been so careless.

"That's love grass that one's traipsing through," Dari said. He kept his voice low to avoid her scolding him. "Plume grass over there. It's a little different."

Annja wondered if he was trying to impress her or was just babbling because his nerves had kicked in. She wished she'd talked him out of coming along, even though she appreciated the company. If the tracks she was following led to some of the men who'd shot at her, she would need to call her sword. And Dari didn't need to see that.

"Should have done a lot of things differently," she said too softly for him to hear.

"Hard to see it. Not much light," he continued. "But that's kangaroo grass to your left. And there's some love creeper. Looks like it's dying back a bit. It likes the heat. Love grass, love creeper, lots of love in this place."

Annja didn't hear the things that she wanted to— sounds of insects that could take the fall chill, owls and small animals scuttling along the forest floor. It could be that she and Dari had unnerved them—or that the men they were tracking had spooked them into silence.

They hadn't traveled more than another dozen yards when she lost the tracks. The game trail disappeared, and thick ground cover spread out in all directions. She pressed on, angling toward where her inner direction sense suggested the dig was. Their footfalls were almost silent with only the occasional *shush* of thick, wet leaves moving as they passed through. The moss was soft and springy; she could tell that even through the soles of her tennis shoes. And it was slippery. She had to move a little slower than she'd like just to keep her balance.

Through gaps in the ironwoods to her right, she could see a stream, the moonlight glinting off its surface and making it shimmer like molten silver. Something splashed in the water, and she stopped and listened. A fish or a frog, she decided, finally continuing on.

Eventually, she came to a bend in the stream. It was wider and the current fast. More like a small river, she thought, the banks swollen slightly from the night's downpour. A log stretched across it, and from scrapes in the bark, it looked as if something, or someone, had used it as a bridge. Maybe the men from the SUV. A search of the bank confirmed that; she spotted two sets of boot prints.

"Still want to come along?" she asked, noting Dari's uneasy expression as he stared at the water.

"No worries. I'll go first." He removed his leather boots and held one in each hand, as if using them to balance him. "A mite cold, this is." He put one foot in front of the other. "Slippery, too. Wish my bike hadn't gone cactus. We'd have found a friendlier way to go."

In the moonlight she could see his toes curl around the wood, as if he'd had some gymnastics training in his youth. Dari certainly is an interesting soul, she mused. Yet for all his smoothness, the log swayed beneath him. He took a half-dozen steps and stopped, steadying himself and waiting for the log to stop quivering before he took another half dozen.

She waited until he was nearly across before she took her turn, keeping her shoes on. Indeed it was slippery, and for a heartbeat she expected to fall into the churning water. But she slowed her breathing, as she'd learned in her martial-arts training, and she closed her eyes and relied on her feet alone to carry her across. Annja felt the log wobble, too, and at the same time sag; it was rotting from all the moisture.

Once on the other side, she waited for Dari to put on

his boots. Then she was quick to find the tracks again and follow them. The ground was uneven, and roots from the stringybarks poked up here and there as if they were trying to purposely trip her. There were gullies hidden by the ground cover, one of which sent Annja to the ground. She picked herself up before Dari could help, and she tested her ankles—the right one was sore. Sprained maybe—she'd be able to tell after she'd walked on it some more.

In some places the ground cover was so thick and high that Annja had to push her way through it. The men had come this way, too—she found prints in the rare bare spots of ground.

"They're going to Dr. Michaels's camp," she said.

"Should've brought guns along," Dari said. "Nate told me I should buy one for the op shops, for when I take the money to deposit. I think I'll buy one when I get back," he said quietly.

Ahead the trees thinned and mist rose from the clearing like a cloud come to ground, the earth warmer than the air. Tendrils swirled with the breeze, and Annja imagined ghosts dancing. She paused only a moment to appreciate the serenity of it, and then she walked faster, feeling a slight burn in her leg muscles from the exertion, and a stronger burn at her right ankle. She checked for tracks on this side of the fog, and then looked for them again after she had passed through.

"Nothing." She'd lost them.

There were pieces of moss-covered shale, and in the moonlight she'd expected to see where patches had been smeared from someone walking over them. Clearly the men she'd been following had done nothing to hide their tracks; someone with no training at all could have followed them—up until this point.

Dari studied her as she followed the edge of the fog bank, looking for scraped moss, broken twigs, heel imprints.

"Nothing," she said again.

It was as if the two men had vanished, but she knew that wasn't the case. It was simply night, and she'd reached a stretch of the forest that was so littered with rock shards that finding boot prints was difficult.

Annja considered redoubling her efforts, and asking Dari for his flashlight. But it would take a considerable amount of time, and reaching Dr. Michaels was more pressing. She got her bearings and pointed toward a tall copse of white stringybarks.

"I'm pretty sure the camp is over there. It shouldn't be much farther."

"Hope not," Dari said. "Not used to all this walking. My feet hurt. My legs hurt. Hell, I'm aching all over." He dropped his voice again when he caught her scowl. "I can't turn back, though. I'm not tin arsed. I'd get myself lost. Besides, I might miss all the good stuff, eh?"

It niggled at the back of her mind that she'd lost the tracks. Annja didn't like that she had enemies around and couldn't tell where they were. She knew with certainty the men were up to no good, or else they wouldn't be here on this sodden night.

An hour later they saw a light. The forest spread away to the north and south, as if the trees had come upon an imaginary line that they were not allowed to cross. It was a natural break in the woods, Michaels had explained to her on the first day of her visit. There'd been a few trees cut down for the site, but only a few. This extensive clearing hadn't had anything grow in it for centuries, he'd said. "Since perhaps the Egyptians had come."

The tents were large and elaborate. There were five of them, one more of a canopy than anything, with tables under it for sifting and arranging artifacts. A dying fire burned in front of the nearest tent, and that was the light Annja had spotted. She stared at the fire, caught up in a memory that wasn't hers, and a shiver traveled down her back.

Dari nudged her. "I think we took a few wrong turns out there. I think we could've gotten here quicker and with less wear on the feet if we'd not gone through that fog patch."

Annja didn't reply. She glanced away from the fire and to the ridge behind the dig, which separated the tertiary site from this one. The moonlight created shadows in the rock, making it look like the cracked and leathery face of an old, old man. There were no lights on in the tents.

"Everyone's sleeping." Dari stated the obvious.

"Not for long," Annja said.

Moments later she and Dari were inside the Michaels's tent, Annja rapidly telling them about the assault at the hotel.

"So you think we saw something?" Wes Michaels sat cross-legged on his cot, unmindful that he was dressed only in pajama bottoms. His wife had thrown on a robe before allowing company in. "Or uncovered something so valuable someone would kill for it?" He rubbed his hands together as he thought.

The tent was large enough to contain two cots, a small table and four folding camp chairs. There was a trunk that likely held clothes and such, a refrigerator—the size that might fit in a college dorm room—and a small generator that powered the fridge and the light that hung above the table. Close and homey, Annja thought, just like the tents on the television show *M*A*S*H* that she'd watched as a child.

Dari had a hard time folding himself into one of the camp chairs. He'd selected the one facing Wes, so his back would be to Jennifer.

It was dry inside, save for right around the tent flap where the breeze still gusted and sent a little water onto the rug. Annja took off her jacket and hung it on the back of one of the chairs. She crouched at the foot of the cot, her ankle throbbing and letting her know it was indeed sprained.

"That jade ankh," Jennifer said. "It's the most valuable piece we found. I wouldn't want to guess at what it's worth. But it's not here. It was crated up yesterday and sent to the city. If thieves come looking for it, they'll be disappointed."

"But maybe the men who shot at you don't know it's not here," Dari said.

Annja closed her eyes and pictured Sute again. She remembered being on the ridge with Oliver, looking through his camera and seeing Sute and the others.

"No. The more I think about it," Annja said, "the more it seems that it's not what I saw—what Oliver and I saw— but *who* we saw. I can't shake that notion."

Dr. Michaels uncurled his legs and set his feet into moccasins conveniently placed by his cot. "And you think maybe Jenn and me, and the others, saw this person, too?" He shook his head. "We've not had many visitors lately, Miss Creed. You and your crew. Our funder checks in from time to time. Sometimes we have a man bring supplies in, but more often Jenn goes into the city to get what we need."

"Gives me a break from Wes," she said. Jennifer yawned and rubbed at her eyes. "Can't imagine us seeing anyone who didn't want to be seen. Least of all anyone who'd want to kill us for seeing him." She waggled her fingers as if trying to dismiss Annja's notion.

"No one came out here tonight?" Annja persisted.

"Just you, Miss Creed, and..." Wes looked to the dripping biker.

"Darioush," he said. "I own three op shops in Sydney." He paused then added, "And I'm thinking about building another one."

Wes raised both eyebrows.

"I gave her a lift out here," Dari explained. "Well, part of the way. Painter hauled us most of the rest."

Jennifer slapped her hand against her knee and yawned again. "That sounds like a story." She stretched to a camp stool that served as a nightstand and looked at the clock. "It's almost midnight. How about we bunk the two of you in with—"

"I can't even think about sleeping." Annja rose and reached for her jacket, seeing that it was snagged and the embroidery ripped—no doubt from the tree limbs and bushes of the preserve. Strings of seed beads had come loose, and there were paint speckles on the back of the right arm. She put it on. "I'm going to check the other camp."

"The uni's?" Jennifer's voice rose in disbelief. "Girl, it's almost midnight, and that's a good trek up that rise and over even in broad daylight. Not that it's all that far. The rocks just aren't all that friendly."

Annja offered them a slight smile. "You have a satellite phone here, right?"

Wes nodded.

"Keep it close, in case you need to call someone if there's trouble. And you've two security men, right? That your funder's supplied?"

"In the small tent by the sifting trays," Wes said.

"I'd wake them up," Annja continued. "Put them on alert. They've got guns, right?"

Wes nodded slowly.

"Good. The men who were after me weren't terribly good shots, but they had plenty of guns between them."

Jennifer paled, truly frightened now. "Wes, maybe we better call someone, get some police out here."

Wes shook his head. "Sat phone's been out of juice for most of two days now. I was going to pick up another charger. Should've. I'm always putting off trips into the city. But this all might be nothing, right, Miss Creed?"

Annja bit her lower lip. "I don't know. I'll be back after I check on the university site."

Dari made a move to rise, but Annja shook her head. "Stay here," she ordered.

"I don't need protection," Dari protested.

"But maybe they do." She nodded to Wes and Jennifer and parted the tent flap.

"Here." Dari reached in his pocket and tossed her his flashlight. "Not much, but it might help."

She left the tent, hurrying toward the ridge.

Annja did not look back. Otherwise she might have seen two dark-clad men in hiking boots skirt the camp and head toward the far southern tent.

13

Annja enjoyed climbing, and the ridge that stretched like the spiny backbone of some beast between the two dig sites provided little challenge—despite the absence of even rudimentary climbing equipment. Still, the slick rocks made her cautious, and so she paid attention to selecting her hand- and footholds and kept her mind strictly on the task. There was an easier way up the ridge—one she and Oliver had taken yesterday, but that would not give her as high a vantage point as she wanted this night.

She knew there was a path some way to the north, which cut through a low section of the ridge. The students and the Michaels crew traveled it once in a while to visit each other's dig. But for some reason she didn't want to take that route, either; it would take her too long, and she preferred this unanticipated, untraveled way.

Her fingers wedged into a narrow horizontal crevice and she pulled herself up. The shoulder where she'd been grazed stung; she'd opened up the wound that had been attempting to heal. Her ankle bothered her more than a little, too, and she was careful to put most of her weight on her left foot as she pushed herself up to the next crevice.

A chunk of stone snapped off in her right hand, and the muscles bunched in her left arm to keep herself steady. Her lungs were warm and her throat was growing tight from the exertion, but she welcomed the sensations, and she looked forward to the exhilarated way she would feel when she reached the top and rested a moment.

Halfway up, she thought she'd heard something below her. Dari? she wondered. The tall, bald biker had fancied himself something of her protector, refusing to leave her when the painter had dropped them off at the service road. Too bad about his bike, she thought. It would have gotten them here faster and by a better route, and she wouldn't have sprained her ankle traipsing through the soggy woods.

She heard a noise again, and she looked down, the moonlight showing nothing but upthrusts of rocks and at the edge of her vision the tops of the archaeologists' tents. The tent canopy that covered the artifacts and sifting tables looked like some giant bird with its wings spread, water pooling and making part of it sag. She couldn't see anyone moving about, but despite the moon it was too dark to see much directly around the tents.

She climbed higher, hoping Dari hadn't decided to come protect her. He seemed athletic enough, but unless he had climbing experience, tackling this section of the wet rocky ridge would be a bad idea. Looking over her shoulder again, she saw only the light and shadows of the ridge, and she no longer heard any noise.

It wasn't until she'd nearly reached the top a few minutes later that she heard a sound again, scree shifting and gravel falling below. She knew she hadn't been responsible for it.

"Dari?" she called out.

No answer.

"Dari! Wes?"

Annja scrambled to the top and waited. Someone was following her, and she would meet whoever it was up here. A part of her hoped it was Dari, that he'd ignored her request to stay with the Michaelses. She fervently hoped it wasn't Wes coming to help; he did not strike her as terribly agile, and she worried that he might fall.

A heartbeat later, she learned it was neither man. A dark-clad stranger pulled himself up on the ridge a few yards south of her position and crouched, arms to his sides to balance himself. He had on something like a ski mask, so that only his eyes and part of his nose showed. He didn't blink as he regarded her.

There was little sound up here; the breeze was still strong and stirred the leaves on the trees below, causing them to rustle with a faint noise like children whispering. But Annja's senses were so acute that she could hear the stranger's breath, steady and slow despite the climb.

"What is this about?" She knew she would fight him, had already touched her sword with her mind. But she prayed he would talk to her first. She desperately wanted answers.

"What is this about? It is about your death, American

fool." His voice was slow and soft and heavily accented. Arabic, she guessed, or some other Middle Eastern dialect. "*Kelbeh*, it is about your painful and quick death." He made no move to approach her, wanting the advance to be hers.

"Why must I die?" Annja sensed the sword just beyond her reach. She was anxious to call it, but she held back, knowing that when it appeared the time for talking to this man would be done. "Why do you need to kill me?" she asked.

"Because my master commands it, *kelbeh*, because you saw—" He stopped, eyes flickering for a moment.

"Saw him?" A flash of the stranger's eyes confirmed to Annja that it was a *who* not a *what* that she'd seen. The jade ankh, though immeasurably valuable, was not behind this. "And he didn't want to be seen, your master," she continued, still keeping the sword in limbo. "At least not by a television crew that could inadvertently send his picture into people's living rooms. That's it, isn't it? All of this is about Oliver taking a man's picture," Annja said, hoping her guess was correct.

"My master prefers…" The man trailed off, and Annja could tell he was having difficulty searching for the English words. "Secrecy." He paused. "To be as one anonymous, pretty *kelbeh*." He spit out the last word as if it were a rotten piece of meat. "You are *khanzeera al matina* to him," he hissed.

"Charming, you are," Annja whispered. "What about the students? Do they have to die, too?" she asked loudly.

"Everyone dies, *kelbeh*. No one escapes such a fate. You, however, will sooner than them."

"Did you follow me from the Cross?" Still she kept the sword from appearing.

His answer was an unseen grin that tweaked the fabric of his ski mask into a crooked fold.

"Wasn't it enough that you killed Oliver and took his cameras? No one else can see your master now. You have all the evidence."

He shifted from his left foot to his right when the breeze gusted stronger. The top of the ridge was not wide, and he was being careful to keep his balance.

"Wasn't it enough?" Annja repeated. Her anger was showing, something she tried to keep in check. The sensation of the hilt teasing her hand was becoming more pronounced, but still she kept the sword at bay.

"He begged for his life, I was told, the American with the big cameras and the blue eyes," the man replied. His voice was even and without emotion. "He did not suffer much, I was also told. There was no need for undue pain. There was only the need for his eternal silence." The man finally shuffled toward her a few steps, anxious that she was not coming to meet him. "You do not need to suffer, either. You need only to die."

If she leaned forward, she could reach him with the sword. The blade was starting to materialize, a length of ghostly silver. Annja had gained much control over the sword's coming and going over the past several months. Her mind still kept it from fully forming, but the air shimmered in anticipation. *One more question,* she thought.

"Where is Oliver's body? My cameraman? At least give me that much."

"Such knowledge would do you no good, as you will soon join him."

He sprang forward then, and the sword materialized. She heard the wind gusting stronger still, heard his breath coming faster and louder, the scree trickling down the side of the ridge as he'd dislodged it. She heard her own heartbeat angrily in her ears, and she heard the sword whistle as she lunged.

"Where's Oliver's body?" she repeated, though she knew she'd get no answer. "Where, where, where?"

Annja swung wide and extended herself, slicing him across the chest, careful not to inflict a death blow. His blood speckled her face, and she drew the sword back in a reverse arc, lower this time.

"I'll give you once last chance to tell me!"

He spit at her. "Where did the sword come from, *kelbeh?*" He held a hand to his chest, as if trying to keep the blood inside him. "No matter, I can kill you anyway."

He reached to the small of his back and retrieved a gun. In response, she stepped in closer and lunged again, cutting deep through his belly. He fell dead at her feet and the gun clattered down the side of the ridge and out of sight.

Annja was fast, accurate and powerful, had been so before she inherited Joan of Arc's mantle. But since she'd been passed the sword, all of her physical attributes had become even more honed. She could sense things most people would not notice.

She spun to face the second man. She'd heard him clawing his way up the ridge, trying to be silent so he could come at her from behind, but loose gravel had given him away. He had no doubt thought that she'd given all her attention to his companion. But he was about to find out how dead wrong that assumption was.

"Kelbeh," he said, using the same derogatory term his fellow had favored. *"In'al yomak!"* He was dressed differently than the other man in that in place of a ski mask he wore a tightly wrapped turban and a pair of night-vision goggles.

He'd give her no more information than his friend had, she knew. In fact, he might not even speak English.

"In'al yomak!" he repeated. *"Yin'al mayteenak!"*

"I don't even want to know what that means." Annja let out a low breath and brought the sword up parallel to her torso.

His eyes on the blade, he skittered back, agile as a cat. He hissed at her and raised his hand, bringing it down in an instant on a slab of stone at his feet. It was a demonstration of his skill. He cracked the slab in half with one blow, looked up and met her eyes.

"Impressive," she admitted. "A brick can withstand almost seven hundred pounds of static load. So you know how to split bricks like a good martial artist. I can do that, too, but I've no reason to show off and chip a nail for the likes of you," she said.

His expression—all she could see was the lower half of his face—didn't give a hint that he understood her. The goggles were aimed straight at her, as if the eyes behind them were measuring her mettle. His pants were tight, almost like a leotard, and so she could see his leg muscles quiver ever so slightly, the only suggestion she had that he was going to move.

He leaped at her, anticipating where she would swing and landing crouched under it, driving his elbow up into her abdomen and knocking the breath from her.

Annja managed to hold on to her sword, but she reeled from the blow. The elbow, almost all bone, could be a devastating weapon, and he employed it again before she could retaliate, this time striking higher and cracking a few of her ribs.

"Damn you," she cursed under her breath. She brought the pommel of the sword down, intending to hit the top of his head and crack his skull, but instead landing the blow on his shoulder. He was moving again, coming at her from the side now.

It was a deadly dance they performed on the narrow ridge, the moonlight setting her sword to glimmering and revealing every move the two made.

He certainly was a more skilled opponent than his friend, and probably better than the ones she'd fought at the hotel. He was new to her, not being one of the men she'd spotted in the Cross or on the sidewalk this morning before she'd leaped onto the bus. She decided to leave the attacks to him, opting for defense to wear him down and to protect her throbbing ribs.

If he had a gun, he'd made no move to draw it. Guns were loud and could wake both camps, and she'd noted that his companion had only pulled his at the end in desperation.

So they don't want to wake the camps, she thought. Maybe they had no plans to hurt any of the archaeologists. Or maybe they'd planned to kill them stealthily, slipping from tent to tent. The rest of her thoughts disappeared when he moved again.

He clearly respected her as an opponent, stepping in and then back, his gaze flitting between her eyes and the blade, careful not to get so close that she could skewer him. He said something to her, in a language she could not understand, and then he crouched and waited for her to come to him. When that didn't happen, he took the offensive once more.

He raised a hand above his head, hoping to draw her eyes up. Annja knew better and kept watching his face. Then, just as she drew the sword above her head, he shot forward, right leg kicking and straight as a rod. She recognized it as a long-range power kick, a martial-arts move used for both defense and offense, a way to hurt your opponents while at the same time keeping them from you. She brought the sword down and stepped to the side just in time. His foot brushed her jacket, and her blade struck his leg and bounced off as if it had struck armor.

Next, she twisted and pulled the sword back again, brought it down, intending to cleave his leg off at the kneecap. But he was fast, perhaps faster than her. He'd moved out of her range and her sword whistled in the wind. Before she could raise it again, he put his weight on his uninjured leg and kicked out with the other, this time catching her hip and spinning her. Annja felt her right foot slip on the scree, and the dull ache in her ankle became a fiery brand that brought a cry from her lips.

She cursed as she regained her balance, raised the sword above her head again and watched him dart in so close she couldn't effectively bring the sword down. He grabbed her arms with both hands, fingers digging in and with a surprising strength keeping her arms high. He brought his face in inches from hers, and she could smell his breath. It was foul and brought to mind the scent of rotting leaves.

He said something else, soft and muffled so that she couldn't make it out, then he stepped to the side and tugged her arms down, raised his knee in a jackhammer movement and buried it in her stomach. She nearly lost her grip on the sword.

A small part of her admired the move. From her training she knew that a well-delivered knee strike could exert about two tons of force. This one had certainly been enough to make her gasp and set her cracked ribs on fire. She fought for air and distance. She needed to get her opponent back so he couldn't neutralize her sword again. And yet she could not give him an opening for his long-range kicks.

She matched him for style, forcing the pain in her ribs and her ankle to the back of her mind. He employed Muay Thai, she recognized, a specialized mastery of martial arts taught in Thailand. She was reasonably familiar with the Hanuman technique and Chaiya forms. In the latter the arms drive the fists, and so she used them to drive the sword forward, making the blade an extension of herself.

She bobbed and weaved as he tried to get inside to use his knee strike again. All the while he avoided her blade.

"Yin'al mayteenak!"

Annja didn't offer any retort, saving her energy for her swings. She finally landed a solid blow on his right arm, the blood arcing away. He didn't cry out, but the pain and surprise registered on his twitching lips. Though she'd drawn blood, he continued to fight as if nothing was wrong. She pressed her attack, and he brought up his wrists and elbows, blocking the pommel of her sword and keeping the blade from cutting him again. He was strong and pushed her back.

Her chest felt tight, from the trek through the woods and up the rise, and from the blows he'd landed against her, and her lungs felt as if they had become a well-stoked furnace. She sucked in breath after hot breath and kept sparring with him, waiting for an opening he was disinclined to give.

He was supremely skilled, she admitted, clearly able to master the pain from where she'd sliced him and able to avoid her well-aimed blows. He continued to use his wrists and elbows to keep the sword from reaching him, and she continued to keep him from getting inside. She had no idea how long the fight was taking, minutes probably, though it felt like hours, her legs and arms becoming lead weights that took considerable effort to move.

On your terms, she thought. I will try this on your terms. She took a deep breath and held it, willed the sword away and noted the astonishment on his face. Annja had learned the rudiments of Muay Thai from a man who'd fought in the Thailand arenas in his youth and who had opened a gym in New York with the proceeds from his winnings. A brutal sport that often led to serious injury and sometimes death, she normally avoided using it. The art left little room for her sword and was not as graceful as other forms.

This time she let the man in, using his own move against him. She grabbed the front of his heavy shirt and pulled him down with all her might, driving her knee up in the same motion and landing a solid strike to his chin. She heard his jaw snap and felt him sag momentarily against her. Then she pushed him back and brought up her leg, kicking him in the stomach and watching him sway on his feet.

To kill him? Annja preferred leaving her opponents alive if possible. But she doubted she'd get anything useful out of him, and hadn't heard him speak one word of English—or of any other language she recognized. Killing him would keep him from coming after her, yet he hardly seemed a threat now.

He fought to keep his balance, face looking broken and deformed, wet with his blood. His eyes looked unfocused.

"We can stop this," she said. She took in a few deep breaths and shifted her weight to her left leg. "I don't have to kill you."

"Yin'al mayteenak," he repeated, though this time there was no power in the words, and it took effort to speak them. His chest rose and fell irregularly and he fought for breath.

"Yin'al yourself," she retorted. Her mind reached for the sword again. She would make this quick like an execution.

But before it solidified in her hand, he rushed at her. Unsteady, he nevertheless tried to continue the fight. He'd appeared to make himself look more injured than he truly was. He spun and kicked, his foot hissing against the satin fabric of her jacket. He managed a second spin kick, this time slamming the toe of his hiking boot against her left thigh. A third kick and she reached down and grabbed his ankle with both hands. She pulled up, setting him completely off balance and pitching him to the ground.

She followed through by driving her heel into his chest. She felt his ribs cave in, and she kicked him again. With a deep breath and a step back, she lashed out at the side of his head with all the strength she could summon. His neck snapped.

Dropping to her knees, Annja reached behind her and grabbed her right ankle. It was swollen and pulsed with pain.

She sat and tugged off the shoe, then reached over to the man she'd just dropped. His tight-fighting pants were made of something similar to leotard material. She ripped them along the seam, and then tore off a strip. It wasn't as good as a bandage, but it was better than nothing. She'd sprained her ankle a few times before and knew how to wrap it. She used a second strip to reinforce it, then she jimmied the shoe back on. It barely fit over the makeshift bandage and the tongue rode up and lolled out. She had just enough lace to tie it.

An Arab schooled in Muay Thai, she mused, and in Australia trying to kill me because of someone I saw. Interesting and awful.

She felt the lower part of his leg. There was no fat on it, and she could feel calluses from the knee down, strong like a length of iron pipe. She recalled her own Muay Thai instruction, where she kicked a padded pole to strengthen her shins. Her instructor said he'd been forced to kick bamboo trees until he could no longer stand.

"Who were you working for? And what did you do with Oliver's body?" She gingerly prodded her ribs and decided that two were cracked for certain, and a third was likely. "A lot of pain and woe I've had for shooting a program on fringe archaeology."

Still sitting, she leaned over and felt his pockets. "Nothing." She turned him over and found one on the back of his pants. "No wallet. No ID. No gun, though your companion had that covered." But there was a twenty-dollar Australian bill. "For emergencies maybe?" She nearly stuffed it back into his pocket, but then she put it in her jacket pocket instead. "You're not going to need it anymore."

She pulled off his goggles and scowled. He was a complete stranger to her, and she wondered how many goons this "master" had working for him. "How could you and your friend have followed us so quickly from the Cross?"

But maybe he hadn't followed her, she thought. Maybe he'd simply come out here to wait for her or to wait for further instructions. Or maybe he and his partner had passed her and Dari on the highway or taken a different road, passed them when they were at the gas station or riding in the back of the painter's truck. She looked at his hiking boots. The treads were caked with mud. She pushed herself up and gingerly tested her wrapped ankle, walked to the other man and looked at his boots, too. Annja wanted to make sure these were the two she'd tried to track through the soggy woods.

She turned this man over and searched his back pocket.

"Bingo." She pulled out a thin wallet and leafed through it, holding it out so she could see in the moonlight. There was a driver's license and three credit cards.

"Finally some identification." But the name would do her no good at the moment, and it might not even be the man's real one. She put the wallet in her jacket pocket and then checked the pockets on his shirt. "Bingo again." She found a set of keys, one obviously to the SUV, the other small, as if it fit a lockbox or padlock. These went in her jeans pocket.

Annja waited only another few minutes before starting down the western side of the ridge. From her vantage point the differences between the two sites were stark. Dr. Michaels's staff had large tents with some of the comforts of home. The students' tents—three of them in total—were much smaller and looked as if they'd been purchased from a used-sporting-goods store. There was also a canopy tent, and though Annja couldn't see what was under it, she assumed it was for sifting tables and any artifacts they'd found. And where Michaels's archaeologists had been working on a long section of midden that practically ran the length of this section of the ridge, the student excavation was much smaller.

She suspected there was no security, just students on a campout who had no doubt signed waivers to hold the university harmless should anything happen to them.

A light burned in one of the tents, and Annja could see two forms silhouetted. A man and a woman, sitting opposite each other, she noted, the woman small but well endowed. As Annja continued to pick her way down the ridge, she saw the woman lean forward and remove her shirt, then the man edged closer.

No security, and no staff supervision, she thought. While that made it easy for the archaeology students to have a tryst, it also made it easy for Annja to move about unnoticed.

In a handful of minutes she was at the base of the ridge. Okay, I'm here, she thought. What's the next step?

Talking to the students, certainly, trying to figure out who the men were at the site yesterday, which one didn't like his picture taken. Get some names, then get back to Sydney. She had transportation now, an SUV courtesy of the men on top of the ridge who would no longer be driving anywhere. She would contact the police and tie everything up in a neat little bow and fly back to New York. The skeletons of the giant penguin-things in South America could wait a few more days.

"If only things would turn out that easy," she whispered.

Annja kept to the edge of the ridge. With the moon almost directly overhead, the shadows from the rock effectively cloaked her. It wasn't that she didn't want the students to know she was there, she just wanted to do a little exploring first before she made her presence known, make sure there were no more Arab assassins skulking around.

She crept to the canopy tent and noted that they had only one sifting table, and it was not nearly as well constructed as Dr. Michaels's. A second table had shards of pots spread out, labels under some of them. She glided close and retrieved the small flashlight from her pocket. Using her body as a shield, she flicked it on and looked from one object to the next.

One pottery piece showed a rendering of what was clearly Anubis, an ankh held at his side. Another was of a kangaroo. Most of the pieces were so small and weathered that little could be made of them. No wonder the uni-

versity was given free reign here; all of this was interesting, and should be recovered and documented, but it was
not near the scope and value of Dr. Michaels's find.

She retraced her steps to where she'd come down the
ridge, traveled a little to the south and found three pieces
of canvas stretched out on the ground and held in place
by tent stakes. It only took a little effort to pull the stakes
loose. She glanced behind her to the three tents.

What is so special about this site that would draw this
man who wants me dead? Annja had to know.

No one was stirring—save the couple intertwining
themselves in front of the lantern. Annja pulled up a
corner of the canvas and saw a slab the size of a manhole
cover. There were lines of hieroglyphics—half-closed
eyes, stylized birds, cats, cow-headed men. Now this was
something significant, she thought. She wondered if Wes
Michaels had seen it.

The other two canvases covered similar slabs, one twice
the size and in excellent condition with deep etchings that
marked it an important find. Good for the students, she
thought. She hadn't seen a piece this large at the Michaels
site.

Time to wake someone up, she decided. She started
toward the closest tent, when she caught movement out
of the corner of her eye. With so many shadows, she
hadn't seen the figure hiding. It had bushy hair, and it
moved a little awkwardly, so Annja didn't think it was one
of the Arab assassins.

"You, stop!" Her voice was commanding but soft, not
wanting to alert the entire camp.

But the figure didn't stop. It hurried to another collection of shadows and disappeared. Annja let out a frustrated breath and followed.

"What's this?" Annja figured she'd be practically on top of her target, but instead found only rocks. The shadows from the ridge stretched out and practically covered all of the ground. But the moonlight revealed a metal spike, tall and driven into the ground, and this drew her curiosity. Had her eyesight not been so keen, she wouldn't have noticed it. She edged closer and saw a second spike, and a rope ladder affixed to them and leading into a tight crevice.

"I bet you went down here, didn't you?" she whispered.

As if in response, she saw a light bobbing below.

"Definitely interesting." And definitely a place she would have otherwise explored in daylight, after she'd talked to the students and reported to the police. But the presence of the flashlight-toting stranger forced her hand.

She gave another glance behind her. No one in the tents stirred. People were in there, though. She heard faint cries of passion from the one tent, snoring from another.

I could take a quick look, see if I can find you, whoever you are, she thought. Annja had an inner sense about things, and it was telling her this could be connected to her troubles. Besides, she had a flashlight.

She held the flashlight between her teeth, just as Dari had done when he worked on the bike. She lowered herself over the side and started to climb down, the darkness reaching up and swallowing her.

14

Annja descended slowly, holding the small flashlight in her teeth and keeping both hands on the rope ladder, which swayed precariously.

She didn't see another light below, and so she thought the mysterious figure might have turned it off, opting to hide in the plethora of shadows.

This is stupid, she thought, coming down here without any equipment. The flashlight in her mouth certainly couldn't qualify as equipment, and she was in sorry shape with cracked ribs and a sprained ankle.

The flashlight's beam was so narrow it didn't reveal anything other than a rock face about ten feet past the ladder. Dari had probably bought it just for its tight beam so he could work on his motorcycle engine, she realized.

I should climb right back up and talk to the students, leave my mystery man to this hole, she told herself. She'd herd the students together with Dr. Michaels's group and go to the police. The problem was, Annja realized, that this whole thing was one big mystery. And once she'd gotten hold of a mystery, she didn't want to let go. Like a dogged sleuth out of a good paperback thriller, she needed to puzzle it out, which included finding the figure that disappeared down here. I should climb right back up this instant and…

But she kept going down, and after what she guessed was about a thirty-foot climb, her feet touched solid rock. Just a little look around first, she thought, provided she could see anything with the tiny flashlight. Maybe I can find him…or her. Maybe it's a student, she thought.

"Hello?" Again she kept her voice hushed. "I'm not going to hurt you. I just want to talk." Oh, that's pretty lame, she chided herself.

She didn't hear anyone walking, and no one was close enough so she could hear breathing. The floor was slick from what rain had come in. She shuffled to the wall straight ahead, brushing aside the rope ladder as if it was a curtain. The floor was even, and she paused to look down, bending over and holding the flashlight close. She ran her fingers across it.

"Natural and unnatural at the same time," she pronounced it. It was granite, but it was polished as if it had been worked by men. Not quite to the standards one would find on the floor of a government building or museum, but definitely not something Mother Nature had done on her own. "Curious and curiouser."

She went to the wall, finding it had been worked, as well, and was covered with hieroglyphics. In her amazement, she momentarily forgot about her quarry. "I wish

I could read this," she whispered. Annja mentally added hieroglyphics to the list of subjects she intended to study—when she had time.

She ran a hand through her hair to brush it off her forehead. It was still wet, and the bun she'd twisted it into earlier had come loose. It was tangled with leaves and tiny branches, and she brushed out a clump of dirt.

Annja tried to study the carvings the way she'd read books when she was a kid with a flashlight under the covers at the orphanage. Line by line.

There were images of birds, looking as if they were walking backward, and there were other birds that faced cow-headed men. There was a cow-headed woman figure that was larger than the other figures. Annja recognized her as Hathor. Again the goddess had upraised arms, as if to welcome the sun. The carvings were deep, hardly weathered, the cave protecting them from the elements and time. Annja withdrew her fingers, not wanting the oil and dirt from her skin to mar the images.

Dr. Michaels didn't know about this. She was sure he would have told her in his excitement. She suspected hardly anyone knew about them. The crevice opening was small, and would be shielded by the shadows from the ridge even during daylight. She wouldn't have noticed it herself if the moon hadn't glinted off one of the spikes holding the ladder. But the students knew about it, and maybe the "master," and certainly the mysterious figure she'd pursued down here.

Once more she told herself it was time to go back up, that she'd have a chance to explore this later. If the stranger she'd followed didn't want to be found, she certainly wasn't going to be able to find him with her dinky light. But the wonder of this hidden place held her, and she continued to look at the hieroglyphics.

The previous night in her hotel room she'd surfed some of the Internet sites about Egyptian deities, specifically Hathor. She was typically rendered as a cow with a sun disk between her perfect horns, or sometimes as a cow-headed woman in resplendent garb. The latter was how she was shown here.

Annja remembered reading that Hathor's name was sometimes translated as "the House of Horus," which associated her with the royal family, as Horus was associated with kings. Some saw her as the mother goddess of the entire world, and unlike other Egyptian deities, her priests were male *and* female. Typically, a male deity had male priests, and a female deity, female priests.

Music and dance were part of the prayer rituals. The figures Annja studied seemed to dance under the narrow beam of her flashlight, and the breeze that found its way down faintly whistled as if in homage to the goddess.

Some saw Hathor as the veritable incarnation of dance, Annja recalled, and the goddess was said to have danced before Ra when he despaired or was lost in melancholy. Artists prayed to her seeking inspiration for their creations. The offerings to her included twin mirrors—one for the goddess to look upon herself and one for the worshiper to see his or her own beauty.

Hathor was worshiped throughout all of Egypt, and apparently in Australia, as well, Annja mused.

"The seductress, lady of turquoise, and lady of malachite," Annja said. Hathor was called those things among her many titles. "Mining. There was something about mining." She mentally called up one of the Web sites she had visited. Hathor was worshiped by miners and was associated with precious metals and gemstones. If a miner held Hathor's favor, he would have good finds to help support his family.

Annja saw carvings that might have symbolized a mine. That would fit, Annja thought. And there were other shapes, a goose, lion, cat, a tree. Hathor was a goddess who was represented by many shapes, including those. The tree would be a sycamore fig, she thought.

Why a cow? Milk? Nourishing? Life? Hathor embodied beauty, life, security, health, warmth, and Annja figured a cow might be associated with those things…certainly with sustaining life. And a fig tree could exude a milky substance.

She'd read that the goddess was also tied to fragrances, particularly myrrh, which was especially valuable and precious to the Egyptians.

"Like this site must be precious to whoever wants me dead," Annja muttered. "Hmm…what's this?" Her light glinted off something in the wall, and she moved it closer so she could see better. "Brass? No, gold." Just a trace of it, she discovered, inlaid as a piece of jewelry around Hathor's bovine neck. Wait until Wes sees this, she thought.

There were more traces of gold in some of the other carvings Annja spotted, these at waist height; she'd been looking at eye level and higher until now. The carvers must have taken strands of gold and pounded them into the cracks to inlay it.

There wasn't a lot of gold—at least not that she could

see with her tiny light. But the presence of gold marked it as different from the hieroglyphics at the larger dig.

She pressed her face near the stone and smelled its age. There was a mustiness to the cavern, and despite the breeze that brought a little fresh air down, what she breathed had a stagnant odor.

"Just a few more minutes," she said. Then she'd go back up. She'd postpone the shoot in South America and stay in Australia, convince Doug there was far more to this than a one-hour piece on fringe archaeology. She owed it to Oliver to put more effort into bringing these amazing sites to light.

Her flashlight flickered and blinked like the tail of a firefly. Then it went out, plunging her into blackest black.

She put the useless flashlight in her pocket, not wanting to litter the cave, and reached her fingers to the wall. She looked up, hoping to see a little moonlight coming through the small crevice, but there was nothing. The ridge shadowing the area let not even a hint of light in. It was a wonder she'd even noticed one of the spikes holding the rope ladder.

Annja didn't panic. She wasn't afraid of the dark. Rather, she tended to find it sort of comforting. She walked her fingers along the wall and took baby steps, not wanting to trip or to go too far and miss the ladder. She tried to picture the ladder and how far she'd come from it, but she'd become too distracted by the hiero-glyphics to take a good guess. It couldn't be too far, though, she told herself. This cave couldn't be that big.

Sounds came to her as she moved. The chirping of some insects that had made a home in this place, the breeze, her breathing and finally the crunch of some-thing she'd just stepped on. She had gone too far, she realized, as she'd not stepped on anything in her initial explorations. She knelt and felt around her feet, finding thin pieces of wood.

Pencils, she realized as she explored blindly. And pens, a clipboard, and—thank God—a flashlight. It was a large, heavy one, with a square battery beneath it that weighed at least a pound. She ran her fingers across it before turning it on, finding a bulbous light at the back with a separate switch, and a half-globe light at the front that was about six inches across. The latter was what she wanted, and so she found the proper switch.

The beam was bright, broad and welcoming, and it revealed an assortment of things around her feet—the writing instruments that she'd broken; three plastic clip-boards, each holding a thick sheaf of paper, the top pages covered in notes; a six-pack of bottled water, unopened; an open cardboard box filled with pairs of white gloves and plastic and paper bags; and a tape measure. She set the flashlight on the ground and tugged free one of the water bottles; it went down quickly and soothed her dry throat.

Then she picked up the light again and swung it around so she could get an overall look of the cave—and at the person she'd followed there.

"Oh, my." It was far bigger than she expected, so large her light didn't quite reach the opposite wall. Beetles skittered away from the flashlight beam, trying to find refuge in the shadows. A pair of thin brown lizards scam-pered away, too, as Annja continued to try to take it all in.

She saw no trace of the person she'd followed.

Where could he have gone? And just how big is this place?

It was a man-worked chamber for the most part, with chiseled walls behind her and to her right. Walls made of stone blocks carved so precisely they didn't need mortar made up the other three walls. It was a pentagon, though not all the sides were of equal length. And all the sides were covered with a myriad of hieroglyphics, many of them inlaid here and there with gold and decorated with stone chips she recognized as opals. The largest figures were of Hathor, but Horus was present, too, and Anubis. Mixed in with the stylized birds she'd seen at the Michaels dig were renderings of kangaroos and wombats and something that might be a koala.

There were three pillars, and whether they were necessary to help support the ceiling or were for decoration, Annja couldn't tell. They were ringed with half suns, cow heads and more kangaroos. There were symbols in rows and columns that she knew could be translated into words. A few of the symbols she recognized from pieces at Dr. Michaels's site and from books and Internet sites she'd perused.

Near one of the pillars two lights stood on poles, like those a photographer might use to illuminate a person posing for a portrait. They'd be used to bathe the cave in light, which was something she'd like to do just to get a better look. Cables ran from them to a small generator that sat between two large, intact urns.

Incredible relics, she thought, looking at the urns. What an amazing, amazing find. One of the urns was covered in elaborate engravings of ankhs, half suns and kangaroos, some of them painted. The other was partially covered, as if someone had started work on it and then stopped.

She moved closer to the urns so her flashlight beam might reach the wall behind them. She was rewarded by seeing two more pillars, but these had collapsed into a jumble of broken stones that had become coated in places with lime. The small brown lizards she'd seen earlier had escaped there, and they scurried into a crack in one of the larger pieces. More beetles hurried into the shadows.

"Don't mean to disturb you," Annja told them. "I'm just looking." Maybe an earth tremor had brought the columns down. She tilted the light upward and saw cracks in the ceiling where the tops of the pillars had been. She also saw more hieroglyphics. They appeared to cover every inch of the stone ceiling. "They were very busy here, the Egyptians," she said.

She only glanced at the symbols; they were similar to the ones on the walls. Then she continued to shine the light around the cave, seeing if there was a niche where the mystery man might be hiding. Chamber, she corrected herself after a moment. She'd only thought it a cave when she came down with Dari's tiny flashlight. *Temple* perhaps would be a better term, she mused, as so many of the symbols were of Hathor.

There was a stone head to the east, about the size of a compact car. It was in the shape of a cow's head with forward-facing human-looking eyes. The top of the head had been chiseled and polished into a flat surface so it could serve as a table or an altar. Annja glided toward it, her light reaching out to more of the chamber beyond.

Maybe the man's hiding behind the cow head, she thought. She'd grab him and then they'd both go up. She'd go talk to the students and find her way to the police. She'd come back down here and turn on the larger lights, bring a camera and get some shots of everything.

A half-dozen yards beyond the cow's head, the longest of the five walls was revealed to have niches in it. Annja approached them, shivering when she saw the contents. In each niche—and there were dozens—she saw the remains of birds and rodents, all apparent failed attempts at mummification.

No natron, she thought. They tried to use something else, and it didn't work. There was a fusty smell to this section of the chamber, but that was more from the age of the place than anything. The animals had given up their scents centuries ago. She skirted the wall, grimly fascinated by the collection of bones and strips of cloth. She guessed that she was well under the rock ridge at this point, and that the chamber was easily two hundred feet across at its widest point.

She turned to go back to the rope ladder, thinking perhaps that the man had climbed the ladder while she was lost in the dark. Her flashlight beam struck a slash in the wall that she at first thought merely a discoloration in the stone. But it was more than that, and she hurried toward it. The slash was a passageway, hewed into the rock and rimmed with carvings of Anubis, god of the dead.

"He went this way. He must have," Annja whispered. She didn't hesitate; she aimed the flashlight forward and went inside. It was a hallway, more like a tunnel, she thought, considering that it was narrow and the ceiling no more than six feet high. She felt a little claustrophobic, but she kept going, and she tried to picture where she was headed with respect to the ridge and the two dig sites. She could tell she was descending, though only at a slight angle, and after a dozen yards the trail curved gently to the east. After a dozen more yards it swung back to the west, ending at a set of steps that led down. On the walls on each side she saw faint carvings of Anubis, life-size, with the god's pointed ears touching the ceiling.

She tested the first step, finding it solid. She didn't want her weight to cause anything to crumble. Have the students been this way? she wondered. After a moment she answered that. Someone had to have come down here. I can practically see their boot prints. My mystery man. The light bounced with each of her footfalls, showing that dust had been disturbed ahead of her on the center of the stairs.

Why had they kept this a secret from Wes Michaels? She answered that question almost immediately. If the university thoroughly explored and recorded this on its own, it would gain all the credit and could profit financially and garner worldwide attention. And they'd not leaked a word of this yet, or there'd be at least some publicity on the archaeology sites.

Who's involved with this? she wondered. Someone beyond the university, certainly, as otherwise Annja would not be the target of Arab martial-arts masters. University of Sydney professors didn't strike her as the types who would bring in hired assassins.

The stairs narrowed to the point her shoulders brushed

the walls. She walked sideways to the bottom, which she put at another twenty feet down from the chamber above. Again there were life-size images of Anubis.

She stepped out into another chamber, this much smaller than the first one. It smelled ghastly, and a pan of the light showed why. The ceiling had spiderweb cracks in it. Water had trickled through and had ruined the goods arrayed on the floor—long-rotted animal hides, bodies wrapped in cloth, which from their outlines looked to be nothing more than skeletons, jars that had been filled with grain and other foodstuffs and now contained only mold.

The smell was so intense, Annja fought to keep from gagging. The coolness of the depth and the lack of fresh air likely had kept everything from turning to dust. Her stomach roiled and she cupped her free hand over her mouth. Still, rather than retreat she played the light along the walls, seeing more hieroglyphics, though not nearly as elaborate as the ones above.

She saw another doorway, and then a second one—this one leading to another tunnel that appeared to slant up.

Which one did he take?

She hurried toward the first doorway, picking a path around the jars and corpses and finding the air even worse when she poked her head through. She bent and retched until her stomach ached and her cracked ribs burned. Then she glanced in.

The chamber beyond was natural; the Egyptians had not carved a single image into it that she could see. Water trickled down one side and flowed across the floor in a straight line, and she guessed there must be an underground stream running through the ridge above. There was a pool roughly in the center, which the water ran to, reminding her of cisterns in Aztec and Mayan ruins. The Egyptians might have used this place to get freshwater while they worked on their underground complex.

The water certainly was no longer fresh. Littering the pool's surface were hundreds of small dead fish, their eyes bulging and their bellies white in the beam of the flashlight. They were responsible for the incredible stench.

"Ugh," Annja pronounced. Now it definitely was time to leave.

She spun and blinked furiously, meeting another beam of light—this one aimed right at her eyes.

"Put your flashlight down and put your hands up!"

Because the light had practically blinded her, Annja couldn't see the speaker, but she guessed it was the man she'd followed. He'd gotten behind her and hid, waited for the right time to approach.

"Do it now!" he ordered.

Annja complied.

15

The doors were locked after 8:00 p.m., so Hamam used his key card to enter the building. The hall before him was shadowy, as only every fourth bank of overhead lights was on at this late hour to conserve electricity. "The tomb," the other professors who frequented the offices at night referred to it. Hamam was amused by the reference.

There were only two other instructors here this evening, both from the arts department; he'd spotted their cars in the parking lot. Their offices were on the floor above his, at the opposite end of the hall. They were no doubt working late grading term essays that students had started turning in over the past few days. Hamam had essays on his desk, too, but he had no plans to peruse them. He would be gone from the university before he was supposed to hand grades over to the department head.

Hamam enjoyed the gloominess of this building at night; he thought the dimness made it seem properly eerie and gave the place a little character. Modern structures were usually so sterile and uninteresting, nothing like the ruins he relished, or his home north of Cairo. He listened to his own footfalls as he went, the leather soles of his expensive Italian shoes gliding across the recently polished floor, the heels clicking slowly and rhythmically. The night janitor had already passed by; Hamam could smell the residue of the cleaning supplies. He would not have to put up with the man's overly loud classical selections. It wasn't that Hamam didn't appreciate a good orchestra. He truly did. But the janitor's taste tended toward popular baroque, and the orchestras hailed from cities such as Boston and Cincinnati, lacking the musical refinement of the European symphonies with their most excellent conductors.

He fumbled in his pocket for his office keys. While the building's outer doors had been fitted with mechanisms to read key cards, Hamam doubted the university would ever spend the money to replace the simple locks on the individual offices and storage rooms. He smiled—in a week or so the university's funds and locks would be irrelevant.

Hamam's movements were ritualistic. He opened the door with his left hand, reached in and flicked on the light with his right. Two steps in and he hung his hat on the hook on the wall. A quick turn and he shut the door behind him and flipped the latch to lock it. Unlike many of the other professors in this building and in the others throughout the campus, Hamam never left his door open.

"I expected you some time ago."

Hamam's normally stoic mask was gone in an instant, replaced by wide-eyed astonishment. He gasped, and then his surprise turned to anger, his fists clenching so tight his knuckles whitened.

The high-backed chair at his desk had been turned to face the window, so Hamam could not have noticed that someone was sitting in it.

"I've been here for more than an hour, Gahiji." The voice was sonorous. The speaker waited a moment and then slowly swiveled the chair so he could stare across the desk at Hamam. "Nearly two, I think." He steepled his fingers and rested his chin on them. Like the professor, he was a small man, but he was not quite as thin, and the skin on his face was taut, the lower half of it looking shiny and wet from scarring. His hair was shoulder length, oiled and neatly tied at the back of his head. He had on a gray suit coat, the cut of it and material looking expensive. Beneath it he wore a black T-shirt with a slightly frayed collar.

"Sayed," Hamam said. "I told you never to come here." The professor's eyes were thin slits, and his face was flushed with anger. He clenched and unclenched his fists and drew his shoulders back. "I am paying you enough that you can damn well follow my instructions."

A silence settled between them, neither man wanting to break it. From outside—Sayed had opened the window— a car horn sounded. A moment later there was a burst of young laughter from students walking past on a nearby sidewalk. Sayed leaned forward, the desk chair creaking. Finally, he spoke.

"My apologies, Gahiji, for intruding into your academic world." The words were flat and did not seem heartfelt, and they did little to soothe Hamam's ire.

"You were never to set foot at the university," Hamam softly raged. "Never to be seen in any public places on this continent. Never to be seen publicly with me."

"Because you do not want to be seen with an international terrorist?"

"Yes," Hamam said. "I'm paying you well."

"Indeed. I am satisfied with the amount."

Another silence settled, this longer than the first. Again, Sayed finally broke it.

"The world thinks I am in England or Ireland, yes? Interpol places me somewhere near London. Bombing soccer fields and buses and underground trains." Sayed leaned back in the chair now, making it squeak even louder. "The world thinks I am there because of the news reports, maybe, but the American television woman knows I am here instead. She and the man with the camera saw me yesterday at your camp." Sayed stood, the fabric of his jacket falling gracefully against his frame.

"Dig, Sayed. It is called a dig, not a *camp*."

Sayed shrugged indifferently.

"And the issue of the American archaeologist is being resolved," Hamam continued. "Isn't that correct?"

He strode farther into his office and waited for Sayed to come around to the front of the desk. Sayed took the simple wooden chair intended for students, and Hamam eased himself into the high-backed chair, placing his hands on the arms of it as if it were a throne. "The men that you acquired on my behalf have killed the cameraman and sent me his cameras and laptop. I have destroyed all evidence of your presence."

"The body burned, I assume, this cameraman. My associates are always tidy," Sayed said.

"Burned, I was told, yes. Incinerated shortly after the deed. No trace remains of the man or any of his belongings. The police have no clues, beyond the bodies of your associates."

"And they cannot be traced to us. But the woman…" Sayed's eyes burned, the first real emotion he'd shown since Hamam had come in. "The woman still lives."

"Your remaining men—"

"Have not reported to me of her demise. Nor have they reported to you." Sayed raised his eyebrows in question.

"No, I've not heard from any of them."

"And three of them will never be heard from again. Killed at the hotel—by her, apparently. The bodies you mentioned," Sayed made a *tsk-tsk*ing sound. "It is not good for my business that those I hire are killed. It makes recruiting others a little more difficult and a little more expensive."

"You're asking me for more money?" Hamam asked.

Sayed raised his hands and feigned an expression of bewilderment. Then his icy countenance returned. "Not yet, Gahiji. As you've said, I've been paid well so far. And as I've said…I am satisfied."

Hamam toyed with some of the objects on his desk— a pen holder, calendar, a paperweight shaped like a pyramid. "I've arranged the trucks," he said quietly.

Sayed nodded.

"They should be more than adequate."

"And painters?"

"Already handled. They should have finished earlier today."

"I will need to inspect them and load them, and I wish to do this now."

"They are in an old industrial building not far from the heart of downtown. Here is the address." Hamam took a sheet of paper from his in basket, noted that it was a flyer for an upcoming student art show and turned it over. He scribbled an address on the back in pencil and passed it to Sayed.

"Good," Sayed purred. "And these trucks, they will handle the weight and pressure?"

It was Hamam's turn to nod.

"Very good indeed."

16

"Put your hands up!"

The speaker hadn't been content with Annja just setting down the big flashlight.

"I said put your hands up. Higher! That's it, mate. Now, lace your fingers. Good girl. Put them behind your head. No smart moves. Don't try anything funny."

Annja squinted, trying to find a shape beyond the light. The dialogue was straight out of a B-grade cop movie. The accent was clearly Australian, and that made her feel a little better. At least it wasn't another Arab assassin.

"Who are you?" she risked asking.

"Doesn't matter who I am. Who are you?"

"Annja Creed," she replied.

The light wobbled a moment, and in it she caught a glimpse of two shapes, one the bushy-haired figure that she'd followed down here. The other was taller and leaner. She couldn't make out any more than that, as the light hit her straight in the face again. She closed her eyes.

"Annja Creed from *Chasing History's Monsters?*"

She nodded. "Yes. So we've covered a third of the introductions. Who are you?"

"Jon," came the quick reply. "And this is—"

"Matthew. I'm in charge of the dig."

"Only when Doc's not here you're in charge," Jon quickly added. "Matthew's the—"

"Graduate assistant assigned to Dr. Hamam," Matthew finished. "I saw you sneaking around the camp, followed you into the hole. Trespassing, trying to steal something probably."

Annja sighed. "I came to help. I didn't come here to steal anything. I followed Jon down here."

"Swallowed the spider to catch the fly, huh?" The tone of Matthew's voice showed that he was clearly in a bad mood.

"Can you put the light down?" Annja felt the heat on her face and knew Jon still had it aimed at her eyes. "And, if you don't mind…" She slowly unlaced her fingers, held her arms out to the sides and then she dropped them. It hurt her ribs to keep her arms up. "The light, please." She felt the heat finally vanish and she opened her eyes. The flashlight, similar to the one she'd borrowed, was pointed down now.

"And do you mind if we, ah, retreat to better-smelling surroundings?" Annja continued. She got a good look at the two now.

Jon looked like a teenager with his mop of curly red hair and cherubic face. He even had a smattering of freckles across the bridge of his nose. He stared at her, mouth agape. Matthew looked more the part of a collegian, hair short and neat, face showing a bare hint of stubble, which no doubt would be gone with the morning, rimless glasses perched high on a narrow nose. His gaze was more appraising and critical, and the dark circles under his eyes attested to either long hours or lack of sleep or both. Both were dressed in khaki pants, Matthew in a dark sweater and Jon in a green sweatshirt with a yellow platypus on it.

"*The* Annja Creed," Jon stated. "Really? *From Chasing History's Monsters? The* Annja Creed! You don't look all that much like her."

"Of course she does," Matthew said. "She's just a little tidier on the program." He pursed his lips. "You look like you've been through a war, Ms. Creed. Let's get up top and get you something warm to drink." He turned to Jon. "What the bloody hell were you doing down here anyway?" Then, more softly: "And what the bloody hell is Annja Creed doing at our dig? And at this hour? It's bloody well near midnight."

Jon shuffled his feet and seemed to study a spot on the floor. "I was just looking around," he said after a moment. "I couldn't sleep and figured I might as well get some work done. And then when I heard her come after me, I figured I was in trouble, didn't know who she was. Thought maybe it was you or Cindy. So I hid."

"Well, you're about as bright as a burned-out birthday candle," Matthew retorted. He gestured up the tunnel that led from the burial room. "You know you're not supposed to be down here without Doc." To Annja he said, "And I don't give a flat wombat if you're a celebrity, you're not supposed to be down here at all."

It would have been easy to stay silent during the walk up the tunnel, but Annja was concerned for everyone's safety, and so she gave them an abbreviated version of her day.

"So you think somebody here at our dig is trying to kill you?" Jon posed. "There are no Arabs here. Just us, seven graduate students, counting Matthew. Most of us are from Brisbane, actually. But I'm from just north of Sydney. We're all adults—"

"Six of us are adults anyway," Matthew said.

Jon made a face. "So the uni lets us stay out here at night if we want."

"When I'm around, you can stay out here," Matthew added.

"Only for liability," Jon cut in. "That's why you have to be here. Doc slept over a couple of nights, though, a week or so ago. He usually just comes out during the day, 'cept when he's lecturing to undergraduate classes. And then he doesn't come out at all."

"That would be Tuesdays and Thursdays that he lectures. Friday, he was here in the morning," Matthew said.

"With some guys," Jon added. "Dark, maybe Arabs, like you mentioned. But one was Korean. Or Japanese." He paused. "Maybe Chinese."

Matthew let out an irritated sigh. "He was Korean, and I heard Doc call him Kim. He didn't talk much. None of them did. Doc just showed them around. I figured they were benefactors or something. Doc's always making noises about applying for this or that grant."

It was Jon's turn to sigh. "Every prof at the uni talks

about getting grants…if you'd listen, Matthew. Doc's not permanent, anyway, so the grants won't help him much."

Annja raised her eyebrows and stopped. They'd just entered the main chamber again. "A visiting professor? He's not part of the regular staff?"

"From Egypt," Matthew supplied. "An expert Egyptologist, not just an archaeologist. He's here for two or three years, I think, came because the uni let him have charge of a dig. He's great."

"Dr. Hamam…" Annja prompted.

"Dr. Gahiji Hamam. Taught at the University of Cairo," Matthew said. "He's written books."

"I've heard of him," Annja admitted. In fact, she had at least three of his books. Her favorite was on the Bir Dunqash dig, where Hamam and his team uncovered an Egyptian complex of three rooms with redware shards ringing it. Hamam managed to date the shards to Byzantine times.

"We're real lucky to get Doc. He's ace." Matthew smacked Jon on the side of the head. "And Doc doesn't want us down here without him. Good reason for it, I guess. Doesn't want anything disturbed or damaged. Jon's the proverbial poster child for—"

"That's enough, Matthew." Jon made a face.

Annja flicked on her flashlight again, the beams from two lights doing a far better job of illuminating the section of the massive chamber.

"Doc's afraid, I guess, that some of us might take something," Jon said. "I'd never take anything, but…" He sucked in a breath. "I maybe know a student here who might pocket something small and shiny."

Annja let Jon's prattle drift to the back of her mind, and again she studied the walls. "Has any of this been translated?" she asked.

"Sure," Matthew said. "One whole wall, nearly. But that's it as far as I know. Doc's been taking lots of pictures so he can work up the translations later. He's translated the slabs up top. And he's packed up all the portable relics and shipped them to his office for cataloging. Except the pieces we have on the tables under the tent. But those came from above, and most of them are broken."

"What sort of relics? The ones taken from down here?" Annja meant to bring the conversation back around to the Arabs and the Korean, but her curiosity slipped out.

"Statues, vases, pots, all small," Jon said. "But in remarkable condition just because they've been down here, and for the most part out of the wind and weather. There's lots of stuff we found intact. So many other sites, here and in Egypt, you find only pieces."

"The uni has a museum with Egyptian relics," Matthew said. "It'll get all the stuff recovered from here. Doc'll get quite a feather in his hat."

Jon made a huffing sound. "We'll get credit, too."

Matthew pointed to the ladder. "C'mon."

"These Arabs," Annja said. They paused at the huge cow-head altar. "Can you tell me anything more about them?"

"Well, they were only out here two times," Jon said.

"Three," Matthew corrected. "The one of them anyway was out here three times. Twice he was out here by himself, only talked to Doc and didn't stay long. He was here yesterday, too. Never looked at a single piece on the table. He didn't seem too interested—"

"Yeah, I remember," Jon interrupted. "He's the one with the scars. Gave Cindy the shivers the way he looked at her. He was the only one I heard talk. 'Course we keep pretty busy out here, and Doc and them guys, the grantors, they didn't stick too close to us. Didn't catch any of their names. You don't think they're the guys you fought on the spine?"

"The preserve ridge," Matthew said to be more precise. "I doubt that any men Doc is involved with…"

"I don't know if they're the same men. But I think you're in danger, too. Something one of the men on the ridge said indicates that," Annja said. That everyone dies, she thought.

Matthew nodded to the rope ladder. "Ladies first."

Annja flicked off the flashlight and sat it near the ladder. She started climbing, finding going up more painful than her trip down. Her side throbbed from where she'd been kicked in the ribs, and despite the makeshift wrap on her sprained ankle it burned when she put weight on it.

"I bet Doc doesn't know those Arabs might be up to something," Jon said. He started up when Annja passed the halfway mark. "He's not going to be happy to hear it."

"And he's not going to be happy to find out you were prowling down here by yourself," Matthew said.

"Pigs, I wasn't prowling. And he doesn't have to know."

"Oh, he has to know," Matthew returned. He flicked off his flashlight and crooked it under his right arm, using his left to help him climb. "And I'm going to relish telling him."

Annja breathed deep when her head cleared the crevice. The stink of the dead fish and the burial chamber still clung to her nostrils. She heaved herself out, noticing there were lanterns glowing in two of the tents now.

Jon was out quickly behind her, then on his feet and jogging toward the dark tent. Annja stood, hands on her hips, scanning the area, still concerned there might be more of the thugs around. "How many men did Dr. Hamam have out here who weren't part of the university?"

Matthew answered as he climbed out of the crevice. "Just the three. No, four with the Korean."

"And one of them was the scarred man?"

Matthew nodded, and then realized Annja couldn't see him. "Yeah. Looked like he'd been in a fire and that part of his skin had melted. Not right to judge by appearance and all, but he was creepy looking."

Arabs and a Korean, and the Arab on the ridge proficient in Muay Thai. Such an interesting mix, Annja mused. Which one of the men who'd been in the camp was the "master," as the men she'd killed had referred to him?

"Was one of them in charge?"

Matthew stepped past her, shrugging. "Grants are nice and all, but not my business. I'm just a graduate assistant. I really didn't pay much attention to them." He looked over his shoulder to make sure she was following. "I'm gonna roust the others for you." He started toward the tents again, and then stopped, his shoulders sagging. He turned.

"Look, Ms. Creed, I've seen you a couple of times.

Chasing History's Monsters isn't exactly serious programming, you know. I'm pleased to meet you, though not under these circumstances. I'm not sure I believe all of your story, but I'll err on the cautious side and gather my mates here. I'm responsible for them, you know. At least when Doc's not around. And I don't want any Arabs shooting at them—or at me. This is just a little weird, you have to understand. No, it's a lot weird. Only thing that makes me think you're right with me is that you look like hell." He opened his mouth as if to say something else, then closed it and shook his head. He turned back toward the tents, angling toward the tent where Annja had seen the two lovers.

A lantern was lit now in the third tent, the one Jon shared with one or two other students. Two students, Annja confirmed, noting the silhouettes. She saw Jon gesture wildly, his form easy to pick out because of the bushy hair.

"This has been a long day," she said, following Matthew, but letting the distance grow between them. "I look like hell? I feel like hell." But despite the master's orders to have me killed, I'm still breathing.

Matthew poked his head in the tent, and a quick and heated exchange ensued. Next, he went to the other tent, shaking the canvas and hollering, "Get up and get dressed." Then he joined Annja, crossing his arms and sticking his hands in his armpits. No shadows reached her and he could well see her in the moonlight. "Nice jacket, Ms. Creed. I've never been to the place myself. Not my sort of entertainment. But if I had, I don't think I would've advertised the fact by wearing…"

"Matthew!" Jon had emerged from his tent, two men following him, both of them in sweatpants and T-shirts, and both grumbling about being woken. "I used the sat phone and called Doc." He jogged toward Annja and Matthew, holding the phone out in front of him.

Matthew raised a scolding finger.

"I only talked a minute. I know the limits. I told him Annja Creed was here and that some men had tried to kill her. Told him that—"

"It was my place to call, Jon," Matthew said.

Jon gave him a lopsided grin. "I know. But I had the phone in my tent. I guess I'd forgotten to put it back. Anyway, Doc was all excited that Annja Creed is here." He moved close to Matthew and whispered, but his voice was loud enough that Annja could hear. "Doc said we should keep her here, come up with some reason. He said he's gonna send someone out."

"Wonderful," Annja muttered. To Matthew she said, "You're the boss here, right? Get them dressed—better dressed—in a hurry. We're getting out of here. And bring that phone. We're going to need it."

Matthew's perturbed expression melted into one of concern. He looked a little pale in the moonlight.

17

Annja led the seven graduate students over the ridge, picking a spot that looked reasonably easy to climb, still staying away from the path the students usually took when visiting the other site. She figured if she was going to run into anyone dangerous, it would be on the path, and so it was to be avoided. Also, climbing made the students work and for the most part forced them to keep their mouths shut.

In the several minutes it had taken to muster them she'd had to deal with questions piled on top of questions.

"What's Annja Creed the famous archaeologist doing out here?"

"Ninjas? There were ninjas shooting at her?"

"Are we going to be on television?" This came from Cindy.

"Is Doc involved?"

Then there were the mutterings of disbelief, suggestions that this was all some ruse to get them away from their dig site and their precious find that hadn't been reported yet and would make them all famous.

"Doc's gonna spit the dummy over this."

"Yeah, you just don't lob in on our place and tell us we've gotta leave."

"Who does she think she is anyway?" This came from Jeff, the one student who'd never seen an episode of *Chasing History's Monsters.*

Annja offered only a few replies, letting Matthew order them around. She thought he was enjoying his authority, despite the predicament she'd put him in.

"If this all turns out to be nothing," he cautioned her. "If Doc isn't involved—"

"Then I'll be grateful, and you'll all be safe," Annja interrupted.

She adopted a fast pace and the students had to work hard to keep up. When she crested the ridge she saw lights on in all of the tents and people moving around. She knew there were a dozen people to account for at the Michaels dig, including the two security guards and Dari.

Faint sounds came to her: a murmur, which must be the archaeologists chattering; a dog barking, perhaps a dingo loose in the preserve; the breeze gusting and rustling the leaves on the trees beyond the site. She also heard the students behind her grabbing this or that rock, their shoes pushing scree down the other side.

"We're going here only for safety in numbers, right?" Matthew joined her at the top of the ridge, looking down at Dr. Michaels's camp.

Annja nodded.

"Then Dr. Michaels doesn't need to know about the temple to Hathor we found," he said.

"It's not my place to tell him," Annja admitted. "But I don't care much for secrets." Except the ones I'm forced to keep, she thought.

The trek down was relatively easy, the moon revealing a course that wasn't terribly steep and had few granite upthrusts. She'd spotted no dark-clad men on the ridge or down below in the camp, but the moonlight didn't keep all the shadows at bay, and so she remained on guard.

Several minutes later they were in front of Dr. Michaels's tent. The other archaeologists had pulled out extra folding chairs and mats so everyone had something to sit on. Annja took a head count while Jennifer welcomed the students.

"Where's Dari?" she asked after she double-checked her number.

Wes looked worried. "He left right after you did. We told him we could well take care of ourselves, and he was concerned about you traipsing off on your own. I thought he'd caught up to you."

Annja couldn't suppress a groan. Now she'd have to go looking for him—finding one man in this preserve at night might be like looking for that proverbial needle in a haystack. She just hoped she wouldn't find his body and that the men who'd attacked her hadn't first gotten to him.

"Perhaps we could form search parties," Jennifer suggested. "We could—"

"Not a good idea." This came from Matthew, the only student who hadn't accepted one of the offered seats. He rocked back and forth on his heels and looked from the archaeologists to the ridge to Jon. "We're going to have company. This dill here called Dr. Hamam, and he's sending someone out for Ms. Creed. She thinks we might be in danger."

Dr. Michaels stroked his chin. "Are you really going looking for him, Annja? He's a big boy. He can't find you—he'll come back."

"If he's able," Annja said. "But I've got a very bad feeling about all of this."

"It's not my fault," Jon told Cindy. He tried to keep his voice low, but it carried. "I called Doc 'cause he needed to know Annja Creed had come calling in the middle of the night. Doc's got nothing to do with any ninjas with guns. This is Doc's dig, and he had every right to know we had a visitor. A famous one."

Cindy yawned and leaned into another one of the students. "It's all kind of exciting," she said. "But I'll be bummed if nothing dangerous happens."

Annja rolled her eyes and took visual stock of the site. Nineteen people were clustered around the tent, including herself. Only two of them—the security guards—had guns. Only the security guards looked wholly alert, though the students were perking up; the climb had helped enliven them. The coffee might help, too. Jennifer was passing out mugs and paper cups and pouring from a big pot.

"I've got more brewing," she told them. "But this is for starters."

Annja didn't consider the camp very defensible. She could put them all in the woods and tell them to be quiet, but she doubted some of the students would cooperate.

Someone would hear them out there. Best keep them there, with the security guards posted.

"Matthew, give Dr. Michaels the satellite phone." The graduate assistant hesitated only a moment. "Call the police, whatever police services this place," she ordered.

"And tell them what?" Wes took the phone and stared at it.

"That there's ninjas with guns on the ridge," Cindy snickered.

"That there could be trouble," Annja said. "That there are two dead men on the ridge. That more men are coming." She couldn't help but glance Jon's way. "Get the cops out here quick." She told the students, "Stay here and stay close. Try to stay quiet—"

"Look, Miss Creed, I'm having a hard time swallowing all of this," Wes said. "You've no reason to lie to me or make something up, but ninjas and guns."

"Wes, I think I heard shooting a while back," Jennifer said.

"That was somebody opening their lunch," Wes joked. "I suppose there's no harm in calling the authorities. We've not had them out here before." He rubbed at his eyes and shook his head. "Just all of this is a little much to take in. But I'll call. It'll take them awhile to get here, you understand. We're pretty much—"

"In the sticks, the boondocks," Annja cut in. "I know. Just make the calls and keep it quiet so you can listen."

"So we can hear if anyone's coming," Wes finished. "There's an access road to the west that we take. Our cars are parked there. Anyone driving in would come that way."

No, Annja thought, they could take the road where the

painter dropped her and Dari off, come at the site through the trees.

"And there's a road that comes in from the north," Matthew said. "That's the one we use. It snakes around the narrow part of the preserve ridge. But I bet we'll not hear anybody drive on it…not from way over here."

"Just keep your eyes and ears open," Annja cautioned. "And start calling." She nodded to Wes. She turned to Matthew. "And when I get back, I want you to tell me all about your Dr. Hamam."

Wes Michaels was placing a second call by the time she'd jogged past the sifting tables. The moonlight made a stretch of mud slick and revealed a set of boot prints. They weren't grooved, like the assassins' boots.

"Dari," she said. "And so I must rescue my knight in shining armor. This has been just a lovely, lovely day."

Once more, Annja started up the ridge.

18

Dr. Gahiji Hamam put on a pair of white gloves and surveyed the relics on the table, which were illuminated by a flickering fluorescent light that hung directly above.

> The gods that gathered together told Thoth who dwelled in Khemenu—that which comes from thy mouth will be called true.

Hamam had memorized passages from the *Book of the Dead* and enjoyed quoting his own translations of them while he worked.

> The scribe whose word is true is righteous. He has not sinned or called evil upon us. Ammut the Devourer will not be allowed to prevail over him. We shall grant him meat offerings and admittance to the holy presence of Osiris.

There were dozens of small pieces—more on the table
behind him. But for the moment, Hamam concentrated
on these. He had recovered most of them from the underground temple to Hathor, which he suspected at one time
sat atop the earth—at least a portion of it.

If when coming to the Seven Arits he enters the
doors, he shall not be turned back before Osiris. He
shall be made blessed among the spirits and granted
dominion among those ancestral followers of the
great Osiris. He shall be like a lord of eternity, as
one with Osiris. No one can contend against him.

Several pieces were jewelry, twisted strands of gold
decorated with opals—valuable for their materials alone,
but made much more so by their age and origin. The
largest necklace had a fob hanging from it that was a
piece of stone similar to turquoise, but it was a gem he
wasn't familiar with. He would have to consult a book or
the Internet when he got back home; perhaps it was a
stone mined locally rather than one brought from Egypt.
The fob had a thin gold wire twisted around its top and
bottom, affixing it to the much heavier gold chain. He
found it striking and wondered who'd worn it.

The piece was not particularly feminine, and he'd not
seen an indication that any Egyptian women had ever
been there. So he guessed it was worn by the man who'd
been in charge of this ancient expedition. Hamam fancied
himself like that man—descended from Egyptian royalty,
a leader, admired, an admirer and an appropriator of fine
things. He ran his gloved finger across the stone. But

unlike the ancient Egyptian who'd brought his kinsmen here, Hamam would be able to return home.

In passing the Pylons of the House of Osiris, the correct spell must be spoken before continuing.

Hamam searched his memory for the rest of his translation.

The great Osiris said you have come here, and you shall be favored Osiris Auf-ankh, who speaks truth, son of Shert-en-Menu, who is also truthful.

Hamam carefully wrapped the necklace, then another piece; this one was not so heavy, but was of equally expert craftsmanship. He concentrated on all the jewelry first, wrapping each piece with extreme care. The work kept his temper in check. He was upset that Annja Creed still lived—the most vital witness to his meeting with Sayed. He was upset that the men he'd hired through Sayed had not killed her. He'd hired nearly fifty, for various tasks he'd lined up—including slaying Annja Creed and now all the others out at the digs.

He hadn't wanted to devote so many to tying up the loose ends at the sites. There was much other work to be done. How could the terrorist have recommended such incompetent fools! She was just one woman, and according to Jon, she wasn't even armed.

May you appear in happiness wherever we go. Let whoever is listening be satisfied. Let there be heart-

felt joy. Let there be no lies told against me before
the great one, the lord of Amentet.

Hamam was pleased Jon had called to tell him Annja
Creed was at the dig. He in turn called Sayed, who guar-
anteed the woman's imminent demise. Sayed needed her
dead just as badly as Hamam did; he wanted Interpol to
keep thinking he was in England.

But he was also saddened about Jon's revelation.
The immature graduate student had become his favorite,
and he had hoped to have him killed last, or perhaps
even spared and brought along to Egypt and incarcer-
ated, if necessary, as an assistant. Now Jon would have
to die with Annja Creed, quickly before he started
piecing things together. Jon was a tad juvenile, but he
was very, very bright. He might figure out Hamam's plan
and tell someone. Curious Jon had seen the fish, after all.

Hamam continued to translate.

The place once closed is open. The place sealed is
truly sealed. That which rests in the sealed place is
opened by the Ra-soul residing inside. I am delivered by the eye of Horus. I walk, a journey over a
long, long road. The road of souls is open to me.

Hamam concentrated on the small pieces of pottery
now, bowls that might have been for broth or for some
religious ceremony—possibly the latter as they were
found in the temple. The clay was thin and fragile, and
despite his careful efforts, Hamam worried that some
pieces might break during transport.

"Can't be helped," he said. "Worth the risk."

He continued to work until everything was wrapped, and then he began placing the pieces in a crate filled with straw and shredded newsprint, making sure to put the jewelry on top. He would have preferred better packing material, but it was what he could find in the museum's storage closets, and searching elsewhere might draw undue attention.

The museum curator thought these objects would eventually go on display—after Hamam and the department's other archaeologists had cataloged and photographed them. Hamam smiled at how gullible the curator was.

Hamam's reputation had helped gain him access at any time to the museum—he was in the basement of it now—without having a security guard hovering. Hamam was considered one of the most renowned Egyptologists in the world, and no nefarious activities had been publicly linked to him. Hamam's illegal deeds had been low-key up until this point; he'd given no one a reason not to trust him. And those few who had asked too many questions were no longer among the living.

He moved to another table, this with larger pieces, all of them taken from the niches in the *cave* as his students called it. In Hamam's native Egypt so many of the tombs and temples that had been excavated had already been stripped of their treasures—by grave robbers from centuries past. But the cave had not been touched before he and his students had discovered it, and so the relics were as pristine as time allowed.

"All of this priceless, and all of this mine alone." He selected a large bowl to begin with, nearly as big across as a dinner plate. It was painted inside and out, and though the paint had faded considerably, hints of color remained. The images were of half suns and stiff-looking birds, with a border that might have been a serpent. Hamam intended to inspect it—to inspect everything—under better light when he got home.

"Doctor, I've loaded nineteen crates now. Any more?"

Hamam nodded to the crate he'd just packed on the table behind him. "Thank you, Kim."

The man was Korean, so powerfully built that his shoulders strained the seams of the janitor's uniform he wore. His face was all angles and planes, and the sheen of sweat on it made his skin almost glow in the fluorescent lighting. Kim was Hamam's man, not picked by Sayed. He'd come over with Hamam, independently, and was quick to find janitorial work at the university. Hamam had two other such associates working upstairs in the museum, packing more crates.

"I'll have this crate finished shortly, Kim," Hamam continued. "I will need three more crates for packing, for the rest of these relics. Then I will be finished here." He paused. "Do you realize how precious these things are intact, perfect?"

Kim carefully picked up the packed crate. "What about the museum?"

"The pieces I've marked are being crated as we speak and loaded onto the second truck. We're only taking one of the mummies."

Kim made a snorting sound. "The museum is open tomorrow. I thought we were crating those after hours tomorrow night. Everything's closed Sunday—nothing would be found missing until Monday."

Hamam placed the wrapped bowl in the bottom of another crate and started to wrap a pitcher with kangaroos and cows' heads painted on it. "I had to move up the event, Kim. The American television star has forced my hand."

"This Annja Creed that you mentioned?"

Hamam snarled. "Yes, this Annja Creed."

"That is why you had us buy the plane tickets today." Kim snorted again and left, his heavy feet thudding dully against the concrete floor.

Hamam placed the pitcher in the crate and moved on to another piece. He was working faster than he would have liked, but Annja Creed had brought this about. If anything chipped or shattered in the move, it would be her fault. She would be paying soon enough—for her past and any future transgressions. Sayed had promised.

He inhaled deeply, wanting to pull the history of these objects inside himself. It was rare perfume to him, the odor of the ancient clay and preserved wood. It was his history and his ticket to life among the gods, and it lulled him into a state of euphoria as well as any narcotic could.

Hamam was so caught up in the relics that he didn't hear footsteps approach, until someone was almost on top of him.

"What's going on here?"

The words startled Hamam, and he dropped an idol of Hathor he'd been wrapping. The clay figurine landed on the table and broke in two.

Hamam whirled, his eyes daggers aimed at the intruder.

It was a campus security guard. He didn't think they ever ventured into the museum basement. Had he started upstairs? Hamam's heart seized with worry that his associates had been caught.

"I am packing up relics," Hamam answered. "Have you been upstairs yet?"

The guard narrowed his eyes and shook his head. "I always start my rounds in the basement."

Hamam wrapped the two broken pieces of the idol; he would have them repaired at home. He placed the pieces in the crate and went on to a vase.

"What are you packing all of this for? Weren't they just unpacked?"

"From the dig?" Hamam worked faster. "Well, yes, they were just unpacked. But that is because they were first packed by students out there, not packed professionally, and certainly not for any sort of voyage." He placed the vase in the crate and eyed the other objects, determining what would go in next.

"Where are they going?" This particular security guard had seen Hamam a few times before in other parts of the museum.

"Why are you curious? I have authority to be here. You know that. The dig, and these relics, they are under my aegis," Hamam said authoritatively.

The guard shrugged and relaxed his shoulders a little. "No worries. Have to be careful," he said. "It's my job. These things are valuable. The museum's a showpiece for the university."

"It's good that you're careful," Hamam said. He settled on another bowl, this one with an uneven lip that suggested it might have served as a cup. "You can never be too careful with relics such as these."

"So where are they going?" The guard was persistent.

"On loan," Hamam answered almost too quickly. "To a place not terribly far from Cairo."

This seemed to satisfy the guard, and he turned to leave. Hamam placed the wrapped bowl in the crate and picked up a wooden ankh about a foot long and half that wide. It looked to be carved from a white stringybark, engraved with miniature ankhs and half suns and lacquered with something that had worn off along a stem that was sharpened like a stake. Hamam had found a few of these and guessed that they were intended to be driven in the ground to mark something. The wood was still hard, preserved because it had been in a high niche and moist air had not touched it.

"Is there paperwork on this?" The guard had stopped in the doorway. "I saw someone carrying crates out to a van."

"You don't need to concern yourself with paperwork," Hamam replied. "That's for provosts and the curator, not for you."

"Have to be careful," the guard repeated. He stepped back into the room. "This just doesn't seem right." He reached for a walkie-talkie on his belt. "Probably everything's filled in triplicate somewhere, but I want to make sure. You understand. There are rumors of layoffs, and I don't want to give them an excuse."

Hamam moved surprisingly fast given his age and the close confines of the room filled with tables. Before the security guard could thumb the control, he'd driven the sharp stem of the ankh into his stomach.

The guard hollered and fell to his knees, dropping the walkie-talkie and clawing at the ankh that Hamam pulled out and thrust like a dagger again and again. Then Hamam stepped back as the guard fell forward, blood pooling around the limp body.

It had been some time since he'd killed a man, and though necessary in this instance, it was nevertheless distasteful. Hamam stared at the bloodied ankh, bent and wiped it on the back of the guard's shirt. Some had soaked into the wood, where the lacquer had worn off. It would be difficult to restore, Hamam knew. He stood staring at the body and the ankh for several minutes. Kim's return stirred him.

The big Korean did not hide his surprise at seeing the dead guard.

"It was necessary," was the only explanation Hamam offered. He pointed to a big roll of plastic along one wall. "That will help," he said. "There's an incinerator in the basement of the arts building, where my office is. You can dispose of him there. Quickly."

"And then come back here to get the rest of the crates?"

"Of course, Kim. Hopefully, we will not have to leave anything behind."

"Nakim and Harold, they were starting to load the ones from upstairs when I came down. The trucks are nearly full."

"Good, good."

"You will be leaving soon?"

Hamam nodded. "The crates I've scheduled to fly out before dawn. We've three hours to get them to the airport. You have your ticket?"

"Nakim and Harold, too. They were expensive."

"Last-minute flights always are. I will cover them. When do you leave?"

Kim had ripped free a large sheet of plastic wrap and was working to roll the dead security guard in it.

"Tomorrow afternoon. It was the earliest we could get."

"It will do. They'll discover the museum robbery in the morning. And they will not discover the other until it is too late."

"We will be away from the campus long before then, waiting at the airport." Kim struggled to sling the guard over his shoulder. Blood pooled between the uniform and the plastic, looking like hamburger that had bled out in the package at the butcher's.

"The cameras were disabled before we came in, and all the sensors," Hamam said. "No one will tie you to this."

"And you?"

"I will be away shortly. And I do not believe anything will be traced to me. I arranged other robberies this night, from two museums in the city. Clues there, and here, are being planted to direct suspicion away from me."

"If anyone lives who cares to be suspicious." The big Korean smiled as he started down the hall. "They will have other things to worry about."

"And Kim?"

He paused and turned slightly so he could see Hamam.

"If you're going to shower tomorrow, do it very, very early."

Kim nodded knowingly.

19

Annja stood on the ridge between the two camps, looking down at the university dig. Wispy clouds had drifted across the moon, cutting the light and making it more difficult to pick out the details. She hadn't found Dari, but then the ridge was long and dark, and she had no intention of calling out for him. She'd listened intently during her climb, thinking she might hear him scrambling up the slope or moaning if he'd slipped and hurt himself. Of course, if he'd *really* hurt himself he might not be making any noise at all, or if he'd been killed by her assailants.

The breeze had died down since her previous trip, and she was sorry for that. The cool wind had been invigorating and had kept her from sweating. She unzipped her Purple Pussycat jacket and flapped the edges of it to cool her. She shouldn't be so warm, she thought, and so she felt her face.

A fever, like I need that on top of everything else. It

was probably a result of the cracked ribs and the sprained ankle, and not giving herself a chance to rest. She usually healed quickly—if she afforded herself an opportunity to do so. She put her weight on her good ankle and scanned the site. Someone had left a lantern on in one of the tents—Jon's.

"Can't see enough to—" Annja smiled with an idea and climbed higher, to where she'd encountered the two assassins. It took her several minutes to reach the spot, and only a minute more to find what she was looking for—the night-vision goggles the Muay Thai expert had been wearing. "Perfect," she pronounced.

She fitted them on and tightened the band so they wouldn't fall off. It cast the world into a landscape of blacks and greens, like something out of a science fiction movie. She'd used something similar before, and so it didn't take her long to adjust. Then she started looking along the ridge for Dari.

"This is nuts," she whispered. "I should be back with the students and Wes." She felt responsible for them. But she also felt responsible for the biker she'd dragged into this because she needed transportation. She hesitated, looking down the slope and to the students' tents. Then she was looking beyond them, to a vehicle that was cutting across the ground and driving up to the canopy where the sifting tables were. Vehicles weren't supposed to come right up to either dig site, she knew; there were designated places for them to park some distance back.

Annja crouched, seeing four men spill out of the vehicle while at the same time seeing a lone figure emerge from one of the smaller tents. "Dari," she said. She could tell that by the outline and the smooth-shaped head. "Keep your head down," she whispered, as if willing the words to him.

He'd obviously heard the car approach, as he clung to the side of the tent, trying not to be seen. The four men spread out across the camp.

"No. Oh, please no." Before gaining her sword and being plunged into one perilous adventure after another, Annja had known little about guns. Now she could easily identify them.

One of the men toted an assault rifle, an M-16 by the look of it. Another carried an Uzi. The remaining men had M-14 Minirifles and pistols, the latter probably 9 mm P-85s from the silhouettes. She took in a breath and held it, steadying her nerves, and then she started down the rise, intent on getting Dari out of there. She touched the hilt of the sword with a thought, ready to call it into her hand in a heartbeat—not that the sword would do her a lick of good unless she was in close.

She was halfway down the slope when she saw Dari start up several yards to the north. The man with the M-16 was coming around the side of the tent and had spooked him. Annja skidded the rest of the way down, summoning the sword as she went, and clamping her teeth shut swallowing a cry of pain. It felt as if someone had shoved a hot poker against her ribs.

The M-16 cracked, a bullet narrowly missing Dari. It struck a rock at the base of the ridge. A second shot followed, the muzzle flaring in her night-vision goggles. She couldn't tell if Dari'd been hit. But he was still moving.

Chaos ensued. The other three men were alerted by

the gunshots and came running. One man raised his pistol in his left hand and fired into a tent as he went. The man with the Uzi sprayed another tent.

So many men sent to kill one woman, she thought. She swallowed hard as she realized they weren't just sent out here to kill her. A hit team this size would be sent to kill everyone, and maybe do a little fast cleanup work afterward. Annja realized that she'd been right to pull the students away from the dig.

"Annja!" Dari had spotted her and was crab-crawling toward her, sending bits of rock and clumps of mud up in his wake.

"Get down!" she hollered as the rifleman drew another bead. "Drop! Now!"

Two of the gunmen fired just as Dari took her advice. The bullets thudded into the rise, rock shards ricocheting, just as Annja managed to reach Dari.

"Where'd you find a sword?" Dari let her tug him up. The two started weaving up the ridge.

"In the rocks," Annja lied. She found an upthrust of granite and stuffed Dari behind it. She tucked herself next to him as more shots ricocheted off the rocks.

"Sword's nice," Dari admitted. "But we need a gun."

"A gun would be nice," Annja said. "Maybe I'll take one of theirs."

"Find those goggles in the rocks, too?"

"Yeah." At least this time she could answer truthfully. "Listen, Dari, I'm going to draw them away. You need to get up and over to the other camp and warn them we have company."

"I can't leave you alone—"

"Yes, you can," she hissed. "There are eighteen people in that camp. I'd rather that not turn into eighteen bodies."

Dari nodded.

She saw his Adam's apple bobbing nervously, as if he was constantly swallowing, and his hands clenching and unclenching. He wanted a little adventure? He had it in spades, she thought, hoping he'd live to tell Nate and the rest of his friends about it.

He started to say something, but she was vaulting away, tumbling down and drawing fire.

Annja thought she had a slight advantage in that her assailants were not wearing night-vision goggles. She was fast and constantly changing direction, making herself a difficult target. Of course, she was outnumbered, and they had guns. Lots of guns.

A bullet whizzed by her head so close it sheared off a lock of her hair. Another sent gravel flying against her goggles. They were better shots than the men at the hotel, she grimly mused as she cleared the bottom of the ridge and dashed to the closest tent. Bullets from the Uzi chewed up the ground behind her. She ducked behind the canvas and caught her breath, then sprinted to the next tent as more rounds ripped into the canvas where she'd been a heartbeat before.

Wes and the others had to be hearing this, she thought. The ridge couldn't cut all the sound. She spun and then flattened herself on the ground behind Jon's tent. Bullets chewed the canvas and burst the lantern inside. She instantly smelled smoke and realized the oil from the lantern had spilled on something and caught fire. The growing light registered painfully in her goggles, and she looked away.

Fine, she thought, I've successfully drawn the attention of all four of them. I've bought Dari some time, but how much time do I have? She squeezed the hilt tight in her right hand. Her left palm was pressed against the ground, tiny shards biting into it. In lulls in the gunfire, she heard the men reloading and talking among themselves. Some of it was in a language she couldn't understand, but two of the men spoke English.

"Has to be the Creed woman," one man said. "Hamam and Sayed want her dead."

There was more gunfire and Annja sprinted to the south, drawing them toward what she hoped was her salvation. She shrugged out of her jacket as she went, transferring the sword from hand to hand so she could pull out her arms. She was careful not to run too close to the slabs covered with canvas. Errant gunfire could ruin the ancient carvings.

"Kill her!"

Now there's scintillating speech, Annja thought.

"Shoot her now!"

Bullets sprayed in her wake, and she dived into the shadows, dropping the jacket strategically, then rolling and coming to a rest on her stomach, sword flat against the ground, and little rocks biting into her. She breathed shallowly and through her goggles kept her eyes trained on the men. Her side hurt fiercely, and she hoped she hadn't done any further damage to her ribs.

The two with pistols and M-14 Minis approached from the northeast, her left. They were almost shoulder to shoulder and of similar builds. They weren't amateurs;

she could tell that in the way they moved and how they constantly looked around for a target. Trained by some military or in a mercenary camp, she guessed.

"She went this way," one of them said, his voice carrying in the stillness.

"Into the darkness," the other replied.

So these were the two who spoke English—and with actual English accents. Annja dug the fingers of her left hand into the damp ground as they moved closer. They were about fifty feet away.

The other two appeared, skirting the ridge and deep in the shadows. She might not have seen them were it not for her goggles. They were about 250 feet away, maybe a little less. The one with the Uzi jammed another clip into it, tossing the empty one on the ground. He was wearing gloves and so had no fear that fingerprints would draw the authorities to him. The other leveled the M-16.

Annja hunkered down, sucked in her lower lip and bit down, hoping the competing pain might take her mind off her fiery ribs.

If they weren't walking in pairs, Annja knew she would try to take them now, come at them one by one, fast with her sword. This wasn't like in her hotel room, where the confining space worked to her advantage. As her gaze flitted back and forth between them, the ones with the pistols coming dangerously close, she saw that one of the English-speaking men pointed at the ground.

"I almost fell in that!" he said.

His companion knelt. "There's a rope ladder. Think she went down?"

"I would," the first answered. "Where else could she

have disappeared to?" He pulled a flashlight from his belt, flicked it on and aimed the beam in the crevice. "I'm going to check it out. There's a purple jacket caught partway down. It's got blood on it. We might've hit her." He clipped the flashlight to his belt so it lit up his leg. Gripping the pistol in his right hand, he started down, using his left to help him climb.

Of course the jacket's got blood on it, Annja thought. It was blood spatter from the men she'd fought and killed on the ridge.

His companion stayed up top and waved to the two others. "Remy is checking out a cave. He thinks she's down there. He found her jacket. Hasan, you go with him."

Annja held her breath as the one with the Uzi looked around and cursed softly. He slung the subgun over his arm and followed the first man down the rope ladder.

"We'll stay here," the Englishman told the one with the rifle. "Just in case she's still around the camp and tried to throw us off track."

"Dig," the rifleman corrected. "Sayed calls this a dig. Says the professor doesn't like it called a camp."

"Whatever. We just need to kill her."

"And everyone else out here. The students have to be hiding somewhere." The man's accent was thick and exotic sounding but he also spoke English. "Kill the students, Sayed told me. Then kill the archaeologists to the east. The professor wants no witnesses. He wants it to look like thieves after the artifacts. And the one of us who kills the American girl will get a bonus. If she is down in that hole, Hasan will get the money. His Uzi will turn her into pudding."

Annja chose that moment to rise and rush at the two men standing near the hole. Engaged in conversation, they were less alert to their surroundings, and too confident that she'd escaped into the cave. It had been just what she'd wanted them to think, and it was why she'd dropped her jacket.

The one with the M-16 looked up first, bringing the gun up in the same motion. He'd heard her feet slapping across the ground and tried to draw a bead. He saw her and he squeezed off a round just as she leaped at him, sword leading, body parallel to the ground.

The bullet slammed into her right arm and through it, and this time Annja didn't manage to stifle the cry of pain. But it didn't stop her. In the passing of a heartbeat the pain lessened to a bee sting and triggered an adrenaline rush. There was a momentary sensation of numbness that stretched to her hand and made her fingers tingle, but she redoubled her grip on the sword.

She landed in a crouch as he fired again, the bullet screaming above her head. She rose, knocking the M-16 back with her shoulder as she lunged forward, both hands gripping the sword now. The blade sunk into the gunner's chest. She'd aimed for his heart and was certain she'd hit the mark. The M-16 fell, and he toppled backward as she yanked her blade free.

His companion was swinging around with the pistol, squeezing the trigger as she dropped and rolled past him, jumped up and came at him from behind. She swung the sword as if it were a baseball bat and she was aiming for the perfect pitch. There was so much strength behind her swing that when she cleaved into his waist the blade went through to his spine. His cry was agonizing and terrible, and Annja couldn't pull the sword out with a simple tug. He fell forward, legs and arms quivering, and she planted her good foot on his back to give her leverage so she could retrieve her sword.

He continued to shake, blood gurgling in his mouth as he cried again.

"Mercy to you," she said as she jabbed him in the back, the blade hissing between his ribs and finding his lungs and heart. "Though you'd have granted me no mercy."

She heard shouts from below and spun to look into the crevice. The man with the Uzi had been climbing back up and was nearly to the top.

"No, you don't." She pulled the blade free and swung it again, this time at the rope ladder held by the metal spikes. One slice at each side was all she needed, her sword was that sharp and she was that strong.

The man fell, shooting on his way down. Bullets sprayed up, chipping the stone around the opening and causing Annja to dance back. She heard the gun clatter on the stone below, and the heavy thud of his body hitting the bottom.

She took a moment to catch her breath, and then she looked into the crevice. Directly beneath her was the broken body of the man with the Uzi. Standing over him was the other man who'd climbed down. She watched him feel for a pulse and shake his head, then turn the flashlight on the coil of rope ladder. Finally, he aimed the light up, and Annja withdrew.

20

Annja willed the sword away.

She knew the man was trapped below, and when the authorities arrived, they could deal with him and find a way to get him out. She prayed he didn't damage anything in an attempt to escape; even though the small relics had been removed, the temple itself was priceless. For a moment she considered using the M-16 to finish him—it would guarantee he not harm the ruins.

But that wouldn't be a fair fight. That would be murder.

She felt her right arm. It was slick with blood from where the bullet had passed through. She'd been grazed in that same shoulder early in the morning.

"What an amazing day," she said, as she worked at the left sleeve of her blouse until she ripped it free. She wrapped it around her wound and tied it tight, but not as tight as a tourniquet. She just wanted to staunch the blood. She figured Dr. Michaels would have alcohol or disinfectant. The students probably had some first-aid supplies, but she wasn't going to take the time to look for them. She needed to get back to the archaeologists.

She snatched up the M-16 and reloaded it. Then she stuffed some extra ammunition in the back pocket of her jeans. She took a pistol, too, and extra rounds. Neither man had identification or a wallet, though one had a wad of Australian money rolled up. Annja didn't consider herself a thief, but she knew the dead man had come by the money for doing something terrible. She shoved the roll in her pocket and checked the jacket of the rifleman. He was the smallest of the quartet, and so his jacket would prove the best fit. She still felt feverish, and so she knew she needed to keep warm. Annja found keys in an inside pocket as she put it on. She wouldn't have to hoof it back over the ridge after all.

Annja spotted three more M-16s in the back of the jeep, an M-14 Minirifle along with an AK-47, a large box of ammo, an empty duffel bag, a small carton of grenades and a satellite phone. She grabbed the phone and slid into the driver's seat. She dropped it on the passenger's seat, along with the M-16 she'd taken off the dead man. She laid the pistol in her lap and started the jeep. The engine purred as she backed up the jeep and turned it around, trying to disturb the ground around the dig as little as possible.

How did these men manage to get all these guns—and the grenades—into this country?

"Silly question," she answered herself. "How do they get guns into any country?" There are always illicit channels for those who look hard enough and grease the right palms with a significant amount of cash. She'd run afoul of too many of those kinds of people in recent times.

She kept her night-vision goggles on as she drove, carefully and not as fast as she would have liked.

There was no road here and she was not used to driving sitting on the right side of a vehicle. She kept the headlights off and relied on the black-green sci-fi world the goggles showed to her. Maybe there would be a way to trace this jeep to someone. At the very least the authorities might be able to get something out of the man left alive in the underground temple. Perhaps he would tell them where Oliver's body was…and the name of the mystery man who hadn't wanted to be seen and who was behind all this chaos.

"Or do I already have the man's name?" Annja searched her memory. She'd heard the men talking, about the professor, whom she was certain was this Dr. Hamam the students mentioned. And the men used the name Sayed. "What, what, what?"

Something niggled at the back of her brain, something familiar that was hanging just out of range. She slapped her hands against the steering wheel in frustration.

"What am I missing?"

Maybe Wes would know. Maybe this Sayed was important in archaeology circles in this part of the world. She hit a rut and the jeep jumped, jarring her and knocking her teeth together.

"I'm going to need a vacation when I'm through with this," she groaned.

But she wasn't close to through yet. She saw head-lights coming in her direction, two pairs.

"The police," she said. That's who she wanted it to be, but she wasn't certain. There were high grasses ahead, and she pulled into them and killed the engine. Just to be sure, she told herself.

The vehicles passed her, only one of them close enough for her to get a decent look, and she had to stand to do so, risking being spotted. It was another jeep, or something close, dark colored and driving too fast and carelessly through the preserve. There were no roads so it was bouncing over the uneven earth and digging up bushes and ground cover in its wake. She cringed at the destruction. Four men were inside, at least two with rifles. She saw the silhouettes of the guns sticking up in the back.

Definitely not the police. More goons from Dr. Hamam and Sayed.

She could try to take them out. She had rifles and ammo and her night-vision goggles would give her the edge. But there were four of them—and more in the other jeep. Bad odds. Still…she plucked the rifle up from the seat beside her. But before she could bring it to her shoulder the jeeps were gone, bouncing toward the dig.

They'd find their dead fellows, and maybe the one in the cave below. For a heartbeat she considered following them. But there were the archaeologists and the students to consider. What if there were more than these two jeeps coming? And what if a team of thugs was descending on the other site even now while she just sat here? She started the engine and cut through the tall grass, taking the route another jeep had so as to limit the damage to the preserve.

She mentally pictured where the Michaels site was with respect to the ridge. Her course took her around the northern edge of the spine, where she caught what at first she thought was an access road. But it was too narrow, a hiking trail then, or a road from years ago that had been allowed to grow over. She took it, and then drove across a wide, fast creek, the jeep having no trouble with the jagged terrain. She spooked a trio of kangaroos, as well as some owls that had been nested above her. She caught a quick glance at one of the owls, pale and no larger than a rock melon. Its head took up half of its body, and its wings looked so short she was amazed it could fly.

The adrenaline rush was wearing off, and the pain was surfacing in her arm to compete with her other aches. She fought a wave of dizziness and applied a little more gas when she emerged from a copse of small white stringy-barks and ironwoods. She saw four vehicles at the edge of her vision, two of them SUVs. From her trip here yesterday she knew they belonged to Dr. Michaels and his crew.

"I'm close." She breathed a sigh of relief. It wasn't a far walk, and she nearly pulled up next to an SUV with the intention of hoofing it the rest of the way. But then she drove past it, finding a gap between two stringybarks and a stretch of uneven grassland. She'd been this way before, on each of the three days she came out with Oliver. The jeep rolled up and over a fallen tree, bouncing her again and rattling the guns in the back. She leaned forward in the seat, nerves jangling and listening for gunfire, screams, anything that might tell her there was trouble ahead.

"Nothing," she said. "They're safe for the moment." But not for terribly long, she knew. The other men at the student dig had to have found the place deserted and the bodies. They'd be coming this way next. If they haven't already been here, she thought grimly .

Annja's eyes widened in terror as she made out ruts in the grass ahead—deep and muddy and very, very fresh.

"Please, God—" She didn't finish the thought. She pressed the accelerator and bumped toward the dig, seeing the tops of the tents ahead courtesy of the scant moonlight that came through the clouds and her night-vision goggles. She also saw another jeep, just like the one she was driving.

She roared into the camp, front left wheel clipping a tent post and bringing down one of the archaeologist's tents. She grabbed the M-14 Mini in one hand and the pistol in another and jumped out of the jeep. Something glowed in the camp, casting a ghastly, ghostly green that was almost painful to look at.

She scuttled forward, guns in hand, and slipped behind Dr. Michaels's tent and peered around a corner. She blinked furiously and flipped up her goggles with her forearm. In the center of the site, near the large canopy tent, a fire roared.

A broad-shouldered man stepped out from behind another tent and started firing at her. He shouted words she couldn't understand, and gestured with his head to get the attention of his companions.

Several yards behind him, three men with rifles stood as if at attention, backs to the fire and facing the archaeologists and students.

"Kill her!" one of them shouted. "We'll take care of the rest."

Annja ducked to avoid the gunfire, and then instantly poked her head back out, returned fire and quickly counted. Seventeen—there should be twenty with Dari. Dari's face was a bloody mess, as was one of the security guards. They'd put up a fight, Annja thought, and were beaten as punishment.

She fired again and missed the man shooting at her; she'd been distracted by the scene behind him. Now he was moving, crouching as he ran, using the shadows of a tent for cover as he came closer. She squeezed off another shot and dropped him.

All but Dari had their hands in the air. She raced forward and saw that his hands were tied in front of him. Then she saw two men raise their rifles to their captives, while the third had turned his attention to her.

Annja felt as if her stomach were rising into her throat. The men intended to execute them! She spun and grabbed cover near the body of the gunman she'd just dropped. Bullets whizzed into the ground near her.

She far preferred her sword to a gun; she was simply better with it. But there was no time, and too much distance, and so she raised the rifle to her aching shoulder, stood to get a clear shot, and squeezed off three shots. She dropped the man who'd been moving toward her, and one of the others, hitting one in the head and one in the neck. But she missed the third.

He'd fired at the same time.

Screams erupted, just as Annja ran forward, aiming as she went and firing. The gun jammed and she tossed it, bringing up the pistol as he dropped to a crouch, obscured behind the bonfire.

The archaeologists and students broke their line and huddled, one still screaming—Annja recognized Cindy's voice. Others wailed and called to her. She didn't hear any more shots, and so she knew the gunman was fleeing.

Her mind whirled. She knew she needed to see to the people; from their cries she knew at least one of them had been hit. But she couldn't afford to let the gunman get away. She swung around the fire, feeling its heat against her face, and registering that chairs and tables fueled it. She ignored Wes calling to her and kept running, seeing the man's boot prints in the muddy ground and following them. He was running toward the trees.

"I will come back," she called to them.

If I was him, I'd circle around and get to the jeep, Annja thought. Probably has a walkie-talkie or a satellite phone there and will call his buddies. And I can't let him do that.

His tracks ended where the grass began at the edge of the site, but Annja could hear him thrashing through the brush. She flipped her night-vision goggles down and followed him in, moving as quickly as she could. She realized her injuries were slowing her, and she brought to mind one of the martial-arts techniques she'd learned to help block out pain. It was difficult to concentrate on that and on pursuing the man, but she managed. And she closed the distance.

The world was an intense mix of green and black in the woods, and she registered myriad small heat sources moving away—ground squirrels and mice, so many mice! She vaguely recalled watching a nature program about Australia's problem with rodents, and then she shoved the errant thought aside and focused on her quarry.

Finally she spotted him, just as he was swinging a pistol around to shoot at her. She fired first, missing him by several inches and shredding the bark on a small tree. She got off a second shot before he could get a good fix on her, and he fell. It wasn't like in the movies, Annja had come to learn, people flying back when hit in the chest with a bullet.

She kept the gun out and advanced, ready to shoot again if he so much as twitched. He was definitely dead, as she noted blood running from his mouth and chest, and he wasn't breathing. She prodded him with her foot to be certain. Then she knelt and looked for identification, which she knew she wouldn't find.

"C'mon, I can't just leave you out here. You'd be too hard to find, or some animal will come and eat you. You're coming with me."

She fought a wave of dizziness and picked him up in a fireman's carry, moving fast because she wanted to get back to Wes and the others. She managed to lug him a few hundred yards when the pain in her side and her ankle became too great and the dizzy sensation returned. She dropped him and started pulling him by his ankles, still not slowing, but when she reached the edge of the dig site she let him go. "Good enough," she pronounced.

Time to round everyone up and pass out the weapons, she thought. There were two more jeeps full of men who might be heading their way.

She was halfway to the bonfire when she collapsed.

21

Annja blinked and woke suddenly.

She was about ten feet from the bonfire, on a cot that someone had pulled out of a tent, a blanket draped over her. There was a cool rag on her forehead, which fell into her lap when she sat up. Instantly, she felt dizzy again.

There was more gunfire, and she swung her legs over the side of the cot, getting them tangled in the blanket. She struggled with it for a moment, before she won and balled the blanket on the end of the cot. Then she stood, carefully, so the dizziness wouldn't send her to the ground again.

She saw the jeep she'd driven into the camp, and the tent next to it that she'd taken down with a tire. Dari, Cindy, Wes, Jennifer and two security guards were using the jeep and the collapsed tent as cover and were firing at something she couldn't see. A quick look around the rest of the camp showed that the students and the rest of the archaeologists were near the canopy tent, on the other side of the bonfire.

Annja started toward the jeep, setting her feet in time with her pounding heart. She must have collapsed earlier, and someone had put her on the cot and tried to take care of her. Her arm had been dressed. And then the rest of the hit squad must have shown up from the other dig site. That six people were shooting meant that they must have retrieved some guns from the jeep.

And more than guns, she realized after a moment. Dari lobbed a grenade, which thundered and spit up chunks of dirt when it hit. Cindy cheered and kept firing, and Dari threw another one before Annja could reach them.

"Dari's got blood worth bottling!" Jennifer exclaimed. "He got one with that last throw."

"Let me toss one!" Cindy reached into the back of the jeep and pulled out a grenade, but Dari grabbed it from her.

"I don't want you blowing us all up," he said.

Cindy made a face and started firing again. It looked as if she actually knew how to use a pistol.

Through the smoke from the grenades, Annja finally saw what they were shooting at—the men who had driven toward the student camp while she was driving away.

"How long was I out?" Annja asked as she shouldered up between Cindy and Dari.

No one answered, but Jennifer reached behind Cindy and passed Annja an M-16.

"I used to target shoot when I was in college," Jennifer said. "Haven't lost my touch. I nailed one of the bastards!"

Indeed, as Annja fitted the rifle to her sore shoulder, she saw two bodies. One was sprawled across the hood of a jeep, and the other one was on the ground in pieces from the grenades. She fired, shattering the windshield of the closest jeep. Not military grade, she thought.

She fired again, just as tires squealed and the jeeps pulled back. The remaining men—three in each jeep that she could see, returned fire, but the archaeologists had excellent cover and knew when to duck. Within the passing of a few heartbeats the vehicles were roaring away.

"Hated to throw those grenades," Dari said. "I don't want to hurt the preserve."

Dr. Michaels slapped him on the back. "Saved our necks, you did. The government can replant. And you kept them from entering our site."

For the first time Annja saw deep lines on his face, from worry and fatigue, and maybe from loss. She looked at him and met his sad gaze.

"They killed Josie," Wes said.

"And Matthew," Cindy said. Her eyes were puffy from crying. "They wanted to know where you were, and when we wouldn't tell them—honestly because we didn't know exactly—they shot Jeff, and then Matthew." She dropped to her knees and put her head in her hands, her shoulders shaking from the force of her sobs. "How could something like this happen?"

"Shot Josie for the same reason, mostly," Wes said. He was the calmest of the bunch, but Annja suspected that was because he hadn't let himself absorb the gravity of everything. "They shot her in the head like an execution. They wanted to know if we'd left the sites any time yesterday or today, or if we talked to anyone."

"Because one man didn't want to be seen," Annja said

dully. "Or maybe two men didn't want to be seen together."

"Dr. Hamam," Jon said. The student had shuffled up behind them. He was white from fear, his eyes unnaturally wide. "Dr. Hamam was with that man with all the scars. I didn't like that man."

"The man is called Sayed," Annja added.

Jon stroked his chin, his lip quivering nervously. "Sayed. That was the guy with Doc, right?" It looked as if Jon might topple at any moment, his legs trembling so much the fabric of his pants made a *shooshing* sound.

"Creeped me out," Cindy said. She raised her head, face a red mask of anger and disbelief. "Good reason why, I guess, if these were his men. But Doc wouldn't've had anything to do with this. Just that creepy Sayed fellow. Bet Doc didn't know he was a bad dude." She started crying again.

Annja didn't blame her. It was as if the students and the archaeologists had been dropped in the middle of a skirmish, something they were all totally unprepared for.

"God, please don't let them come back," Cindy said.

Annja couldn't hear the jeeps anymore; they were out of range. The sounds of the woods came back—owls and night birds mostly, and something that sounded like a cricket.

"Sayed, huh?" Jon knelt next to Cindy and stroked her hair. "Name sounds familiar somehow."

"Sayed Houssam," Annja whispered, as it suddenly came to her. "A very bad man."

Cindy continued babbling about how innocent Doc must be and that "this horrid Sayed person" must have duped him into thinking he was a grantor or investor who really only wanted to steal gold from the dig.

"Sayed Houssam, the international terrorist. A murderer a hundred times over." That's what had been tickling the back of Annja's thoughts. It wasn't that she was well informed about everything going on in the world, but she did read newspapers online, and she had read several articles about bus and subway bombings in London. Who hadn't been transfixed by all the terrorism reports? she thought. Sayed Houssam—the Sword—had come up amid the reports. He was an international terrorist whose name had been associated with bin Laden and Saddam Hussein and others of their ilk—someone for hire and who supposedly had his own agenda. She'd seen his picture in the online papers.

Why hadn't she recognized him when she looked through Oliver's camera? Because they were far away and she didn't get a good look at him, she reasoned. And because she certainly wasn't expecting to see an international terrorist at a student dig in a forest preserve northwest of Sydney. Last she'd read he was in London, having bombed the bleachers at a soccer stadium.

He certainly doesn't want anyone to know he's here, she thought. And either he doesn't want to be connected to Dr. Hamam, or Dr. Hamam doesn't want to be connected to him.

"This isn't just about Egyptian relics," she said, talking to herself and not realizing at first that she was speaking aloud. "The Sword bombs things—he doesn't steal artifacts. At least I don't think he does."

"Then what's it about?" Wes asked. "I'd bloody well like to know why Josie had to die."

"And Matthew." Cindy started blubbering, and Jon put his arm around her. Both of them shook together.

"I don't know," Annja answered. "But I will find out."

"And why Jeff had to get shot," Jon put in. He looked up at Annja, tears coming down his face now, too.

Jeff, they'd mentioned him before. "Shot? Someone's hurt? They left someone alive? Jeff is alive?"

"Yeah," Jon replied. "They shot him in the knee. Said they were going to shoot him in the other knee and then cut off his fingers one by one if he didn't tell them where you were."

"But then Matthew put himself between Jeff and that horrid man," Cindy added. She stuffed her fist in her mouth and the tears came faster. "And Matthew took the next bullet."

"They shot Josie just after," Wes said. "They were going to shoot Jennifer next, maybe shoot all of us. Hell, certainly shoot all of us, but you showed up."

Wes leaned against the jeep. He hadn't let go of the pistol. He peered out into the darkness and sniffed. The air was thick with the smell of smoke from the grenades and had an acrid stench from all the gunfire.

"They're not coming back," Annja told him. "We killed too many of them. They're going back into whatever hole they crawled out of."

"So we're safe," Jennifer said, her shoulders slumping in relief. She hovered over Jon and Cindy, gently touching each one. "I'm afraid, too," she whispered. Her hand shook visibly. "And so very, very angry."

"Safe?" Jon asked. "Really?"

"I didn't say that," Annja cut back a little too sharply. "But those men won't be back, at least for a while." She turned to Wes, who still hadn't moved from the jeep. "You did call the police?"

He nodded. "And before this second wave of bastards showed up I also called for an ambo."

"For Jeff," Annja said.

Another nod. "And for that fellow Dari walloped the crap out of."

Annja's eyebrows rose. "You have one of them? Alive?"

Dari finally spoke. "They raced in here in their jeep, the first batch, jumping out and shouting at us. Well, one of them shouted anyway. Only one spoke English from what we could tell. Then another started waving a gun in my face, and I tackled him."

"And hit him in the throat!" Jennifer cut in. "I thought Dari killed him at first, broke his friggin' neck."

Jon got up and tugged Cindy with him. He dug the ball of his foot into the ground. "That's when they beat Dari up." He pointed to the bald biker's face. "Then they lined us up like we were gonna all be shot by a firing squad, shot Jeff in the knee."

"And killed Matthew and Josie," Annja said. "And before that, Oliver."

She stepped away from the jeep and turned toward the bonfire. The blaze had died down a little, and she could no longer make out the outlines of furniture, only pieces of burning wood. She walked toward the cluster of people beyond it. Jeff would be there, no doubt tended to as someone had tended to her. And hopefully the man Dari had hit in the throat was there. Finally she had someone alive, and she intended to get some answers from him.

22

Annja looked in on Jeff first. He was under the canvas next to a sifting table, on a cot that Jennifer said was the only other one the men hadn't pitched on the bonfire.

"He's in shock," Annja said. She felt his forehead; he was cold, clammy and pale, and his lips had a slight bluish cast.

"Yeah, I know that." This came from an archaeologist named Sulene. She was the youngest of the professional crew, a wisp of a woman with thin, wheat-blond hair. "I've had enough first-aid courses in my closet to tell me that. Not just from loss of blood, though. We pretty well have that stopped, though maybe he's got some internal bleeding going on. He's conscious, barely, but he's not talking."

Sulene pulled back the two blankets that were covering Jeff so Annja could see his bandaged leg. His clothing had been loosened to make him more comfortable. She quickly replaced the blankets and tucked him in again.

More blankets were draped over two bodies just outside the canopy. Annja didn't need to look to know that Josie and Matthew were under them.

"He needs to be in a hospital," Sulene continued, nodding to Jeff. "An ambo is coming, but it's still awhile out, I'll wager. Dr. Michaels got them all coming with one call to the emergency operator—NSW state police, local police, fire brigade probably and the ambo." She nodded to her other patient, stretched out on the ground a few yards away. He had not been given a blanket, and two archaeologists stood over him, one with a gun pointed at his head. "He needs a hospital, too, but I could give a wombat's ass if he gets one. I only made sure he was still alive and straightened him out a bit so he could breathe better. His neck might be broken."

"Thank you for tending me." Annja assumed it had been Sulene who had dressed her arm. She obviously hadn't discovered Annja's cracked ribs, but then there was no outward sign of that injury.

"You could do with an ambo yourself," Sulene said. "Bullet went right through the fleshy part of your arm, but there could be infection. Ankle's all swollen, too. But I didn't do anything for that. Didn't have time." She stepped back from the cot. "You should take Dari with you, to the hospital. I'm out of bandages and alcohol. His face should be looked at. Probably needs at least a few stitches."

Annja walked past Sulene, aware that most of the assembly was watching her. She stopped a few feet back from the man on the ground.

"Has he said anything?" She put her weight on her left

leg, and glanced around for a chair. Probably all of them had been pitched on the fire.

Both archaeologists watching him shook their heads.

"But he will say something." Jennifer came up, right hand in her pocket and a mean look on her face. "I can guarantee you he'll talk."

"We don't even know if he speaks English." This came from the archaeologist holding the pistol on him.

"He speaks English," Annja said. "Or at least understands enough of it. Look at his eyes. He's following our conversation." She knelt next to him, glad to be off her sore ankle. She wasn't worried he'd attack her; she'd noticed that his wrists and ankles had been tied with the wiry twine they used to secure packed crates. Not even his fingers were twitching. His neck might indeed be broken.

Jennifer squatted next to Annja, brandishing a pair of pliers that she'd been holding tight in her left hand. "I stuck the end in the fire," she said. "It's nice and hot like a brand. I've watched enough spy shows to know how to torture a man. Make him hurt enough and he'll talk."

"That might not be necessary," Annja said.

Jennifer's eyes narrowed and she clacked the pliers. "Josie's dead, and one of those students. Josie and I went back twenty years. I don't understand why they had to die, or why these men had to come here. I don't understand why they wanted you so bad that—"

"Because I got a look at their boss, like I said. The Sword—Sayed Houssam—if that's his real name. I suspect it's not, too close to Saddam Hussein, probably picked it for that reason." Annja made a huffing sound and fluttered her hair. She realized the night-vision goggles had been taken off her head. "Funny thing is, Oliver probably had no clue that he got a shot of a terrorist."

Annja leaned so close to the man that she could smell the stink of him. Despite the cool weather, he'd been sweating, perhaps hadn't changed clothes for a while, and there were blood spatters on his shirt, though it didn't look to be his blood. She pulled back.

"If they hadn't come after Oliver and me, no one would have known that the Sword was in Australia. We were only shooting a one-hour segment, and there wouldn't have been any room for shots of the student dig and Sayed. Oliver just likes—*liked*—taking lots of pictures." She brought her face inches from his. "He's dead, isn't he?"

"Your cameraman?"

"He does speak English!" one of the archaeologists cut in.

"Yes, my cameraman. Oliver." One of the assassins on the ridge had told her that he'd been killed, but she wanted confirmation.

"He's dead," the man said. "The American with the blue eyes and expensive cameras." His voice was raspy, perhaps naturally or because Dari had punched him in the throat. It sounded as if it was difficult to get the words out.

"Where is his body?"

"Gone. Nothing but ashes. Nothing to find, and nothing to bury. And you should have joined him." He tried to spit at her, but he couldn't work up the saliva, and apparently he couldn't turn his head.

Jennifer leaned over him and clacked the pliers. "I want to know why you killed Josie and that student." She leaned back and held her free hand to her mouth. The smell of him was intense.

"She told you," he said, adding in a string of ugly-sounding foreign words. "The Sword did not wish to be seen in this place. No witnesses."

"The world thinks he's in England," Annja said numbly.

"Yes," the man answered. Again he seemed to struggle to get the words out. "Unfortunate that the Sword came to this desolate hole on a day when someone was shooting pictures."

Unfortunate for Oliver and Josie and Matthew, Annja thought.

Jennifer choked back a sob and gripped the pliers so tight that even in the scant light Annja could see that her knuckles were white. The woman clearly wanted to hurt someone, she was so angry and distraught over Josie's murder. Annja reached up and took the pliers from her.

"The Sword does not want Egyptian artifacts," Annja said. She watched the man's brow furrow. "What does the Sword want here?"

"His cause is just!"

Annja made a snarling sound. "I read the papers. The Sword rarely has a cause beyond money. He doesn't bomb stadiums and blow up buses to make a political point. Someone pays him to do those things."

The man snarled, but still his head did not turn. "The people he works for have causes. That is enough. Their cause becomes his cause!"

"For the right price." Annja sat the pliers down; she

noted that Jennifer's eyes were fixed on them. "And what is Dr. Hamam's cause?"

The man looked straight ahead, up into the face of the archeologist with the gun. He set his lips into a thin, defiant line.

"I can make him talk," Jennifer said. Her words came out a whisper, no power behind them. She gulped in air and fought the tears that threatened the corners of her eyes.

Annja leaned forward again, put her hands on his shoulders and put all her weight on him. "You will tell us."

His eyes seemed to fix on a spot far from the clearing in the forest preserve.

"What does Dr. Hamam want with the Sword?" For good measure she jabbed her knee into his side, noting that he didn't even flinch. Annja detested the notion of torture, but Oliver's face loomed large in the back of her mind. "What foul, foul thing is the Sword up to here?"

He remained silent. Sounds came to her, someone talking to Sulene, Jon talking to Cindy, Jennifer giving in to her sobs, the crackle of the still-burning fire. Faintly, she heard sirens.

"You'll tell the police, then," Annja said. She jabbed him again and then pushed off him to help her stand. "And I'll tell them all about the Sword being in Sydney."

"He is the wind, American," the man said. "He cannot be caught."

The archaeologist holding the gun lowered it and pulled back on the trigger. "I'm betting, mate, that everyone here will say I shot you in self-defense."

"I don't know what the Sword's ultimate work here is," he spit, "but it will be glorious and deadly."

Annja turned away, disgusted and frustrated. "He probably doesn't know," she told Jennifer. "Lackeys like him are usually not let in on the prize. They're merely brought along to help obtain it."

Moments later, a police van drove into sight. There was another car behind it, back by where the archaeologists parked their vehicles, and a truck that looked like a SWAT wagon. Annja could see the flashing lights, and she heard someone talking loudly over a police radio.

There were more headlights coming through the trees, two more police cars judging by the height of the flashing lights, and after a moment, another truck. She heard the sound of a helicopter. It seemed that Dr. Michaels had been able to lure a small army of police.

The side of the van read Cessnock Correctional Centre. Two officers got out, guns holstered, but the snap off them so they could be pulled quickly. The taller one pushed his hat back and took a look around. Wes and Jennifer were quick to meet him.

Annja held back and listened.

"Not easy to find the road," the tall officer said. "But your directions were good."

"I used to drive cabs when I was in college," Wes said. "I know how to give directions." Then he started to explain what had happened at the site, Jennifer interjecting about the shootings.

"No ambo yet?" This came from Sulene, who continued to worry over Jeff.

"No, not yet," Annja told her. "But the police are a start. The ambulance shouldn't be far behind."

"I hope not for Jeff's sake," Sulene said. She took a glance at the cops and then looked back at Jeff. "I wish that friend of yours—Dari—killed that son of a bitch rather than just cracked his neck."

"There's been enough killing. Besides, if his neck is broken, might that not be worse than death?" Annja yawned. Despite her nap in the Purple Pussycat, she was feeling the effects of the ordeal, and knew she could do with some more sleep. And maybe a trip to the hospital wouldn't be such a bad idea after all, she thought. Grazed, shot, cracked ribs and a sprained ankle…a little professional mending might be a very good idea. "What a thoroughly rotten day this has been."

Dari joined her, watching as four more officers, these state police, joined the two from the van. After a few moments, Jennifer led them to the injured killer and gestured at the two bodies.

The bald biker's face looked much worse than Annja had realized. Close to the fire the flames revealed every cut. The gargoyle tattoo was obscured by a smear of blood, and the fleshy ridge above his right eye was torn where one of the men had ripped out his silver hoop. The diamond stud had likewise been ripped out of his nose.

"Where's that sword you were swinging?" he asked her. "The one you found on the ridge?"

Annja shrugged. "I must have dropped it somewhere."

"Pity. It was a beaut," he said. "That would have been a souvenir worth keeping."

A brief silence settled between them.

"Sorry about all of this," she said. Annja didn't know quite what else to say. She'd inadvertently dragged other innocents into her adventures before, but rarely did they get beat up so badly. "Sulene's right—you need to go to a hospital."

"I'm in better shape than you," he returned. "At least I wasn't shot."

"At least we're both alive." Annja's voice trailed off as two of the police officers looked under the blankets at the bodies. A third went to Jeff's cot.

The remaining three continued to talk to Wes and Jennifer, all of them hovering around the intruder. Jennifer talked about the two jeeps filled with the men who drove away. Then she pointed to Annja, and the police looked her way.

"You going to talk to them?" Dari raised a bloody eyebrow. Annja could see where bruises were starting to form on his cheeks. They would be large and would cover most of his face.

"I guess I'm going to have to," she said. "But they're not the ones I need to talk to. Those guys are back in Sydney."

"Where this Dr. Hamam teaches?"

Annja nodded and shuffled toward the three policemen.

"Those men were looking for Annja Creed," Jennifer said, waggling her fingers. "The woman who was doing a television special about our dig."

Annja heard more sirens, and hoped it was the ambulance.

"Ambo's coming," an officer announced. "And so's a medi-evac chopper. It's just trying to find a close place to land."

Annja stood next to Jennifer and told her side of the story, leaving out her sword, but leaving nothing out about Sayed and Dr. Hamam.

The police listened, one of them taking notes, one of them asking questions, and the third appearing to keep an eye on the Arab, but carefully taking in her story. She was surprised that they seemed to believe her, and at the same time she was glad that none of them had heard of her before or had watched a single episode of *Chasing History's Monsters.*

Somehow she'd expected at least one of them to accuse her of being partly responsible for the carnage; she would have accused herself if she were in their position. And she half expected to be asked to "come downtown with us, ma'am." Instead, the lead officer told her simply to stick around the country a few more days and let them know where she would be staying. He passed her a card with his name and contact numbers on it.

"And contact the Sydney police first thing in the morning," the lead officer said. "They'll want to ask you about the incident at the hotel. State investigators are going to want to talk to you, too."

"Of course," Annja agreed.

"You really should have talked to the Sydney detectives right away, ma'am," he said.

"I realize that now," she said apologetically.

"Yeah, hindsight really is twenty-twenty. Take care of yourself ma'am."

Then he left her to call in a preliminary report.

Annja breathed a sigh of relief. She knew she could

well be wanted in the Sydney hotel matter, and word of it hadn't trickled out to police forces in other towns.

Annja learned that not all of the area police had come from Cessnock, but it had a prison, and Wes had told them there were a lot of men who needed locking up—hence the Cessnock police were asked to bring a prisoner transport van. One of the officers looking at the bodies grumbled that they didn't need to bring their van for one live prisoner, adding that instead the archaeologist should have called for multiple ambulances.

Moments later an ambulance arrived, and Sulene waved frantically to get the paramedics' attention.

"Jeff should be going on the helicopter," Sulene said. "You can put that bastard on a backboard and take him in the ambo. I want Jeff on the helicopter."

Annja wandered back to Dari.

"You should go with them, Dari."

"Look, Miss Cr—"

"Annja."

"Are you going? You were shot."

She didn't answer. She stared at the flames.

"The ambo's from Cessnock, Annja. You'll like the town. They call it a city, but it's a spit of a city next to Sydney. It's not too far north of here. Don't think it has more than twenty thousand folks. But you can't call it a woop woop, either." He crossed his arms. "Used to be a mining town, but the coalfields all closed down some years back. Now it produces wine. The Darkinjung tribe settled it a few thousand years ago, then the Europeans came and wiped out a lot of the indigenous folk with their diseases. A lot of history there, that's what you'd like about it."

"I might visit it when I come back for a vacation," Annja said.

"So you're not going in the ambulance?"

She shook her head.

"You're going to see Dr. Hamam, aren't you?" Dari asked.

Annja nodded sadly.

"Seems like you're more than just a television archaeologist," Dari said.

"And you're more than just another bloke from the Cross," she replied with a smile.

"You look me up next time you're in Sydney. Easy enough to find me through one of my op shops," he said.

"I promise." Annja felt in her pocket for the keys to the SUV. She had her own ride to the university.

23

Fortunately, one of the police officers drove Annja to the end of the service road where the SUV was parked. He just assumed the car was hers—it was a rental after all, and she had the keys for it. Though she'd been pretty complete in her descriptions of the fight on the ridge, and the subsequent one in the student camp—including telling them about the man trapped in the underground temple—she'd neglected to mention lifting the keys. She'd wanted transportation without having to ask someone to chauffer her around.

Unfortunately, the tank was less than a quarter full, and so another stop at a gas station was in order. Perhaps not so unfortunate after all, Annja decided, as she left the highway and exited into what Dari had called a woop woop. The town might have been small, but the gas station doubled as a convenience store.

Annja bought a bottle of pain killers, a comb, a brush

and hair tie and a brown sweatshirt that displayed a picture of an Australian cattle dog. The other selections featured sharks, Tasmanian devils, boomerangs, aboriginal flags and various coats of arms and were in colors bright enough to add to her headache. Then she visited the restroom and turned on the tap, filling her hand with cold water and swallowing two pills before tackling anything else.

She looked into the mirror and shuddered. Annja had been in plenty of scrapes before, but she couldn't recall when she'd been in so many fights within such a short amount of time.

"Who told me I looked like hell?" She shook her head. "I look worse. God, do I know this person staring back at me?" Tangled hanks of hair pulled out when she combed it, but after several minutes she'd managed to make it presentable, and she twisted it back into the tie.

Her face was another matter. She scrubbed it and scowled at a bluish bruise on her cheek, and another on her jaw, the latter turning a vivid purple. Her lower lip was a little swollen, but maybe no one would notice that. There were five small bruises on her neck, where one of the men must have grabbed her and squeezed. She stared closer. It looked as if she had the makings of a black eye.

Another trip to the cash register resulted in a travel-size stick of deodorant and overpriced makeup that covered up most of the evidence of the fight.

A vial of perfume completed her purchase. She dabbed some behind her ears and on her wrists to get rid of some of the stink she'd acquired from her ordeal. She used a liberal amount of the deodorant and threw the rest away.

Then she tossed her blouse in the garbage, along with the jacket she'd taken from one of the men. She put on the sweatshirt and decided she looked acceptable enough.

"At least I look more like a human and less like something a big cat dragged in. I guess I clean up pretty good." She no longer resembled the gaunt, haunted, battered-looking woman of a few minutes ago.

Annja knew that in her previous state she likely wouldn't be able to talk her way past any security guard—and that's what she'd likely need to do. She'd looked like a homeless person.

A third trip to the cash register bought her two ham-and-cheese sandwiches, a carton of milk, a big green apple and a handful of candy bars. She took them out to the SUV and started eating before she pulled back onto the road. She'd paid for everything with some of the money from the roll she'd taken off one of the men. It couldn't have been helped, she knew; the gas station didn't take American credit cards and she'd been pretty well tapped out after paying the painter for a lift in his pickup.

She spotted a speed-limit sign as she pulled back on the highway and pointed herself toward Sydney. Annja didn't look down at the dash to see how fast she was going; she knew it was above the limit. She just didn't want to know how much above.

Annja feasted quickly, both because she was famished and because she was nervous. Something was up, and she hadn't put the pieces together. But she knew it had to be bad to involve the Sword. The police had heard of him, and the officer who'd given her the lift said a bulletin was going out immediately. The police had seemed reluctant to consider Dr. Hamam a threat, especially when Cindy and Jon came up and reiterated how the professor couldn't have realized what sort of company he was keeping.

"Oh, he knew," Annja muttered as she slugged down the milk. "But what are the two of them up to?" She stashed the wrappers back in the bag and set it on the passenger's side of the floorboard. Then, hunkering down and still keeping her eye on the road, she reached under the passenger's seat. "Lovely." She pulled out a gun and immediately cut her speed. "I so do not need to be pulled over and have the cops find this."

She scolded herself for not searching the SUV thoroughly at the gas station. The gun might come in handy, but she still preferred the sword. She put it back, contorted a little, and reached under the driver's seat, finding a map folder, but no more weapons. The map, she reasoned, would come in far handier than the gun.

Annja turned on the radio, curious if she'd hear a breaking-news bulletin about Sayed. Instead, she heard the DJ announce a power hour of heavy-meal bands. "No, thank you," she said as she turned it off. She put both hands on the wheel and watched the miles go by.

When she neared Sydney she fished out the map, finding one detailed enough of the city to show the university. There was a light attached to the rearview mirror, and she turned it on.

"Interesting," she said.

There were five circles on the map, drawn in thick pencil. Did they mean something? Or were they drawn by the rent-a-car place in response to a previous driver's questions for tourist stops? She abandoned the map and let her thoughts whirl until she turned off into the city.

Taking a side street, she pulled over and looked at the map more closely, holding it up to the light. The places marked were near the intersections of George and Argyle Streets in the Rocks area not far from Circular Quay and the harbor; another at Harris and Miller; the smallest circle at Bulwara Road and Mary Ann; one at William and Forest, not far from Kings Cross; and the fifth obscured the street names but sat in the middle of a triangle formed by Chinatown, Capital Square and Paddy's Markets. There were three small *X* marks, too, but they were in the middle of squares and not associated with a particular street.

It took her a minute to find the Darlington campus of the university on the next map fold and to trace a route there. That's where she intended to begin, as not a single student at the dig knew where Dr. Hamam lived.

"At the university," Jon had told her right before she left. "If he's not at the dig, he's at the university. He lives for Egypt."

It least it would be a start. Someone at the university would tell Annja where Dr. Hamam lived; she could be charming and persuasive when needed.

Traffic was light, Sydney seemed like a ghost town at this early hour. Residential streets were mostly dark, and Annja was struck by the disparity in traveling only a few blocks. Fine, big houses that were well kept up and that she knew would fetch hundreds of thousands of dollars lined a clean street of manicured lawns. Within minutes she came to a section reminiscent of any large city—run-down places with peeling paint, sagging roofs, broken steps and cracked sidewalks. Sheets served as drapes in one place; next to it was a narrow two-story building with the windows boarded up and a tricycle with no wheels sitting out front.

She came to a small business district that looked as if it had some age to it but was clean and tidy. The lights burned softly in a bakery, and she imagined that people were already preparing the morning's goods. A going-out-of-business banner was plastered across the window of an art gallery. This part of the city reminded her of one of the smaller New York City boroughs she liked to frequent.

She pulled onto one of the university's main drives, and noted it was close to 4:00 a.m. It was a big campus; she could tell that even in the darkness.

"How the hell am I going to find him?" she muttered. A few moments later she parked next to a kiosk, ghostly lit by a streetlight. It didn't take her long to find a faculty directory. "Now why would his office be way over there?" She tapped the map. "Because he's temporary, as Jon said. Just a visitor. And one who has more than worn out his welcome."

She chewed on one of her fingernails and twisted the hem of her sweatshirt with her other hand. Whatever Dr. Hamam and the Sword were planning would happen soon; she just knew it. And that meant she didn't have a lot of time to track them down and end it.

She got back in the SUV and took Missenden to Parramatta, avoiding the interior of the campus. She didn't see a soul out and about, though she saw quite a few lights on. She took a right on Ross and found Science Road, passed a campus security car that paid her no heed and rolled into a parking lot. The sign said she needed a parking sticker, but she expected to be in and out before anyone cruised by and noticed her vehicle.

She tried three doors and couldn't find anything open, not even a window she could crawl through, and there was nothing she could climb to reach the second floor and try the windows there. Annja went back to the parking lot and looked around. There were four cars. One of them might belong to Dr. Hamam. She went to the door closest to the lot and pounded on it. She paced on the short sidewalk and pounded again, pressed her face to the glass of a small window set halfway up in the door and peered inside to find the hall beyond dimly lit.

Annja bent to get a close look at the lock. She tucked her arm into her side and ground her teeth together; her ribs were reminding her they were still cracked. She could tell the door required a key card, but she might be able to trick it. There didn't look to be any way to pick it, and the window was safety glass, the kind that had the wire running through it. She was too big to fit through it anyway.

A third time pounding, and Annja was just about ready to find campus security and plead her case. But through the small window she saw a man coming down the hall, arms swinging loosely at his sides. He took his time getting to her, and he only opened the door a crack.

She produced her wallet, the way a cop showed his badge on TV shows. It displayed an old press credential card on one side that she'd acquired for doing a series of segments in Europe a few years ago. She'd kept it because it looked impressive and official.

"So?" he said, unimpressed. His gray-green shirt was crisp with creases and had a name tag sewn on it, but she could only make out the letters *Th.* "What can a reporter want at four in the morning? And at this building?"

It wasn't quite four yet; Annja checked her watch.

"I'm with a film crew doing a special on a dig north of Sydney."

"Dr. Hamam's big project?"

Her eyes glistened and she slipped the tip of her tennis shoe in the door.

"Yes, I need to speak with him. It's urgent." She put on a concerned face, forehead scrunched in wrinkles. "It's very important." No pleading in her voice, all businesslike. She met his gaze and didn't blink.

He looked through the window and into the parking lot. "That your car? The big black one?"

She nodded.

"You need a sticker to park there."

"Is Dr. Hamam here?"

"I don't think so. He works late, but not this late. And he doesn't come in this early."

"Could I check? His office?" She worked to keep from talking too quickly, as she sometimes did when she was in a hurry. "It would only take a moment."

"I suppose. Got nothing else to do right now. But you need a sticker for the lot."

"I'll risk it," she said.

"I'll have to go with you."

"Of course."

He let her in and closed the door firmly behind her. Immediately she was assaulted by the smell of floor polish and disinfectant. Thadeus was the name on his shirt.

"You're the night watchman?"

He gave a clipped laugh. "Hardly, though I suppose you could say so. I'm the third-shift janitor for this building, and in another hour I'm going to be heading home for a nice long weekend. So you'll make this quick?"

"Of course. Thank you, Thadeus."

Hamam's office was down a turn in the corridor, nearly at the other end of the hall. They hadn't quite got there when the janitor shook his head and stopped.

"No lights. Told you he didn't work this late, or come in this early. You could try back on Monday."

"I'll have to go to his house, then."

"I suppose so," he said.

She hesitated. "But I don't know where he lives."

"Neither do I."

"But I bet his address is in his office."

He shook his head again.

"And I bet you have a key." She turned on a dazzling smile and prayed that it would work. For a moment it looked as if it was lost on him and that he would boot her back out into the parking lot.

"I shouldn't be doing this," he said.

"I'll be quick. I promise."

He hesitated.

"It's important. Really." This time a hint of desperation crept into her voice. Annja didn't want to break into the office, but she knew at this point she would. Something bad was transpiring—she knew it with every inch of her being, and she was obligated by some unknown force to do something about it.

"All right." He looked at her, puzzled, and fished out a ring of keys. His fingers went to a tarnished one that had Master written on it on a small piece of masking tape. "But you're not to take anything."

"No."

"Then be quick. Neither one of us needs to get in trouble." He opened the door and turned on the light, and after she slipped inside he stood in the frame, arms crossed in front of his chest. "I really shouldn't be doing this," he said again.

She was immediately struck by the plainness of the office. There were no pictures or certificates on the walls, and the bookcases were only half-filled. The desk was uncluttered, with in and out baskets on one corner, the phone and a carefully folded newspaper on another. There was a calendar blotter, and she stepped behind the desk.

She looked up to see Thadeus watching her.

Today's date was circled in green marker on the calendar, but nothing was written in the space beneath. Previous dates had things marked like "Student essays due," "Report to the vice-chancellor," "Evening seminar on the papyrus of Ani." There were also scrawls in hieroglyphics, and Annja wondered if they were doodles or secret reminder notes.

"Find an address?"

"Not yet." She opened the desk drawer and discovered pens and pencils neatly lined up in a tray, every pencil sharpened to a fine point and not a single mechanical pencil in the bunch. There were index cards, sticky note pads and paperclips, all of it orderly. Nothing personal, she noted, no photographs of family members or favorite dogs, no candy bars or packs of chewing gum. She looked in another drawer.

"You know, I've been thinking," Thadeus said. "If I had an office, I wouldn't keep my home address listed in it. I'd know where I lived, and I wouldn't need anything to remind me."

Annja was quick to answer. "I thought maybe I'd find a faculty directory, or some letters that had been sent to his home address that he'd brought in. It would be an apartment, I'd think, him being here as a visiting professor. Though I suppose he could be renting a house near the campus."

Out of the corner of her eye, she saw that Thadeus was getting impatient, his knee jumping and his mouth working. She looked through the next drawer, finally finding something personal—a paperweight of an Egyptian pyramid. She turned it over and smiled: Made In China. There were more office supplies, but nothing of interest.

"Time to go," Thadeus said.

Annja briefly entertained the notion of leaving with him and finding a way to slip back in. She knew where the office was and therefore which window to break now. Maybe she could find something on the bookshelves.

"And what's so important anyway that it can't wait for later in the day? Campus operator can maybe help you after nine or so. Why not wait for Monday?"

"Because I think your visiting professor is involved with an international terrorist and I want to know what they're up to." Annja spoke rapid-fire out of frustration, having resigned herself to looking elsewhere.

The janitor made a huffing sound. "I wouldn't doubt it. He's an odd duck, that one. Strange hours. Strange visitors."

She looked up and studied his face; the janitor wasn't kidding. "What visitors?"

"Aside from you? Well, yesterday, or maybe it was the day before, a Middle Eastern gentlemen—I'd be hard-pressed to tell you what country he was from—thought he'd snuck in here without me seeing. Not much passes by me, though. Small man, but I didn't like the looks of him. Face all scarred. I would've tossed him out, but I just didn't want to—"

"Confront him?" Annja asked.

"Yeah."

Annja dug through the rest of the drawers in a frenzy. "He's a terrorist, that man you saw, and he goes by the name of the Sword." It was all right to reveal that, she figured, as it would be out on the news soon enough if the police took it seriously.

"What's he doing with Dr. Hamam?"

"That's what I'm trying to find out." The desperation and frustration were thick in her voice. "Damn. Nothing."

Thadeus cleared his throat. "He also spent a lot of time at the museum on campus, or so he told me one night. We've quite the Egyptian display. I went through it once, took my middle son."

She looked up again.

"But it doesn't open until noon on Saturdays."

Annja came around the desk, so quickly and clumsily

that she knocked over the wastebasket. Crumpled and burned papers tumbled out. She plopped down on the floor and started going through them. There was an acrid scent to them, as if they'd been burned fairly recently. She thought she should have noticed the smell immediately, but then the scent of floor polish and disinfectant had hung heavy out in the hall.

"Find something?"

"Maybe. Give me just a little bit more time."

"Didn't like the looks of that scarred fellow at all. Wasn't the disfigurement, mind you. My wife's missing her left arm from the elbow down, born that way." He paused and rocked back on his heels, looked left and right out of the office to make sure no one else was about during this ungodly early hour. He leaned back in. "I didn't like the way he walked, all skulky like, and the way he kept his head down. He was dressed too good, an expensive suit like you'd see on a movie star or a politician."

He continued to discuss the terrorist, asking Annja what things he'd blown up and what she knew about him. She didn't answer; she was too caught up in the notes she'd found. The largest crumpled piece had been on the bottom and was charred the least. She carefully opened it.

"What's it say?"

She saw no problem reading it to him, as he'd been so cooperative.

Thoth is the judge of right and truth of the company of gods, all in the presence of Osiris. Hear Thoth's judgment. Osiris's heart has been weighed, and the soul of that heart has provided testimony. His heart has been found right according to the trial in the great balance.

She paused. "I think it's a translation from the *Book of the Dead.*"

"The what?"

"It's not really a book. It's just called that." She continued:

Osiris, no wickedness has been found inside him, and he has not committed an evil act. He is worthy of the offerings that are made in his temples. His mouth does not speak evil words.

She paused. "Interesting, but not useful," she decided.

She looked at the rest of the pieces, not able to make out any complete sentences. Thadeus knelt in front of her and tried to help.

"'Pipe, pump,'" he read. "'One hundred psi, 150 psi.' That's all imperial measurements, not metric. Means pound per square inch."

"But inch of what?" Annja mused aloud. "Water, gas, solid?"

She unfolded a half-charred receipt for truck rentals—three, no clue to the size or the company. Then she found part of an address, which she showed to the janitor.

"That's not all that awfully far from here. It's an old industrial complex. My dad used to work at the Palmen Factory there. But it's closed now."

She stood and paced in a tight circle. "Think, think,

think." Then she paced in front of one of the bookshelves, eyes scanning the titles while her mind continued to whirl.

Ancient Egypt, by Daniel Cohen; *Ancient Egypt,* by Geraldine Harris; *Ancient Egypt,* by George Hart; *The Egyptians,* by Roger Coote; *Ramses II and Egypt,* by Oliver Tiano; *The Nubians: People of the Ancient Nile,* by Robert Bainchi; *Gods and Pharaohs from Egyptian Mythology; High Pressure Pumps Instruction Manual.*

She stopped at the last title and pulled it from its spot, passing it to Thadeus. "What do you make of this?"

He thumbed through it as he stood. "Pretty basic," he said. "Imperial again, not metric, so I doubt he got it here. Tells you how to operate water pumps and connect them to various lines."

Annja's throat grew instantly dry and her breath caught.

Inside the underground temple to Hathor, beyond the burial chamber, was the pond covered with dead fish. She hadn't given it any thought when she saw them—other than noting how absolutely awful they smelled.

"The fish were dead because the water had been poisoned." Annja made the mental leap to that conclusion. "And the manual on water pumps, rented trucks…it means they're going to poison something bigger. A lot bigger."

She wrapped her arms around herself and tried to absorb the enormity of what she guessed was about to transpire.

"I think they mean to poison Sydney's water, and kill an awful lot of people. Dear God why?"

24

Annja glanced at the dashboard clock. It was almost 4:30 a.m. It had taken her several minutes to search Hamam's office and find the clues in the trash—what she hoped were clues, anyway—to his horrid plans. And it had taken a handful more minutes to call the police and try to explain her suspicions.

"Your name again, ma'am?" the officer had asked.

"Annja Creed," she'd repeated. "I'm an American, and I—"

"The television personality. Yes, ma'am, I know who you are. Where are you?"

Annja knew she was wanted by the authorities, bare minimum for questioning. But most likely she was some sort of suspect in the shooting incident at the hotel. Enough guests standing in the hall had seen her fight with the men in her room and kill two of them.

"I'm at the university," she'd answered truthfully,

stifling a yawn. "I'm in an office building off Science Road, Dr. Hamam's office on the first floor. The building has green trim around the windows." Then she had tugged the card out of her pocket and gave him the name of the police officer from Cessnock she'd spoken with a few hours ago. He'd tell the Sydney police about the gunmen at the dig; that would give credence to her story. She rattled off the location of the old industrial park where she thought something bad would transpire, based on the note in the trash, and the intersections circled on the map that she could remember. She'd left the map in the SUV.

At the same time the janitor was in the office across the hall, calling campus security and telling them to locate Dr. Gahiji Hamam.

When the police officer kept asking Annja more information about herself, and when it appeared that he was deliberately trying to stall her, she hung up and left. She was certain she could find the industrial park from the directions Thadeus had given her.

As she drove, her head occasionally nodding in fatigue, she prayed that the officer had believed some of what she'd told him. She intended to call again if no police showed up at the industrial park. She thought it a good bet that some police might go to the university. Thadeus had said he'd wait for them and tell them his own suspicions about Hamam and his terrorist visitor.

I'm tired, so very tired, Annja thought. And on top of that she ached from the top of her head to her very sprained ankle. She felt miserable and could benefit from rest and medical care, but there wasn't time for it.

The campus still looked uninhabited as she drove

through it; not a soul was on the sidewalks or driving into or out of the parking lots. It would be so very easy to fall asleep, she thought, yawning and rubbing her eyes. She still had two candy bars left from her convenience-store stop, and so she ate them, barely registering their sugary taste as she pulled out of the campus gates and headed south.

She followed the janitor's directions, aided by the map sprawled on the passenger's seat. She turned on the radio, again hearing no news reports, though she did find a talk-radio program discussing the soaring prices of aboriginal art. She let it play just for the noise.

"Why would they want to poison people?" Annja asked aloud. She had learned long ago that talking to herself sometimes helped her puzzle out problems. "Innocent people who have nothing to do with Egyptian artifacts—why hurt them? I'm not wrong. That's what they're going to do, this Dr. Hamam and Sayed the Sword. But why?"

There seemed to be no other explanation for the pumping equipment, truck-rental receipt and the dead fish at the dig site.

"And why Sydney?" A big city, sure. But off the proverbial beaten path as far as terrorist activities went—most of those hotbeds were in the Middle East, Europe and the United States. "Why Sydney?"

She slammed the palm of her hand against the steering wheel. If it was to cover a theft, that seemed pretty ludicrous. If Dr. Hamam wanted to steal artifacts from the student dig, he could have done it easily—without exacting a death toll. Some of the graduate students under his auspices practically worshiped him. Take Jon and

Cindy and maybe even Matthew, for example. They would have helped him crate up the pieces and never asked what would happen to them. Hamam likely could have told them the relics were being shipped to Egypt for closer study, and the students would not have raised an alarm. They might have even helped him carry the crates directly to the airport.

Maybe the professor had indeed stolen the relics, or at least some of them. Jon had told her all the pieces from inside the temple were intact, with traces of color remaining, and therefore exceedingly valuable. But as much as Annja revered the past and its antiquities, and recognized the importance of the Australian find, she knew that the artifacts were just things, and not worth killing that many people over.

"He could have just flown away with them," she said, yawning, and then yawning longer and wider. "Why couldn't he have left everything else alone?" A commercial came on advertising discounted day trips to the Blue Mountains, the Three Sisters rock formation and a small zoo in the area with koala bears that could be petted. Annja's head bobbed forward and she dug the fingernails of her left hand into her palm to force herself to stay awake.

"What if Oliver hadn't stood on the ridge less than forty-eight hours past and taken a shot of Dr. Hamam and the terrorist? Maybe he didn't even take any images. Maybe Oliver just looked. But what if he hadn't stood up there? And what if I hadn't joined him?"

She knew if Oliver hadn't walked up the ridge just before they called it a wrap, then the Sword would not have seen him. Assassins would not have subsequently killed him and come after her. And though those assassins might have later descended on the archaeology digs to eliminate potential witnesses, she and Oliver would have been on a plane to New York and oblivious to their nefarious deeds.

And as a result, maybe no one would have been alerted to the poison—before the act. Maybe no one would have known about the powerful terrorist on Australian soil.

"And maybe no one would be trying to stop him." Annja leaned forward in her seat and looked up at a street sign. "Not this one. Gotta be the next." She kept driving south. "Maybe Oliver climbed that ridge and became a sacrificial lamb. Maybe Ollie's sacrifice was to get my attention and set things in motion."

More cars were out on the streets now than when Annja had first come into the city. People were no doubt heading out to early-morning jobs. She saw a station wagon full of kids and suitcases, a family leaving on a vacation.

"Good that they're getting out of Sydney," Annja mused. "This place isn't safe right now."

The dashboard clock read 4:44 when she pulled up to the industrial park. The sky was starting to lighten, and from the looks of the few thin clouds overhead it would be a bright day. The sign at the entrance to the park was old and weathered, and a plank of wood was missing out of its middle. There were several lights on high poles in the parking lots, but only about half of them worked, and those glowed with a pale blue-white. They looked to be the kind with sensors that signaled them to come on at dusk and turn off when the sun rose.

The tall wire gate was pulled closed, but there was no lock on it, only a chain that dangled loose. Annja turned off the radio, left the SUV running and jumped out. She pushed the gate open with little effort—though it squealed loudly—then she slowly pulled into the parking lot, not bothering to get out again and close the gate. Her gaze flitted everywhere.

No sign of any police cars yet, but that didn't mean they weren't on their way. She'd come directly from the university and had not been too careful about obeying the speed limit.

Two small factories, the ones directly to the east, appeared to be closed, their walls made of some sort of rusted metal and rust-stained concrete, and most of the windows broken. Annja spotted seagulls flying out of a hole in a roof. There was a larger factory beyond them still operating, smoke coming from one of its stacks. If there were other complexes, she couldn't spot them from here, and so she drove across a section of a parking lot that was empty of everything save tall tufts of weeds that sprouted from cracks in the pavement.

Beyond the first of the closed factories, which sported fading graffiti and under it the names of the former businesses, was a larger lot that had a few dozen cars. None of the vehicles were new or expensive, marking them as belonging to laborers who likely weren't earning a high hourly wage.

Annja shook her head to rouse herself. The sugar from the candy bars either hadn't kicked in or she was so hopelessly tired that a sugar rush wouldn't matter.

She spotted a one-man shed where perhaps a factory

watchman was posted. It was in the middle of the lot, and she headed there. No sooner had she passed two rows of cars when she veered away.

"So tired I'm not thinking straight," she said. "I talk to him—or her—and let on by asking questions that I'm not supposed to be here, I will probably get bounced." She drove around the southern edge of the factory, not knowing really what she was looking for, maybe a big garage or warehouse where the rented trucks might be, a place to mix and load the poison. An empty place, most likely, she thought.

"Empty and ignored," she told herself.

She turned around and drove back to the two abandoned factories, and she scrutinized them more carefully. The first had been a cement plant, and was the uglier of the two. Its two stacks were corroded, and a thorny vine, dying with the fall, had grown halfway up one of them, birds' nests dotting it here and there. She rolled down her window and leaned out; the air was filled with an unpleasant smell that could have come from this abandoned place or from the operating factory. Her eyes watered.

The building wasn't especially large, and resembled an ugly box, with twisted pieces of rebar sticking out at odd angles like the legs of an overturned spider. There was a roll of something like barbed wire stretched across a bank of windows that had been broken. It would effectively keep most people out. Probably not to keep them from looting the place, Annja guessed, but to keep them from hurting themselves inside and suing whoever owned this monstrosity.

What struck Annja was that despite its horrid appearance, it was *clean*. There were no piles of refuse around it or discarded fast-food bags, no mounds of cigarettes or other detritus from people who'd cruised in the lot.

The building had a wide corrugated door, mostly rusted, that was chained and locked. At least it looked locked from her vantage point. There were a few smaller doors, one with a faded Workers sign above it, another with Deliveries. She thought those might not be locked, so she slipped out of the SUV and tried them. Not only were they locked, but also they were rusted shut, with no sign that anyone had broken in.

She looked through a low window, one the roll of barbed wire didn't quite reach. The interior was thick with shadows; the emerging sun and what glow was left from the lights in the parking lot weren't quite enough to reach very far inside. From what she could tell, it looked as if a jumble of girders had fallen from above, and a metal stairway that stretched out of sight was missing most of its steps. The floor and walls had thick cracks, and all the other details were lost in the darkness.

She hurried to a window on the other side and saw nothing different, save a concrete truck, which immediately set her heart beating faster. Then she noticed it was missing tires in the front; it hadn't been anywhere in quite some time. Annja dashed back to the SUV and went to other closed factory.

Maybe it was nothing, the address in the wastebasket, she thought. Or maybe she'd read it wrong or Thadeus had given her bad directions. She tried to tell herself that she was jumping to conclusions about the terrorist poisoning Sydney's water supply—but that didn't work. In her gut she knew she was right.

She'd take a quick look at this one, she decided, and then she would try another spot marked on the map.

She came at the next building from the rear, where she was surprised to see an open section where part of a wall had been brought down. Jensan's Tile was painted in a repeating stripe around the top, the letters looking dark gray against a pale gray building. She turned off the SUV this time, pocketed the keys and jogged toward the opening.

The structure was a mishmash of material. Part of its skin was corrugated metal, but from the inside she could tell it was over a wood frame, with beams that stretched up about twenty feet. This section must have been a storage area, as the floor was hard-packed earth with tiny gravel chips scattered everywhere. She saw the remains of pallets, some of them charred.

There were no traces of whatever kind of tiles the place used to manufacture, but an open man-sized door set in an interior brick wall hinted that she could find out. She stepped through it into a fairly small room that had probably served as an office. A metal desk was intact against the wall to her left, the chair so much splinters in front of it. There were remnants of other desks and file cabinets, wooden ones that must have been expensive in their day—one brass handle remained attached to a drawer.

She was about to turn and leave to pursue one of the other spots marked on the map when she heard something coming from beyond a closed door.

Annja wished she'd brought the gun with her; she'd left it under the seat in the SUV, and she wasn't about to go back and get it. She glided forward, careful not to step on anything that would make noise and give her away. The door that led away was cracked open, no longer hanging properly from broken hinges. She scowled. If she opened it, it would make a heck of a racket. But would it be heard above the noise that was getting louder?

She peered through the crack and inhaled sharply. Six men worked over a hole they were enlarging in the concrete floor. They were using something like a jackhammer, and it, coupled with the concrete breaking away, was responsible for the noise. There was obviously electricity in the building, to operate their tools—and for the bank of flickering lights that hung overhead. With no windows, they wouldn't have to worry about the light attracting attention from anyone passing outside.

The room had been used for manufacturing the tiles, or at least cutting them. On the far side, Annja could see what remained of conveyor belts, and there was something that looked like a guillotine that might have been used to break larger tile sheets into specified sizes. All of it was rusty and broken, and pools of water on the floor, which sparkled incongruously in the lights from overhead, suggested that the roof leaked in several places.

Craning her neck and forcing the door open just a bit wider, she cringed when it squeaked harshly. She waited but it was not enough, apparently, to draw the men's attention. She saw three vehicles to her left. One was a jeep, with mud thick on its tires and quarter panels, and a shattered windshield from where she had shot it hours earlier.

Another was a small four-door Honda sedan, forest-green and certain to be inconspicuous on the street.

The vehicle that made the hackles on the back of her neck rise was a mid-sized tanker truck that read, Bob's Pools And Water Gardens. A wavy blue line underscored the words, and smiling goldfish in sunglasses frolicked above Water Gardens.

A man perched on top of the truck was draining large jugs into a hole in the top of the tank. A hose ran from a port on the back of the tank and coiled on the concrete a few feet from the men who were maneuvering their drills against the floor.

She nudged the door open wider still and touched her sword with her mind.

Why did I have to be right?

25

Annja wasn't confident she could take them. There were seven men, and though she only saw guns on two of them—pistols shoved behind the waistbands of the men facing away from her—she knew they could all have weapons.

Four of the men were dressed in the same dark clothes the other thugs had worn. They didn't have ski masks—no one to conceal their faces from here. Instead, each had a small black turban that appeared tightly wrapped. The six around the hole were wearing goggles, the cheap plastic kind designed to protect their eyes from the shards of flying concrete. Two wore pressed blue pants and beige shirts. Across the back of one she read Bob's Pools. They'd made no effort to keep their clothes clean, and the pants were dusty from the chipping concrete. The final man, the one on top of the tanker truck, had on jeans and a flannel shirt, a short brown beard and he reminded her of the assistant from *Home Improvement*.

She turned her ear to the door and listened closely. The two men in the Bob's Pools shirts had backed away from the hole and were conversing. One was an Asian man, tall and broad shouldered. She recalled some of the graduate students mentioning a big Korean. The other was darker skinned, and she recognized him from out on the street by her hotel.

Annja knew she needed to act quickly, but she also knew a little more information could prove useful, and a little more time might allow the police to show up and better the odds.

"The first chemical will neutralize the chlorine in the city's water," the Korean explained. "It is very concentrated, so take care not to splash any on you."

"And then we recycle it through the tank?"

The Korean smiled. "The main that runs under this building is old and one of the largest in the city. It will be easy to tap into, and out here no one will notice the smell."

"Except us." The man wrinkled his nose and gestured to another man, who had just put down his drill. "Get us the masks, and then make the connection. It stinks worse than roadkill."

Another man, this one so young-looking Annja thought he should be in high school, pointed to tanks propped up against the base of a broken assembly table. "And these?" He picked up a wrench that was at least two feet long.

"After the chlorine has been neutralized," the Korean answered, "then we use those. Don't you listen?"

The tanks were filled with poison, and Annja knew she couldn't let the men dump them into the water supply. She could not wait any longer, despite the horrible odds.

Where were the police?

Perhaps the officer she'd spoken to hadn't believed her—the tale was a little farfetched, something out of a bad movie. Or maybe they'd already cruised through the lots, as she had, and found nothing amiss. But wouldn't they have noticed her SUV? In any event, she knew enough science to understand time was running out.

Chlorine was used in drinking water to help make it safe. It could potentially detoxify whatever poison the crew intended to introduce. But if the chlorine was neutralized, the poison could work all of its grisly wonders. She was certain it had killed all those fish in the cave. Undoubtedly it could also kill people.

She centered herself and closed her eyes, sought the balance she had learned to achieve through her rigorous martial-arts training. Her breathing even, her heart beating strong and calm, she was ready. Reaching for the sword, she opened the door.

Annja had to yank it hard, the metal screaming against the concrete because it had dropped on its hinges. She leaped through the opening, just as two of the men reached for their guns.

Everything happened so quickly, she tried to register it all. The two men in Bob's Pools shirts darted behind the tanker truck, and the man on top slid off, landing on the side away from Annja. Three of the seven were no longer visible.

That left four to contend with in plain sight—two with guns, and two who were picking up lengths of chain that had been lying on the floor. The teenager was still holding the massive wrench in one hand.

She didn't speak, didn't even consider asking that they surrender. They wouldn't, *couldn't* really, given the gravity of what they were doing. It was an all-in gamble, for which she suspected they were being well paid. If they were caught, something she was certain they believed impossible, Annja was certain Australia's justice system would never let them go free.

The two men with pistols dropped to one knee and fired, both bullets striking the metal door she'd been standing in front of a heartbeat before. She'd run to their left, something they hadn't expected, and darted toward the tanker truck and cover.

"Kill her!" This came from one of the men with the chains. "She was in the forest last night. She is the *kelbeh* we were to kill first."

"Do not hit the truck!" someone shouted.

Annja dropped and rolled beneath the tanker, barely avoiding bullets that whizzed into the floor and sent concrete chips flying.

The men were all shouting what sounded like curses.

I'm glad I don't know your language, Annja thought. I really don't want to know what foul names you're calling me. She kept rolling, keeping the sword protected from hitting the concrete. She came up on the other side of the truck, where the man in jeans and the two in Bob's Pools shirts had hidden.

She leaped to her feet. The Korean was on a walkie-talkie, speaking rapid-fire about her. The man in jeans and the flannel shirt was in front of him. To her right was the other Bob's Pools fellow.

The one in the flannel shirt shouted. He dashed at her,

ducking as he closed in an effort to avoid the sweep of her sword. Annja hadn't intended to kill him with the blade, had merely wanted to entice him into just what he was doing. She had no desire to skewer an unarmed man.

The sword whistling in the air above his head to keep him low, she kicked out with her right leg, heel catching him in the center of the chest so hard she suspected she'd cracked his sternum. The pain in her ankle was excruciating.

The Korean skittered as her first foe fell back. She spun and kicked the man again near the same spot. Not quite as much force in the second blow, it was nonetheless enough to send him hard against the concrete, his head bouncing with a sickly sound at the feet of the Korean, who continued to chatter rapid-fire on the walkie-talkie. He lay unmoving as she pivoted to her right, where the other man in the Bob's Pool shirt stood.

This one had pulled a gun, small enough that it could have come from his pocket. He fired three times in rapid succession, but she'd dropped just in time. She pushed off and lunged with all her might, sword leading and sinking up to the hilt into his stomach.

Through all of this she heard shouting—from the men with the guns and chains she'd avoided by rolling under the truck. She heard the slap of their shoes over the concrete floor, and a metallic groaning noise followed by the clank of something heavy hitting the floor, probably the large wrench.

She whirled to face the Korean, only to find him dead on the concrete; the three bullets his companion had intended for her had found their mark in him instead. The broken walkie-talkie next to him made a hissing, crackling sound.

Four to go, she thought as she vaulted over the Korean and came around the front of the tanker truck. She nearly slipped in a puddle of water, her ankle shooting lances of fire straight up to her hip. The odds still were not good, four against one, but the fellow shooting the Korean had helped. And the siren she now heard in the distance might go a very long way to bettering the odds…provided it was the police and provided they were coming here.

In a split second she assessed the situation. The two men with guns stood between her and the hole they'd drilled in the concrete. The other two had dropped their chains and were working with the hose from the tanker. The teenager had loosened the main connection with the wrench. The way the hose vibrated, Annja could tell something was being pumped through it and into the water pipes.

"No!" she shouted.

"By all that's holy, yes." The voice came from behind her, punctuated by the slamming of the truck cab door.

She'd not had a look inside it, assumed it was empty. She spun, rewarded with another fiery lance up her leg and took in the leering visage of the Sword.

"You're done," he whispered. "Your God is not mine, Annja Creed, and mine will help me win this day."

She hesitated. He was too far away for her to lunge and strike him before he could shoot. His hand was holding steady on the trigger, and his eyes held hers as surely as if they were a tightening vise. He had a presence, though not a pleasant one. His gaze was commanding and frightening, and it complemented a face that was at the same time striking and horrid. She couldn't turn away.

The lower half of his face was shiny and pale, scar tissue from a deep burn. There were scars on his neck, too, the worst a thick ropy disfigurement that snaked into the unbuttoned neck of his Bob's Pools shirt. His cheekbones were high and his nose straight and in perfect proportion to his features. His eyebrows were thin, as if he plucked them, and the narrow mustache under his nose was shot through with a hint of gray.

His hair was oiled and pulled back into a ponytail, the hair lying so tight against the sides of his face it looked painful. It would have been a handsome face except for the scarring, and except for the hateful expression it bore.

Behind her, she heard the men working and heard the thrumming sound from the tanker truck as it continued to pump the neutralizing agent into the water. She had to move, go for the Sword, and leap at him despite the distance. But her legs seemed rooted to the spot.

"It's too late, Annja Creed." His voice had a mesmerizing quality, but it dripped venom and sent a shiver down her spine. "You should have died quickly yesterday, and I should have sent better men to do it. How could I have known that one American woman would be so difficult to slay? There is something in you, Annja Creed, which sets you apart. I sense in you a singular soul, and I will regret—and rejoice—in its passing." To the men behind her, he hollered, "Quickly! The chlorine must be gone from the water!"

A reply came in a language she couldn't understand. Then, in English someone said, "Shall I shoot her, Sayed?"

"No. I want her to taste the poison that everyone in this

city will soon be drinking and bathing in. She is too beautiful to mar with bullet holes or with the cut of a knife." He waved the gun at her. "Put down your sword, Annja Creed, or I will be forced to wound you horribly and make your death slow and painful. Let us give your family something to bury, eh?"

I have no family, Annja thought.

"She should die slow!" This came from behind her. "My brother, she killed him. Let me hurt her!"

The work with the pump and the water main continued until a chuffing sound signaled the tanker was empty.

Sayed smiled, revealing perfect, glistening white teeth. "That sword, Annja Creed. That beautiful weapon. I want you to put it down now."

Let my strike be true, Annja prayed. She made a motion as if to drop the sword, but instead dismissed it to the otherhere.

The terrorist's eyes widened in shock, and Annja capitalized on that instant, pumping her legs as she raced toward him, pushing off and hurling herself toward him. She heard his gun go off, and then she heard the impact of her open hand against his chest. It was intended as a killing blow, a karate maneuver taught only by masters and only to choice students. It was designed to strike the heart and stop it.

He flinched at the last instant, but she struck close anyway, the blow sending him back, gasping and quivering as if he'd been hit by a bolt of lightning. He might die from her blow, but not immediately as she had planned. And she could not finish him now, as there were four other men to think about.

One of them was shooting at her. She bobbed, weaved and whirled so she did not give him a stationary target. She summoned the sword as she went, and the men shouted their surprise, one of them calling her a witch.

She leaped over the felled Korean and the man she'd killed and came to the truck's bumper. She raised the sword above her head and brought it down hard and quick, severing the hose attached to the back of the tank. It might have already dumped its load into the water line, but it didn't need to recycle the mix and dump it elsewhere. And it didn't need to be equipped to dump any poison.

Liquid sprayed from the severed hose, showering her. It stung her eyes and she tried to spit out what had got in her mouth. It burned fiercely.

"Police!" she heard.

She wiped her eyes on the sleeve of her sweatshirt and saw a blurry image of two uniformed officers rushing through the door she'd opened. She dismissed the sword and looked between them and the four men, two of whom were putting their guns down on the floor. The other two were raising their hands. Nothing was quite in focus, the liquid still stinging her eyes and lips.

"You, too! Get your hands up!"

It took Annja a moment to realize they were talking to her.

The police moved into the room, one taking up a position across from the four men, gaze flitting to her. He motioned with his head that she should join the others.

"I'm not with them," she said. But she didn't argue. To the other officer she said, "There are three men behind the tanker, two dead, one maybe dying." Hopefully dying in the Sword's case, she thought. That terrorist does not deserve to keep taking in oxygen.

Four more officers filed in, going straight for the dark-clad men and handcuffing them.

"Those canisters—" Annja gestured to the ones propped up against the old table, blinking furiously trying to clear her vision "—they're filled with poison. And those—"

One of the officers came up to her, handcuffs dangling in front of him. "Turn around," he ordered.

"Those men were trying to poison the water supply." She turned and sucked in a sharp breath. When he yanked her hands up behind her back her ribs protested. "I called earlier. You've got to listen to me."

"Oh, we'll listen, all right. Down at headquarters." He roughly ushered her out the door.

The parking lot was dotted with emergency vehicles, including two white vans that were disgorging people in hazardous-material suits. The bulk of them must have approached without sirens, she realized.

The police officer she'd called earlier had obviously taken her seriously. She let out a guarded sigh of relief. "I've got a map in my car," she said to the one shepherding her. "It's marked with places where they might be dumping the poison right now. I know there have to be at least two more trucks."

"Jamie," the officer herding her called out. "Check that SUV. Keys?"

"Front pocket," Annja said.

He fished for them and tossed them to a tall female officer with a hard-set expression. Then he patted her down to make sure she didn't have any weapons.

"Peabody said he saw you with a sword."

She didn't answer.

"I can't even find a pocket knife." He shrugged and nudged her to a faster pace, angling her toward the closest sedan.

"Have the media been alerted?" Annja tried to slow him, but he persistently nudged her in the direction of the car, nearly knocking her over. "Listen, people need to know not to drink the water, that it's poison and—"

"I'm sure all of that's being handled. Not your worry," he told her. He opened the rear door and gestured. "In you go."

"I'm—"

"I know who you are. Annja Creed, some kind of American celebrity. Got your face plastered all over the squad room. Not in O.J.'s class, but you're wanted on suspicion of a double murder. You'll be the top of the hour on the evening news."

Annja knew she could overpower him, but she wouldn't get far. Not with all these police and emergency-response crews here, and not on her bad ankle.

"Easy, okay?" She gingerly slid into the backseat. He leaned in to help her swing her legs around.

"Hammy! Hey, Hammy!" The officer named Jamie waved and jogged toward him. "We got the map she mentioned. I know a couple of units are already on the Chinatown spot. But she also had a gun under the seat. And two extra clips."

"You're under arrest, Annja Creed," the officer said. "And you're going to be locked up for a very long time. He slammed the door and made a brushing motion with his hands, as if to signal that he'd just disposed of the trash.

26

Sayed Houssam hadn't died in the abandoned factory, Annja learned at the police station. And the man in the flannel shirt would recover—but indeed he had a broken sternum.

The Sword was under heavy guard in the emergency-care unit of St. Vincent's Hospital, and the verdict was still out on whether he would pull through. For all the evil acts he'd perpetrated through the years, she hoped he would die. It had been a long time since she'd wished someone dead.

"Someone will probably give you a medal, Miss Creed. Some idiot out there will think you're a hero." The officer who sat across from Annja was pushing retirement age. He had more hairs showing on his arms than on his head, and he had liver spots on the backs of his hands. He had the bulbous, red-veined nose of a heavy drinker, and his eyes seemed too small for his round, ruddy face.

But those eyes were clear and focused, and they stared at her as if to weigh and measure her and judge her mettle.

He didn't say anything else for several moments. Annja had seen enough police procedures to understand; silence often made people uneasy, and cops employed the technique to get their targets to talk. However, Annja had nothing to say at the moment; all her body wanted to do was sleep.

It had been six hours since the police had stormed the abandoned factory. In those hours she'd learned that the authorities had managed to stop one more of the tanker trucks from disgorging its poison, but the other had emptied half of its load before the police arrived. Two men fled the latter scene and were still at large.

Chemists were hard at work isolating the toxin and finding a way to neutralize it, just as the terrorist had used an agent to neutralize the chlorine.

Bulletins had been issued not to drink the water or to bathe in it, as the toxin could splash in the eyes and mouth and be absorbed that way. One thing the chemists had learned was that the poison was terribly lethal.

Bottled water and soft drinks were flying off the shelves at supermarkets and convenience stores. In some places, riots had been sparked and the police called in.

Police shifts had been extended, and off-duty officers had been called in to help manage the panic. Several vacations had been nixed.

The roads were filled with people leaving the city, and as a result there were dozens of fender benders.

Hospitals and clinics were gearing up to treat poison victims—particularly those who did not hear the news alerts and were oblivious to the hysteria outside their doors.

The police had no clues to Oliver's whereabouts, though more than one of the captured Arabs admitted to hearing that the cameraman was dead. A detective told Annja it was unlikely a body ever would be recovered.

"You certainly have the chest to pin it on, this medal they'll want to give you," the officer said, finally breaking the silence.

Maybe he thought the verbal jab would get a rise out of Annja. She just sat there, exhaustion tugging at her core.

Her ankle had been professionally wrapped by an ambulance crew at the abandoned factory, and her ribs checked. They didn't wrap cracked ribs anymore, and she declined an X ray. Annja had gotten a look at her side in the mirror of the police station restroom, all blue and purple and ghastly—looking not quite as bad as it felt.

She'd taken a couple of painkillers with a soda an officer had offered. Water was off-limits for a while, and so her much needed and coveted shower would have to wait. She'd rubbed the makeup off her face with a dry paper towel, smearing it pitifully, but getting rid of most of it and leaving in its place more bruises and an ugly black eye.

"Yep, someone will want to give you a medal." He tapped his fingers on the edge of the table. "Me? I just want to give you a nice cell. And I want to throw away the key."

She closed her eyes and fell asleep.

Annja was too exhausted to care just how uncomfortable the straight back wooden chair was.

THEY RELEASED HER three days later after extensive questioning, and after Wes and Jennifer Michaels, Dari and several members of the U.S. Embassy staff came forward to speak on her behalf.

"If it weren't for the archaeologists, and that odd-looking bald bloke," the bulbous-nosed officer told her, "and a pair of police sergeants from Cessnock, we might have found something to hold you on. At the very least we could have gotten you on a weapons charge for having an unregistered and unlicensed gun."

Still she didn't answer him; she simply had nothing to say.

"But it looks like you're the hero in all of this, not the villain. Though you're no avenging angel with a sword, like some of the folks at the hotel tried to make you out to be."

Another officer had told her that after a few hours of study, the chemists discovered it wasn't terribly difficult to neutralize the poison, though it was one of the most virulently toxic substances they'd seen—a bioengineered form of botulism. Quick acting and short-lived, it could have killed off a large portion of Sydney's population before it was discovered—if it could have been detected by then. A very short life, the botulism strain had, they emphasized.

The terrorist was still breathing, with the aid of a ventilator, and still in emergency care and under the gaze of a cadre of police.

"Fortunate for the city that a freak heart attack felled him, this Sword fellow," bulbous-nose said. "A bad ticker stopped the number-one man on Interpol's list."

Dr. Hamam could not be found; apparently he'd turned in his resignation to the university, citing family problems at home. He'd taken a red-eye out of Sydney the day of the attempted poisoning. The authorities hadn't yet found anything to tie Hamam to the terrorist plot. None of the men they'd captured in the factory and questioned would link the professor to the acts. The Sword, still attached to a ventilator and under heavy sedation, could not comment.

The Egyptian museum at the university had been robbed, but so had two other museums in the city—apparently the well-planned act of a group of professional thieves. Again, Hamam could not be tied to any of it.

Annja didn't intend to let the professor off. The law might not be able to touch him—yet—but nothing would prevent her. There was the matter of avenging Oliver, Josie and Matthew, and of seeing this mystery through. Annja felt a need to tie up loose ends.

"Why did Hamam want so many people to die?" she asked. The question was aimed at herself, not the policeman.

"Pardon me? I didn't quite catch that." The bulbousnosed cop leaned in close.

"I said thank-you for getting my bags." He'd told her earlier that her things had been gathered from the hotel, including her passport.

"And for keeping your money safe." He passed her a plastic bag with the roll of money she'd taken from the dead thug. She almost didn't take it.

"G'day, Miss Creed," the cop said as he released her.

She left the station and caught a cab straight to the airport.

"I will find you, Dr. Hamam, and you will tell me what this is all about," she vowed.

Less than an hour later she was standing in line at the

ticket counter, using her celebrity and what was left of her charm to find out what flight Dr. Hamam had booked to Egypt. To Cairo, she was told, and she got the next available flight, which was only a three-hour wait.

"How fortunate is that?" The young woman at the counter beamed. "Your lucky day."

I don't feel all that lucky, Annja mused. I feel numb.

She drank two bottles of orange juice in a small restaurant just beyond ticketing and nibbled on a double-thick turkey-and-Swiss-cheese sandwich. There were still bulletins about water restrictions hanging everywhere, and though news reporters had interviewed police officers and chemists touting the safety, people still grabbed the bottled stuff.

She hadn't called Doug Morrell, though she'd had several opportunities, including while she was being held at the police station. She'd call him from Cairo, maybe. She'd definitely call him after she'd found Hamam and settled whatever it was she was going to settle. And she'd make sure that she spoke to Oliver's mother and fiancée personally.

Her lip crooked upward in a sad smile just as her flight number was called. She was living her television show, she thought. She was chasing history's monsters—and Dr. Hamam could quite possibly be the worst monster of all.

27

The pilot announced that it was 10:00 p.m. local time, and that the plane would be on the ground in a few minutes.

Annja recalled little of the actual flight, having slept through most of it. She'd been awake, briefly, for the touchdown and refueling in Frankfurt, and for the few minutes it had taken her to wolf down the meal the airline had provided—she just couldn't recall what she'd eaten.

She'd traveled coach, as business class was full and the roll of money she'd taken wasn't quite enough to cover first-class. She could have charged the trip to her credit card and gotten a more comfortable seat and more room to stretch out her legs in the second row, but on principle she decided to let the terrorist's money pay for the ticket. And so she was crowded near the back.

She still seethed with anger over everything that had happened. Her foul mood was stoked by the crick in her neck and from being a sardine in the tail of the plane.

Why were so many people going to Egypt today? And why did they all have to book this flight? Despite being stiff, she felt better than she had for the previous few days. Her ribs no longer throbbed, and the ache in her ankle was manageable. She still looked like a wreck—with her black eye and bruised face she couldn't get upset that the flight attendant fussed over her the couple of times Annja had woken up. At least Annja had been able to ignore her seat mate, who'd carefully asked, only once, if her husband had beaten her.

Cairo International Airport looked like a giant Christmas display from the air. Annja found it beautiful and wouldn't have minded if they'd been forced to circle a few times. A crew member told her they would be arriving at Terminal 2, and that the airport was about nineteen miles from downtown.

Annja knew that it was a relatively new airport, at least this part of it, and that it serviced a great many airlines from Europe and America, and was a stopover to many other places. Domestic flights were limited to Terminal 1, a much older part of the complex.

She found a shuttle that would whisk her into the heart of Cairo, and she leaned back against the seat and let the small bus rock her. She wasn't physically tired anymore, having slept so many hours on the plane. But she was emotionally worn-out.

She asked the driver to recommend a hotel; it didn't have to be five-star accommodations, but she desired something nice and comfortable. After several days with the Sydney police, and after being shot at so often, she wanted to be pampered—if only for a few hours.

He dropped her at the Four Seasons on Giza Street on the west bank of the Nile. Her room, plush in shades of chocolate, beige and eggshell, looked like a sanctuary. It was worth every penny it would cost her. She only planned to spend one, or maybe two nights there, and they accepted American credit cards.

She stood at the window, wearing the complimentary fluffy robe she'd found in the closet after a long hot bubble bath. It was just past midnight. From this height she had remarkable views of the Great Pyramids, awash in soft lights, and the city's zoological and botanical gardens. In spite of the circumstances she found herself happy to be back in Egypt. She couldn't help but be excited every time she visited.

The bellman had told her the Four Seasons boasted a casino, fitness center, swimming pool and hot tub. She could order a massage, which she did, and could have her clothes cleaned, which she also took him up on. There was nothing fresh in her suitcase to wear—so she gave him everything.

"And don't hold back on the detergent," she'd told him. She had briefly wondered what the laundry staff would think when they came across the blood splatters.

She stood at the window for nearly half an hour, transfixed and relaxed. And she was certain she could have stood there longer, had the bellman not returned with the masseur. He'd explained that most of the hotel's services were available around the clock. Annja tipped him well and let a pug-nosed man with upper arms the size of hams work on her for the next hour. The man did not speak English, but he well understood to leave her mending ribs alone.

Knowing that she could not begin her hunt for Dr.

Hamam until later in the morning, Annja tucked herself into the incredibly comfortable king-size bed. Somehow— despite the hours of sleep on the plane—she managed to drift off again.

IN CLEAN CLOTHES and feeling remarkably well, Annja eyed herself in the mirror. The bruises on her face were several days old and were fading. She used the makeup in her suitcase to cover up the worst of the marks. It wasn't vanity; Annja simply wanted to look presentable on her information hunt.

Though she was desperate to find Dr. Hamam, she'd allowed herself the luxury of resting last night merely because of the late hour. Because he'd left Sydney days before her, the element of a race was gone—he'd already won that part of it. He had to know his pet terrorist was caught, so he certainly had time to go into hiding or set up his defenses. He might consider himself untouchable because he had not yet been linked to the goings-on in Sydney. But Annja was going to bring him to some fashion of justice.

Had her laptop not been destroyed, she would have surfed the Internet after being released by the police, hoping to pick up tidbits about his possible whereabouts and to learn more about the man. She intended to look for the hotel's business-services center right after breakfast. She would use their computers to do a little digging there. Or she could just look in the phone book and call a few of the universities, or call one of the museums— certainly people there had heard of Dr. Gahiji Hamam, probably knew him well.

There was also an impressive library not far away.

"Yeah, I think the library." She hadn't visited one lately; the Internet had been her main research tool. And she couldn't say why she was entertaining the notion now. It just seemed to be the right thing to do.

"The library, then, but after breakfast."

She knew only a little about Hamam at the moment—that he was one of the top Egyptologists in the world, that he'd authored several books, that his students seemed to be terribly loyal and that he'd once taught at a university in Cairo. He'd flown here from Sydney, so Annja hoped he wasn't too far away, that he hadn't in turn booked another flight to who knew where. Annja prayed she could find him soon and gain her answers and her vengeance.

The hotel restaurant was impressive, and offered a menu that made Annja's mouth water. She couldn't make up her mind on what smoothie to drink, and so she ordered two—something called Jet Lag, which was said to be made of yogurt, orange juice, bananas, assorted fruits and orange-blossom honey, and an Alexandria Breeze—pineapple, tamarind, honey and coconut. Both went down quickly.

She followed those with an ample breakfast of Egyptian *fatayer* bread with black honey and *kechta* cream, hash topped with *tameya,* sausage and poached eggs and a plate of local cheeses. The waiter seemed pleased and awed by her ability to put away the mound of food in such a short time. While she ate, she studied a few tourist brochures she'd taken from the stand by the front desk.

She already knew a lot about Egypt, an archaeologist's paradise. Located on the banks of the Nile River, Cairo sat just south of where the river divided itself. The brochure explained that the oldest section of the city sat to the east, and that the western section was modeled after the city of Paris during the mid-nineteenth century and was noted for its wide streets and public gardens.

Annja always found the older section more appealing with its crowded residential areas, ancient mosques and small, twisting streets. Would she find Dr. Hamam there? She doubted the professor had much use for the newer areas.

She knew that bridges linked the islands of Roda and Gezira and the suburbs of Imbabah and Giza. Just west of Giza on the plateau stretched Memphis, the ancient necropolis with its three large pyramids.

"Where are you, Dr. Hamam? Are you somewhere in al-Qahirah?" Annja used the official name of the city. "And what are you up to?" Annja paid for her meal and got directions to the largest library. She walked quickly, her stomach full and her ankle hardly a bother anymore.

Cairo encompassed various districts and once independent historic villages and towns, and altogether claimed a population in excess of fifteen million. It could be much easier finding a very tiny needle in a very big haystack than finding Dr. Hamam in one of the most populous cities on the planet, she thought.

As she walked, taking in all the sights, sounds and the odors of various restaurants, she enjoyed the fact that perhaps more than any other city Cairo was a trip through time. The pyramids, Heliopolis and the Sphinx represented the ancient world, and then there was Saladin's Citadel, the Cairo Tower, the Mosque of Amr ibn al-A'as, the Hanging Church, as well as all the modern constructions.

Annja took the subway after a few more blocks, and sat in the first train car. The first two cars were reserved for women only. She emerged a block from the library. The city had a varied transportation network, from its myriad roads—which seemed as crowded as New York City's streets—to its subway system, boats and ferries and trains. Taxis honked at her, trying to get her attention; she knew that was a common way to attract potential customers.

The library was impressive, and she could have spent the entire day there. More like days, she thought. But she went right to work and found a listing of universities. Several had Hamam listed as a past professor or a visiting lecturer, and one old directory listed him as a department head.

Hamam had studied abroad, she learned, gaining his master's degree from the University of Washington, and working several digs in Egypt and elsewhere before gaining his Ph.D. in Egyptology from Yale. Among his accomplishments was mapping the Theban West Bank through the use of hot-air balloons, and rediscovering the Valley of the Kings, where the tombs of Ramses II's sons were found. His various methods were attributed to producing reams of archaeological data.

Along the way he and his assistants had recovered artifacts, jewelry and mummies, and his books detailed many of the findings of the West Bank and the Valley of the Kings.

She also found a complete list of his works, which she

took a photocopy of, as well as a listing of articles—the one titled "Australian Influence in Ancient Egyptian Culture" caught her eye. Though she was not allowed to copy that because the journal it was in was brittle, she did get to carefully read it, and took it as a rambling piece that Hamam was lucky to get published. The Internet was good for research, but Annja knew that his article, and many of the others she scanned, would not have been available on it.

When she got back to the United States, she vowed to do more of her research in libraries and to cut back on her time online. The computer was convenient, but she'd forgotten just how much she relished the feel of the books and paper and above all of that, the smell of places such as this.

In the Australian article Hamam discussed hieroglyphs found in New South Wales that were in the style of some of the early Egyptian dynasties. Because this particular style was so archaic and able to be translated only by a handful of Egyptologists, people from multiple continents dismissed them as aboriginal scrawling or complete forgeries.

Hamam maintained they were indeed genuine, dated to the Third Dynasty, and chronicled the story of long ago explorers who became shipwrecked, and whose leader— Lord Djes-eb—died not far from the coast. Hamam believed that the expedition was ordered by Khufu, whom he claimed as an ancestor. He also claimed that another, later expedition was sent by Ra-Jedef, one of the reigning kings of the Upper and Lower Nile. Hamam contended that the expedition ordered by Khufu traveled to Australia and made it back, and that it was the subsequent one financed by Ra-Jedef that met with tragedy. Hamam further stated that the shipwrecked Djes-eb was likely a son of Ra-Jedef. There were other Egyptian names mentioned, all of them a blur of letters and hyphens to Annja.

"So no wonder he wanted to lord it over an Egyptian dig in Australia," Annja mused. "He thinks he's descended from Khufu and that maybe some of his ancestors took a trip down under and carved some of the hieroglyphics north of Sydney."

"Shh!" one of the librarians warned.

Annja continued to search for references to Dr. Hamam, finding several articles where he discussed various exhibits at the Museum of Egyptian Antiquities. With a little more digging, she learned that that particular museum was the repository for the most extensive collection of ancient Egyptian relics in the world—nearly 150,000 of them on display, and perhaps four times that many more locked away in its storerooms.

The hair prickled on the back of Annja's neck. Something about the mention of the museum made her uneasy, but more troubling was that she couldn't explain why.

A young but prim-looking librarian who'd noticed her studying "all things Gahiji Hamam," pointed her to the reference section, and from there down a narrow corridor to an old microfiche machine. It was in a room that was dark because of ceiling-high bookshelves that blocked part of the windows, deep maroon carpeting and a three-bulbed overhead lamp where only one of the bulbs glowed.

It wasn't an area for the public, Annja gathered, seeing carts with books stacked in them, file cabinets along one wall and a coat rack that was full and had umbrellas leaning against the wall next to it.

"I will bring you more on Gahiji. Do you know how to use one of these?" She pointed to the microfiche reader. The librarian was clearly a native from her appearance and accent, but her English was impeccable.

Annja nodded and waited, thoughts shifting from Egyptians in Australia to Dr. Hamam and the Museum of Egyptian Antiquities. She realized she was being given special treatment, a stranger, and obviously an American, ushered into a staff room, and all because a prim-looking librarian saw her studying the revered Dr. Hamam.

He stole relics from the university museum in Sydney, Annja told herself. "There's no proof, but I know it. And I think he'll do the same thing here, at the Museum of Egyptian Antiquities. But why? Why why why?" And if the poisoning in Sydney was his twisted way of covering his tracks and distracting authorities while he made his getaway, would he poison people here, too? She felt sick at the thought.

It was one of the largest cities in the world!

"He didn't need to poison anyone in Sydney to steal the artifacts," Annja whispered. "There has to be more to—"

"Here, ma'am, you might find these interesting." The librarian startled her, depositing a yellow box on the table next to her. "These go back about twenty to twenty-five years, when Gahiji, like me, was quite a bit younger, to when he first started his building project. It is not in the city, this great building of his, but the local papers covered it a little back then until he hired security to keep people away and built up the land around it so it's not easy to spot. Tourists would certainly go there if they knew about it. The place isn't exactly hidden, but it's certainly off what some call the beaten path."

Annja put the librarian in her midthirties, so if the building project started twenty-five years ago she would have been about ten.

"Have you ever met Dr. Hamam?" she asked.

The librarian smiled sadly. "Gahiji was a brilliant man then, and more so now, I understand. I know that from all the books he has written that I replace on the shelves, and from all the news articles I have cataloged through the years." She paused. "Yes, I met him. My father took me to the site a few times at the project's beginning, once when Gahiji was there."

"And…" Annja prompted.

"He was exceedingly cordial and shared some cool, sweetened tea with me that he had in a thermos. He talked to me of the glorious Egypt of ancient times."

Annja threaded the material in the machine, and began to read. "Oh, my, in all my poking around on the archaeology sites, I'd never seen this."

"I doubt you'd ever find that on the Internet." The librarian adjusted her glasses. "After those first few articles, it was all hush-hush. There were rumors Gahiji paid high-up newspapermen to look the other way. Oh, there are certainly people who know of it, as he must have quite the staff working there—and perhaps living there. But they know to keep their mouths shut."

"It's a palace," Annja said.

"It is that," the librarian agreed. "And those are just pictures taken partway into its construction. I imagine it's quite a bit more beautiful than what you see there. My father was one of the architects, and that is why he took me to the site. He was proud of his participation in it, and he wanted me to see."

"And did you go back again? After meeting Dr. Hamam that first time?"

She shook her head. "My father was fired the very next day. I heard him talking to my mother, saying that Gahiji was angry that he'd brought me to the site. My father called him Gahiji, not Dr. Hamam. I think they were friends, but all the architects called him Gahiji then. He said Gahiji did not want any more eyes than necessary on his home." She paused. "My father, of course, did not tell me my presence was to blame for his dismissal."

Annja stared at the woman, not knowing what to say.

"But it is good my father lost that job. The three other architects died shortly after the project was finished. Some of the contractors, too, from what I'd heard. I did not pay much attention to death when I was young. My father thought it something like the curse on the archaeologists who first discovered Tut's tomb. Silly superstition."

"You don't like him, do you, Gahiji Hamam?" Annja asked.

"He is a very powerful, very wealthy man. And, no, I do not like him." The librarian drew her finger to her lips, gave Annja a nod and left her to her reading.

"I will find him here, in his secret palace," Annja said, eyes buried in the hood of the machine. "And, no, I do not like him, either."

28

Annja told the woman at the hotel desk that she would be staying at least one more night, maybe two. She ate a big lunch, wanting to make sure her energy was up, and then purchased several bottles of water, rented a motorcycle and headed out of the city.

Worse than New York, Annja declared of the traffic. Driving in Cairo was a dangerous proposition, so many of the locals aggressively weaving from one lane to the next on swarming streets and rarely signaling. Oddly, she noticed that they were more polite around intersections. She thought about Dari as she drove; his bike was far superior to this rental. She hoped he'd been stitched up and was none the worse for wear. She hadn't checked in with him or with West and his wife before she left for the Sydney airport. She'd been too focused on catching up to Hamam.

Besides, she told herself again, she intended to return

to Sydney for a proper vacation. She would plan a reunion with all of them.

She pulled over when she was well outside the city and forced herself to relax, her nerves on edge from what she'd considered a perilous drive and from her upcoming confrontation. She drank one of the bottles of water, saving just enough in the bottom of it so she could splash her face. She didn't care if the makeup covering the bruises smeared. She didn't care what she looked like when she found Hamam.

Annja had two maps with her—one purchased in the city and showing details of the area around Cairo. The other was drawn on a sheet of legal-size paper, the best recollection the librarian had of just where Hamam's palace sat. Between the two maps, she hoped she could find it by nightfall.

The day was beautiful for traveling. It was in the mid-seventies, quite a difference from Australia, and before the afternoon was out she suspected it would reach eighty. The sky was bright blue and looked shiny. The only clouds were high and thin, and the air had a crisp cleanness to it that was a welcome relief from the oppressive scents of the city. The people in the cars that passed her only gave her a glance; there was none of the speed and rudeness and aggressive driving that she'd witnessed in Cairo and its environs.

Her finger traced her route on the map, and she guessed that it would take her perhaps two hours at most to get in the area of Hamam's property, and then she'd have to find the place. Big, the librarian said, though it was nonetheless concealed.

ANNJA CONSIDERED herself good at finding things, but the sun was nearly down before she was able to find anything.

"Kom Ombo," she whispered. Annja had hidden her motorcycle behind a rise of earth and had been exploring on foot, paralleling a twisting dirt trail that had a security fence well back from the main road it branched off. She spotted cameras, too, on the gate and on thin poles that would be difficult to see from a distance.

"This is like Kom Ombo. But more magnificent."

She'd climbed a rise that looked like a sand dune, finding a bowl-shaped depression on the other side. The twisting trail leading down into it was bisected by two security checkpoints and undoubtedly more cameras.

Annja recalled that during the Ptolemaic and Roman periods, stretching from roughly 300 to 80 B.C., a double temple had stood at Kom Ombo. Cleopatra was known to have favored the place, which was dedicated to Sobek, the crocodile-headed god of fertility said to have created the world. It also honored Haroeris—Horus—who at the time was called the sun or war god.

The last rays of the setting sun struck the main structure, making it look golden. Annja was transfixed by its beauty. The complex was nearly as long as two football fields, and would have been visible for miles were it not built in the depression with raised earth ringing it. It would be seen from overhead, Annja thought, though not easily. Its colors purposefully blended in with the grounds. A wide staircase—one hundred or more feet wide—led up to a columned building made of red-brown stone. Various Egyptian gods made up each column, suggesting it was a temple. There was Hathor with her arms raised straight above her head, her hands helping to support the roof. Horus was next to her, and Anubis next to him. Even at this distance, Annja could tell the detail was amazing. About fifty yards to the east of the temple, a thick, stunted tower rose, the top of it almost even with the rise that circled the place. Beyond it was a wall that encompassed a courtyard, and a pool that had been constructed to look natural.

The main building in the courtyard—made of a little darker stone—had a modern touch, windows. Annja saw the failing light glinting off them. She thought she spied a generator beneath the roof of a squat-columned porch, but she couldn't be certain. But a place like this would need at least one, as whoever lived inside would want air-conditioning in the height of Egypt's summer.

"Binoculars," she whispered. "Why didn't I think to buy a pair?"

There was also a large, plain-looking building, and through an open door she saw the front of a truck. It was Hamam's version of a garage with an ancient Egyptian motif.

She had called the whole thing Kom Ombo because that is what the place resembled. She'd been to the ruins at the real Kom Ombo, where, though the structures were larger, they were in decay. This looked pristine.

The real ruins had once been home to hundreds of crocodiles, which the Egyptians there considered sacred animals meant to be protected. Annja had seen mummified crocodiles in what was left of the ruins of the Hathor chapel, tucked away in the temple.

The entire ruins had been excavated in the 1900s, Annja

recalled, though parts of it crumbled into the Nile River when an earthquake struck in the early 1990s. She'd not been able to visit it before the disaster. She also remembered that the massive temple had twin images and offerings everywhere to honor both Sobek and Horus—each god apparently requiring his own tribute. The carvings on the walls there were of Sobek in his crocodile-headed form, and sun disks to represent Horus. There were also carvings of medical instruments and rearing cobras, and hints of murals showing the story of how the laborers cut their building blocks with water and inserts of wood.

She calculated that at least fifteen men patrolled the grounds at this re-creation of Kom Ombo, in what first appeared to be no discernible pattern. But after watching for a while, Annja picked up a thorough routine. They either carried M-16s or AK-47s strapped to their backs, and another rifle in their hands. There were pistols holstered at their waists, and two of them wore flak jackets. They looked military, but some had long hair that hung loose, and others had beards. She crept closer, crawling on her belly, and discovered they were a mix of nationalities—Arab, Korean and perhaps European. So not likely military—more likely mercenary, she guessed.

The odds were horrible, and Annja's fingers trembled with the thought of invading the stronghold. She had options, of course, such as returning to Cairo and contacting the authorities, telling them all of her suspicions and coming back with their version of the cavalry. But Hamam was powerful and rich and perhaps above the law—or far enough above it that she would have to give the police substantial proof of his wrong doings. She could contact the U.S. Embassy in Cairo and plead her case, get the statesmen involved. But that would take time, and she was already several days behind Hamam because of her time sequestered with the Sydney police.

She could study this place some more, and Hamam some more, finding the evidence she needed to get the police to take over. But that would also take time, and Annja didn't have a great measure of patience. She couldn't do nothing, couldn't just walk away and fly back to New York, rest a few days and then delve into the skeletons of giant penguins. It wasn't in her to let something drop.

Besides, something had pointed her in this direction when she met the librarian. Who was she to deny that?

Annja waited until nightfall, drinking the rest of her bottled water and making certain she had the routine of the guards locked into her memory. Then she skittered forward like a scorpion, working to leave no trace over the hard-packed earth and being as silent as possible. Alone, she just might be able to avoid detection.

It took work to make it past the cameras she spotted, and she prayed there weren't any that she hadn't seen. More work to get past the guards and to hide at the temple steps. She hurried up to them when the guards passed, and she hugged the wall where the shadows were thick.

And she listened.

All the sounds were faint but discernible—the soft footfalls of the men patrolling, the shush of their pantlegs rubbing together and the chink of their weapons against their backs and in their hands. She heard a dog barking, or perhaps a fox, from somewhere beyond the wall, and then another. Then there was a soft rattle and hum of a large generator. Pale light spilled out from between columns, and she had to move to remain in the darkness. After a few minutes she moved to another part of the complex and scaled the courtyard wall, using the birds' heads and sun disks molded into the clay and stone as hand- and footholds.

Annja had worn a jacket, but she didn't need it, the temperature was hovering around seventy, she guessed. She was sweating—from nerves mostly. This one-man commando operation she'd launched had set her on a fine, sharp edge. She shrugged out of the jacket when she landed on the ground on the other side of the wall, balled it up and put it behind a bush. Inside the courtyard were the only plants she'd noticed, and these might look like natural growth from the air. The emerging moon showed a few small indigenous trees, such as the date palm, tamarisk and carob, none of them large. Grapes grew along the eastern courtyard wall, and lotus, jasmine and roses grew near the pool, their mingled fragrances heady. To the west she saw a spread of alfalfa grass and a stand of papyrus.

She held her breath when four gazelles crossed in front of her and slowly headed to the pond. A desert fox, one that was too small to threaten the gazelles, hurried to the west when it noticed Annja; that was likely what she'd heard making a barking noise.

She was overwhelmed by the place—it truly was a palace, more than a palace, a piece of history re-created and made magnificent on this hollowed-out stretch of ground in the middle of nowhere. It felt as if she walked in the past, where Egyptians had toiled and worshiped and had left behind artifacts to amaze and puzzle the people of her own time. She wished Wes and Jennifer could see it, wished the world could see it. Annja leaned against the wall and looked up at the tower and the columns of the temple, looked to the north where what must be Hamam's residence sat next to the pond. Lights had come on inside.

"Someone's home," she whispered. "And they're about to have company." As much as she would have liked to continue reveling in the wonder of the place, she had a self-imposed mission to capture Hamam and bring him to justice.

It was for more than the memories of Oliver and Josie and Matthew. It was for the people of Sydney who had nearly died, and for anyone else who might fall victim to the professor's schemes.

Minutes later she was scurrying from tree to tree, spooking the gazelles and getting closer to the pond. She nearly stepped on a lizard, so intent on the building she hadn't been looking down.

"What's this?" She knelt and saw a square of metal the size of a grapefruit. "Uh-oh." It looked to be a motion sensor, and she worried that she might have tripped it— or others—and sent up a proverbial red flag in some monitoring room. She hoped she was small enough, like one of the gazelles, to go unnoticed. Still, she was more careful, keeping lower to the ground and looking for more of the sensors, which were placed next to bushes and rocks to help camouflage them.

Heartbeats later she stood in the shadows of the impressive building. Like the temple, though smaller, its roof was supported by columns, but these bore the likenesses of pharaohs. The center ones straddling thick double doors had Hamam's visage. Annja considered that creepy, and she couldn't suppress the shiver that raced down her spine.

She crept around to the back, finding more lizards and seeing three crocodiles chained to a post like a cruel owner might chain dogs. They paid her no heed, and she kept her distance. Crouching behind a column, she studied the door. It looked old, the wood weathered, probably purposefully, but there was a camera that swiveled this way and that just above it. And it was no doubt locked.

A window, maybe, she thought, though those were likely monitored, too. Apparently Hamam hadn't been content just with being out in the middle of nowhere, in a compound with armed guards and motion sensors. He had to put extra security on his doors.

While she mulled over different scenarios, many of which involved her getting caught, the back doors whispered open and two more guards stepped out. One looked Korean, the other Arab. They conversed briefly, and Annja slid closer. She touched the sword with her mind, but refrained from calling it immediately. She dismissed the notion of summoning it altogether when they stepped to the opposite corner of the building, the Korean pulling out a pack of cigarettes. The doors started to close, and Annja shot through them.

I am so going to die here, she thought. Now her count of armed security guards was up to seventeen, and she was certain there must be more. All those rifles and pistols, and who knew what other defenses Hamam had.

Everyone dies, she told herself. The only thing in this world that matters is what you do with the days you've been granted.

She edged into the room, and her eyes widened in admiration and bewilderment. She'd expected this to be a residence, and perhaps it was, but where she thought she might be sneaking into a kitchen—people so often had them at the back of a house—she'd instead entered a museum.

The lighting was low, like museums she'd been in after hours. But it was enough to give her a hint of the displays. Without realizing what she was doing, Annja started moving down the aisle to her left, looking into case after case.

The first exhibit was ghastly. A mummified head was placed on a pillow, and next to it was a mummified hand and a foot. The tag beneath them stated they were the mummified remains of an unknown wealthy woman, previously wrongly identified as one of the wives of New Kingdom Pharaoh Seti II.

There were mummified birds, too, and Annja wondered where Hamam got his displayed artifacts.

She shook her head, scolding herself. He'd stolen them, of course, from the museum in Sydney or from others, or perhaps appropriated them directly from digs he worked.

He had an impressive wooden image of Horus-sodpu from the Late Period, probably between the Twenty-Third Dynasty and the Thirtieth Dynasty, an image of a Ptolemaic ba—or soul—that was only a few inches high, a plastered linen mask from the fourth century, the card in front of it indicating it was found at Den el Bahn. A wooden mask from the Twenty-Fifth Dynasty caught her eye, as it had retained some of its original paint, and there was a large funerary cone made of red clay, which probably had sat at the front of a tomb, the inscription on it illegible.

There was more—a mud brick stamped with the seal of a pharaoh, a considerable collection of Ptolemaic coins that were slightly corroded but in overall good condition. The images of eagles and kings were clear enough for her to see in the soft light. Coptic coins, a cast of a winged bull and another of an eagle, canopic jars of the style from Twenty-Fifth Dynasty, a bronze head of a Ptolemaic queen, a half-dozen bronze images of Isis and Horus and a wooden statue the size of a doll that was one of the concubines of the dead, possibly from the Twenty-Eighth Dynasty.

Annja was able to stop herself from looking further. Her amazement had turned to ire. Hamam should not have this remarkable collection; it should be on display for the world to see. She found an exit that led to a narrow corridor, so dark she had to feel her way down. There were several oiled-walnut doors off it, with carvings she couldn't see. Incongruous to the outside, they nonetheless were the accoutrements of a wealthy man's abode.

The corridor forked under a pale globe of light, and to the right it became a ramp that led down into blackest black. She wanted very badly to follow it. Something tingled at the back of her mind and urged her to discover what lay beneath this place.

But she opted, instead, for the other direction. She heard voices coming from there, and she smelled incense. There could well be guards, but there could also be answers. She summoned her sword, took a deep breath and started down the hall.

29

Annja stopped outside the doorway and listened. She was pleased the two men just beyond spoke in English so she could take in every word.

"Master Gahiji, Randall discovered a motorcycle beyond the first security post. We have traced its rental to Cairo, paid for two days' use by Annja Creed. She is that woman you told me about. The one who nearly ended everything."

"The devil woman."

Annja knew that had to be Hamam speaking. His voice was rough and sounded forced, as if he suffered a sickness of the throat or lungs.

"I have alerted the security posts, Master Gahiji. The men are fanning out. We will find her. And we will kill her for you."

"No!"

Annja almost jumped at the strained shout.

"I will kill her," Hamam returned. "And in so doing I will discover why she is so difficult to put down, what is so special about one American woman. Sayed and his men could not do it in Australia. She nearly unraveled all of my plans there, as I told you. We almost did not get away with the great finds held captive in the university museum and that I discovered in the temple to my mother goddess."

Annja shuddered. *My mother goddess.* She sensed madness in Hamam. Brilliant, the librarian and his students had called him. Insane, Annja decided to add. They were a dangerous combination of traits and could help explain why he'd chosen to poison the people of Sydney. He was simply nuts.

"Annja Creed," Hamam continued, his voice cracking, "prevented the poison dump into Sydney's water. She ruined the test. But she will not ruin this."

Test? Annja's eyes widened and she tightened the grip on her sword. She breathed shallowly, not wanting to make a sound and straining to absorb every bit of the madman's explanation.

"No, she cannot stop the poison dump in Cairo, my friend."

"Everything is in place, Master Gahiji. I have my men in the city, assembling the tankers and the botulism agent. They will release it tomorrow night at all the stations you indicated. It will be glorious, all the death."

"She will not interfere this time," Hamam stated. "The guards must find her, and they must bring her to me. Look to the temple. She's an archaeologist—she might be there."

Annja skittered back a few steps and pressed herself into a darkened doorway. The man Hamam had been speaking with emerged into the hall. His footsteps were heavy, and she held her breath as he passed. She could make out a few details—he was tall, broad shouldered and barrel-chested, a mix of fat and muscle, and he had a pistol on his hip.

Don't see me, she prayed. Keep going. I do not need every guard in this modern-day Kom Ombo alerted. My life expectancy will pretty much vanish.

He stopped for a moment, as if listening for something, then continued on. When she couldn't hear his footsteps any longer, she edged out into the hall and back to Hamam's door frame.

And if I catch him? Annja thought. What then? I really haven't thought this out. Curse me for taking the knee-jerk approach, for coming out here on my own and for coming in here without any backup. What was I thinking?

She was thinking about Oliver, she admitted, as she sucked in a breath and darted inside, registering everything in a single glance.

Hamam sat behind a massive mahogany desk, the front of it carved to resemble the pillars of the temple outside. Books were stacked on each corner, and in the shadow of the tallest stack were an assortment of pill bottles and a water decanter.

The walls were covered with a mix of bookshelves, all filled, and tapestries of Egyptian life. The rug she stood on was thick and woven with images of stiff-looking birds, cow-headed women and half suns.

He stood, leaning on the edge of his desk and reaching

for a telephone festooned with all manner of buttons. An intercom, most likely, Annja registered, and one that she couldn't allow him to touch.

Three long, amazingly fast steps and she was at the side of the desk, sword arcing down and severing the phone cord. A second swift slash cleaved the contraption in two. A third knocked his cell phone out of reach.

Hamam's eyes were wide with fury and spittle flew from his lips. He tried to speak, but she darted at him, sword held in one hand over her head, her other arm straight out and going for his throat. She had no intention of killing him, despite all the deaths he'd planned and had contracted, but she couldn't let him call for his guards.

He was off balance, shuffling back to get away from her, but not managing that. Her hand closed on his throat even as he tripped and went down. She landed on top of him, straddled him and used her weight to pin him. She sucked in a deep breath, smelling the incense that was burning somewhere nearby and the medicinal smell that hung heavy around his face.

She leaned in close. "You are a madman, Gahiji Hamam. Foul and calculating and worse than the most hideous monsters I've chased through these recent years." She squeezed just enough to keep him from talking, and she kneed him when he tried to get up.

"These are just things, Hamam. All of these relics you've got in your cases. They're just *things,* and they're not worth the lives of people you intend to poison, and no doubt countless people you've already killed."

His eyes bulged as he fought for breath, and she

released her hold only a little. She brought the pommel of her sword down next to his head.

"You've got more relics here than what I saw in your display room, I'll wager." She watched his expression and decided she was right. "In the basement of this place, yes?" His eyes flickered and she figured she was on the right track. "But it's not enough, and you want more."

He started to wheeze, and in his breath Annja detected a hint of decay.

"But why does an old man need more, when there are far fewer years in front of him than behind? What can you possibly do with all this stuff?" She hadn't asked that question to him, just posed it, and still she kept her grip tight enough that he couldn't answer. "Madness and greed are monstrous qualities."

"Pig," he managed to say, the word no more than a whisper.

"What? No *kelbeh?*"

Annja glanced around the room again. Some of the books on a shelf directly in front of her looked old. On the top shelf were rolled pieces of papyrus—originals certainly, not forgeries.

"Why the poison?" Again she relaxed her grip. At the same time she drew the sword back and placed the blade at his throat. "I have to know, Gahiji Hamam."

He smiled at her, a vile expression that set her teeth to hurting. "Blackmail," he croaked. "Don't you see?"

She raised her eyebrows. "No, I don't."

"With Sayed…now with another terrorist, though not one with his qualities…we will poison Cairo."

One of the most heavily populated cities in the world, Annja thought.

"And while the authorities deal with the catastrophe, you cart away the best of the relics from the museum?" The muscles in his jaw worked, and Annja took that for a yes. "But not just Cairo, eh?" She suddenly saw the scope of what he wanted.

"No," he said. "Sydney, Cairo, they are the beginning." He stared at her for a moment before continuing. "Other cities, they will release their Egyptian artifacts to me to avoid suffering the poison."

"Blackmail."

"And sacrifice," he added. "All the deaths I planned… they would be tribute to the mother goddess."

Annja shook her head, her hair fluttering around her shoulders. "It makes no sense. Someone would catch you, just like I've caught you. All these things you've been accumulating and all the things you want to add to your trove. You can't do—"

She took in a gulp of air and held it, then released it in a hissing breath. "The world would not let you get away with this."

"Just for a time," he answered. "I only need the wealth for a time. It will buy me passage to the highest place."

Annja still didn't understand. Even with all of Hamam's resources, he couldn't possibly pull it all off. Some, yes, he'd get some cities to turn over the relics. But the major powers would not cave in. And he wouldn't live free. She found this stronghold, and others knew of it and would eventually tell the authorities. He would be undone.

"Downstairs," she said. "That's where my answers are." Annja dragged him to his feet, holding tight to the waistband of his pants in the back and pressing the blade to his throat. "We're going downstairs, Hamam, because I cannot leave this unsolved."

She shoved him, keeping him off balance. Despite his small stature and age, there was a strength about him, and she didn't want him even trying to escape.

"And if you call out, I'll kill you," she said, though she did not truly mean the threat. "And if what's niggling at the back of my mind is even half-true, I'm betting you can't let yourself be killed here by me."

She waited at the doorway to make certain no one was nearby, and then she herded him down the hall, and then down the ramp that descended into utter darkness. Halfway down, a light came on, a motion sensor she was grateful for. Two turns and another sloping ramp, and she came to a study that dwarfed the one she'd discovered Hamam in upstairs.

Annja wanted to explore every inch of it—to ogle the glass cases and look through the very old books, study the sculptures and carvings under glass domes on pedestals. But she stopped herself. Instead, she forced Hamam to a desk, a duplicate of the one upstairs. It took her a moment to figure out how to use the phone, and in that moment, she was nearly undone.

Hamam reached for a bronze *khopesh* lying on the desk between stacks of books. It was an ancient Egyptian weapon, with a sicklelike blade, the most effective weapon of its time period. He swung it at her, cutting through her shirt and drawing a line of blood across her stomach. He pulled it back and meant to gut her with it, but she moved with lightning speed and brought her sword up and at an angle, and drove it down, pommel first, against the side of his head. He slumped to the floor and she bent over him to make sure he was truly out.

She locked the door to the room and shoved a heavy chair against it and quickly placed several calls, not staying on the line long with each one out of fear that the calls might be monitored and bring Hamam's forces in droves. Through the operator she called the closest police, from Fayhoum, then the Cairo police, U.S. Embassy, and a fire department. She shoved a second chair against the door for good measure, then took a better look around.

From a glance at papers in a top drawer of the desk, Annja learned he'd been accumulating treasures through legal and illegal means for decades, and had kept track of all his acquisitions in paper ledgers.

In the room beyond she saw crates that she guessed had come from Sydney, and more shelves that stretched so far she termed the place an underground warehouse that reminded her of the one shown in *Raiders of the Lost Ark*.

Another room sent shivers through her. It looked like an autopsy room, but with an ancient Egyptian twist. There were tools for mummification, and there were large glass jars labeled Natron and other clay jars that would contain the organs that would be removed from Hamam's body.

"Hamam is dying," Annja said. "And he plans to have himself embalmed."

Beyond the embalming room was a treasure chamber, the likes of which rivaled anything she'd heard of archaeologists discovering in the tombs of the pharaohs and kings.

"And he was going to use his wealth…and his lineage from Khufu…to gain entrance to the place of the gods."

She occupied herself waiting for the authorities by taking a close look at the relics displayed in Hamam's tomb. Among them were stone carvings of pyramid builders and of animals that closely represented kangaroos. She knew these latter pieces had not come from Australia, though she couldn't say how she knew that.

When Hamam came to, he admitted their authenticity. "The kangaroo carvings were uncovered nearly five decades ago from a site east of Cairo. None of the archaeologists at the time paid the animals any notice. They didn't realize the significance, so I liberated those particular pieces from the Cairo museum."

Annja stared at them. "So the Egyptians sailed to Australia…and came back."

"Some of them," Hamam said. "The first expedition. And I trace my ancestry to those first travelers."

"And that line ends with you, Gahiji Hamam." She ushered him upstairs at sword point and waited until she heard the sirens.

epilogue

Henenu watched as one dozen of his men placed a slab above the doorway to Hathor's temple. It was more ornate than his previous carving, and it was decorated with inlaid gold; his brother had discovered veins of gold in a nearby ridge. The prayer that he'd painstakingly carved on the stone's polished surface honored the mistress to the entrance of the valley. A personal prayer that he'd carved on the reverse side, which would not be seen by those entering the temple, begged the mother goddess for a way to take them back home.

He'd ordered the temple to Hathor enlarged, too, something more befitting the goddess. Perhaps she would smile upon them at their effort, allow them to rebuild and sail their ships and return to the blessed land cut through by the blessed Nile.

His brother stood with him, admiring the temple and the crowning stone, the gold inlay glowing in the setting sun.

"It is beautiful, Henenu."

He nodded. With all its angles and planes with squat, wide steps that led up to an entranceway yawning black like the maw of a hungry beast, the temple was indeed beautiful. But to Henenu, it stood as a symbol of the abyss.

"The men have done well, Khentemsemet. This is the finest structure in this accursed land."

"Your words are kind, brother," Khentemsemet replied. "But your heart is not in them. Your voice is sadness itself."

Henenu ground the ball of his foot against the earth and turned away from the temple, looking out over a land filled with riches and wondrous creatures. Other peoples would be glad to call this home. But there was no natron in the soil, and so Henenu, who felt himself failing, would not be properly preserved. He would not be joining the gods at his passing.

His brother touched his shoulder. "The mother goddess, Henenu, will look with joy upon her finished temple."

Henenu continued to scan the horizon, not wanting to meet his brother's gaze.

"The others who came before us, Henenu, they found their way home. They brought with them treasures from this land, and the most unusual of the animals. Like them, we will return to Egypt."

Shimmering waves of heat rose from the ground. It was the height of Australia's summer. The presence of Horus, the god of the sky and of the noon sun, loomed large here.

"I will not be returning, Khentemsemet. Nor will some of the other men who came with us. Some are old, and some have toiled too hard on the buildings. Their bodies are broken and withering. Time is claiming us."

Henenu continued to stare to the west, where a family of kangaroos milled.

"This amazing, wonderful, escapeless hole," Henenu pronounced. "It has caught me in its embrace, and it will keep me from ascending."

JAMES AXLER

DEATH LANDS®

Eden's Twilight

Rumors of an untouched predark ville in the mountains of West Virginia lure traders in search of unimaginable wealth. Ryan and his warrior group join in, although it means an uneasy truce with an old enemy. But as their journey reveals more of Deathlands' darkest secrets, it remains to be seen if this place will become their salvation…or their final resting place.

Available June 2009 wherever books are sold.

James Axler
Outlanders®

SHADOW BOX

A new and horrific face of the Annunaki legacy appears in the Arizona desert. A shambling humanoid monster preys on human victims, leaving empty, mindless shells in its wake. Trapped inside this creature, the souls of rogue Igigi seek hosts for their physical rebirth. And no human—perhaps not even the Cerberus rebels—can stop them from reclaiming the planet of their masters for themselves....

Available May 2009 wherever books are sold.